I0731679

HELIX STRIKE

Sever Squad

Book 2

A.R. KNIGHT

ONE

Enemy Territory

AURORA SNAPPED the bar in half, triggering a meltdown as she slipped the pieces into her mouth. A chocolate taste heaped with artificial elements ran across her tongue and down her throat, carrying all the effective nutrients, plus caffeine, that a battle-hardened soldier might need after waking up mid-mission.

Sever squad had been on Dynas for almost two days now, an adventure starting with a distress call from a planet supposedly inhabited by no one, but actually home to . . . what, Aurora still wasn't sure.

The five soldiers dispensed by DefenseCorp to handle the call had been given a clear objective: find the VIP who'd asked for the rescue, and no clear exit: find your own way off world with the objective in hand.

When Aurora believed Dynas uninhabited, that arrangement didn't make sense. Now that she, Gregor, and Rovo sat in an abandoned tram station beneath what felt, smelled, and sounded like a busy city, DefenseCorp's mission briefing felt like a lie.

Like every other galactic corporation, DefenseCorp

1

existed to make profits for its owners, employees, and various investors. How it stood to make money by sending Sever on a misguided, deceptive assault to nowhere wasn't clear to Aurora, but she knew how she'd get the answers: by shoving Admiral Deepak up against the wall and making him talk to her rifle.

Rovo and Gregor didn't share her fervor. At least, not enough to wake them up on time. They'd each taken a bench on the tram as a bed, and Aurora had given them all five hours to rest. After a blood-soaked and blast-ridden first day, the dwindling adrenaline had left them all feeling hazy, unsure. Drained.

Aurora would be damned if she let her squad die due to exhaustion's ill effects.

Not that Aurora had all her squad. She'd left the squad's band open, set a message on repeat every few minutes asking for Eponi and Sai, the two missing members, to check in. If they had, Aurora's ear piece would've blasted her awake with an alarm.

Nothing had come, which meant Aurora snacked on the nutrient bar and watched the plastic blue-white light parade across the tram station in silence. Relative silence, anyway; above, she could hear engines rumbling, footfalls pounding, and distant shouts calling for this and that.

When Sever had arrived at the station, Aurora and Gregor had done a cursory look that found the station's sole entrance sealed by a locked gate, blocking not only their incoming platform but several others connecting to elsewhere in the city. Other maintenance options were locked too, and while the tram's tunnel continued on, a flimsy metal barrier across the tunnel blaring CLOSED in red-painted letters echoed the surface door's sentiment: nobody would be coming this way.

The why wasn't too hard to figure. The first thing

Sever had found upon their arrival to Dynas had been an outpost overrun with strange half-human, half-fungal creatures. Felix, leading these things, had attempted to infect Sever squad. He'd failed, hard, and Aurora held to the idea that she'd be going back someday to finish that job. Genetic mutants like him were against Galactic law. More important, Felix had tried to hurt Sever, and people who attacked Aurora didn't tend to live long.

Cash. Vengeance. Principles to live by.

Rovo sat up next. Aurora had taken last watch—the rookie had the middle, Gregor first. And while giving up those extra couple sleeping hours meant feeling even more sluggish, being tired beat being dead. Plenty of chemicals could help the former, nothing could help the latter.

The rookie didn't look too bad after his first day as a full Sever. Simulators could do wonders for training team tactics, for practicing your shots, but getting down on a grimy planet with mercenaries loaded for combat stood apart from the screens and the goggles. Rovo had done well. Even gone off on his own for a bit, and while he'd followed Felix into a trap, that could be excused.

Like all rookies, he'd either learn, or he'd die early. Thus far, Aurora felt good about the kid. Not that she had many options if she didn't—Sever only had five members. You had to trust each one to do their jobs.

"No visitors?" Rovo asked as he wandered towards Aurora, sitting off of the tram and on the station's floor.

"Quiet, on all levels," Aurora replied, handing Rovo a protein bar.

Rovo crossed his legs, joined Aurora on the hard, dirty grey tile. His eyes tracked to the stairs heading up, behind Aurora and to his right. Wide enough, with a metal handrail splitting the steps, they seemed designed to handle a big crowd.

"Can't see anyone building a subway like this for a small outpost," Rovo said after he'd sucked down half the nutrient-loaded breakfast. "Has this entire mission been a big surprise, or is it just me?"

"Not you." Aurora nodded down the tunnel, where the tram could, if not for the barrier, keep going deeper into the city. "No way Dynas had the manpower and materials here naturally to make something like this. Whomever built this place had help, and that help came from off world."

"Which means DefenseCorp should have known about it."

"Deepak may not have, but I don't trust that," Aurora said. "So either we've been set up, or . . . "

Aurora and Deepak, the *Nautilus* commander and DefenseCorp admiral who'd sent Sever where they needed to go, didn't have what she'd call a good relationship. He stood fast by the need to play politics, to take top down orders and execute without questions. Aurora, well, Aurora didn't give a damn about authority until and unless obeying it meant the most cash in her account.

Even so, she had a hard time believing Deepak would send one of his best and most morally flexible squads on a pointless suicide mission. Where was the profit in that? If DefenseCorp just wanted to make a show of responding to the distress call, Deepak could've sent scrubs. Rounded up poor-performing recruits and sent them crashing to their swampy dooms in Dynas's depths.

"Or Deepak's hoping we can get out of this," Aurora said as Rovo munched away. "Either expose a secret, or destroy it."

"Sending five people to torch a city doesn't seem like a smart call," Rovo said. "Why not bring the *Nautilus* over and have it roast this place from orbit?"

"Too much noise," Gregor announced, roaming over

from the tram and brushing at bags under his eyes. "Blow up a planet, you have questions. Small team smashes the enemy? Subtle success."

"You're going to smash this whole place with that hammer?" Rovo asked.

"Might smash you," Gregor replied, "if you keep asking questions."

Aurora let them fall into their banter. Good to see the two had developed a bond, though that tended to happen fast on deadly missions. Saving each other's lives brought people closer.

Their armor suits, and Gregor's hammer, were back in the tram. They ought to go back there, squeeze them on and then go tramping up to the city, ready to spit fire and wreak havoc until they found Sai and Eponi. Except the sounds coming from above didn't seem all that menacing.

Walking over to the ramp and up it, Aurora went for another look at the chain gate sealing off the platforms. She felt Gregor and Rovo's eyes follow her, likely wondering what their commander was planning to do in her slim, mission-ready outfit. Meant to slip into the powerful suits, Sever didn't soar into combat wearing street clothes. Which would make her idea tricky.

Aurora didn't consider herself a stealth aficionado. She preferred the soldier to the spy, but charging out from here guns a-blazing would pit three against what could be an entire city. Not exactly good odds.

"We need clothes," Aurora called back down, stopping her climb before she lost sight of the two others. "Ideas?"

"Clothes?" Gregor called back. "We have suits!"

"We're leaving them, at least for now," Aurora replied. "I'm not declaring war on this entire planet until we have to. Our mission is to get the VIP and get out."

"I thought we were doing pretty well," Rovo said.

"They sent a lot after us back at that outpost, but here we are?"

"We lost two people back there," Aurora said. "Against a couple skiffs worth of soldiers. We can't afford that again."

"And you think street clothes are going to—" Rovo stopped as Gregor put a hard hand on the rookie's shoulder.

"Question the commander? You do it up here," Gregor tapped his head with his other hand. "Not from your big mouth."

While Aurora wouldn't say Rovo looked thrilled at Gregor's advice, and Aurora herself didn't think blind obedience often worked as Sever's go-to commandment, she appreciated the big man's interruption all the same. Rovo didn't have the experience, and none of them had enough sleep, to question Aurora's decisions here.

Her plan, to get away from the tram station and find some idea about where they were, where Sai, Eponi, and the VIP might be, without drawing every gun in the city wouldn't have much success if they couldn't get outfits.

Once Aurora explained the idea, and once Gregor had finished his own breakfast, the trio fell in line. First they combed the tram station itself, looking for maintenance gear that might serve. Gregor's hammer broke locks, but they found nothing: the supply closets only had some old tools and random gear designed to mark wet floors and wall off closed areas.

Which meant things would have to get messy.

Aurora, Gregor, and Rovo went up to the sealed door leading to the street. Locked from the outside, the large door blocked the entire staircase with its chain-and-metal bulk.

"Hammer?" Gregor said.

"Too loud," Aurora replied. "We're trying to be subtle here, not scare everyone."

"Much harder."

"Low power lasers ought to do it." Aurora poked at the spot on the gate where an unresponsive panel sat waiting to be woken up by someone with the proper clearance. "Carve right through this part and we'll be all right."

Gregor nodded, but Rovo had a funny look on his face. He stepped up to the door, with Aurora backing away to give the rookie room. Rovo inspected the panel, muttering to himself the whole time.

In a language Aurora didn't know.

"Rovo, what are you saying?" Gregor asked.

The rookie stopped, snapped his head up and had the good grace to blush a bit, "Sorry, I talk through things sometimes. My sisters used to tease me if I got things wrong when I did, so I learned not to do it in Common."

"You are a weird one." Gregor grinned. "But that is okay! We like weirdos."

"Rovo," Aurora interrupted. "The door? You have a better idea?"

"Uh, yeah, I think so. Back with my armor, I took a keycard off a guard back at the outpost. Looks like it might work here."

"And you're still standing there, why?"

ROVO'S INSPIRATION PROVED FRUITFUL: he scanned the guard's keycard and the barrier blinked, then clicked itself loose. They could have peeled the whole thing away, but why invite just anyone down to look at their armor?

"Now, how do we get clothes?" Rovo said as they stood on the barrier's other side, looking out to fitful crowds wandering by in the early, yellow-skied morning.

"Bait," Gregor said, then looked towards Aurora. "Sorry, commander."

"Gregor, why should I be sorry?" Aurora relished the confusion on the big man's face. "It's your turn."

To leave the tram station, find their friends, and rescue the VIP, Sever squad couldn't go to war with an entire city. They'd need to stay undercover, and the best way to do that?

Send Gregor into the open, with no protection, to play the fool.

TWO

That Day

AMID THE STRETCHED, swirling red clouds a new line grew as the ship descended towards their building's landing pad. On the rooftop, a hundred stories above the ground level and the riots, the pad should have been a secure haven for the world's wealthy to wait for their rescue.

Sai stood near the edge, watching smoke climb up this high, watching the black puffs twist its way up the buildings towards and above him. Far below he could see flashes as laser fire, pops as gunfire, broke out between hired security forces and the planet's public. A battle that'd begun on the world's outskirts, that'd progressed further and further as the people, in Sai's mother's parlance, rebelled against their makers.

The moment's politics blurred in, well, the moment. Sai, nearly eighteen, stayed near his mother while the ship approached: an armed passenger shuttle meant to carry them all above the atmosphere to a waiting station. Once they'd left, Sai's mother had promised, DefenseCorp would land its heavy forces and suppress the rebellion.

Sometimes the public could be coerced, sometimes

they had to be defeated. Knowing which method to use was an essential trait in any leader. Sai's father, supposedly, had known that. Just as Sai knew enough not to ask how, if his parents and their friends were such good leaders, their planet was tearing itself apart.

Being a leader, though, did have some clear advantages: Sai's father had left the normal line and taken his place near the head of the waiting groups. He'd gone up front to guarantee his family a spot on this shuttle, and listening to the increasing bangs and bullets from below, that plan made sense.

The shuttle, almost too large for the pad, landed with clunking and hissing, like some mythical, giant creature. A sleek, pointed cylinder with engines bristling out its back, Sai thought the shuttle looked pretty, if lacking in larger weaponry.

They were evacuating, not fighting. They had lost, and this was a retreat.

Sai had to remember that.

An indented door appeared and rose up along the shuttle's side, a stairway dropped down, and the rooftop panic surged forward. Several official-looking people sprang from that open doorway, waving for any luggage to get tossed aside. No space for any large possessions. Every bit would be saved for bodies.

"What about the katana?" Sai asked his mom as the first passengers climbed on board.

"We're taking it," his mom, ever calm, ever stoic, left no question in her voice.

She held the katana in her right hand, Sai in her left. The sword drew some glances, but nobody right there, right then, cared one bit about a blade so long as it wasn't going to be used on them.

Sai took one last look down towards the streets that

he'd walked his whole life, to school, to events, to just explore the massive city's neighborhoods. How many people had he talked to, bought from, or played in the park with were down there, turning rudimentary weapons and righteous fury against Sai's peers?

Orange blossomed, the cracking blast of breaking glass made its way up to the roof and the crowd hunched as they scrambled forward, heading towards the shuttle. Sai, his mother, among them, pressing in.

"Think we'll ever come back?" Sai asked.

"This is our home," his mom replied. "Of course we'll come back. When it's ready."

Sai tried to find his father, but it looked like the man had already boarded the shuttle. More angry noise from below and around the tower pushed the boarding into a full-on charge. Nobody seemed to be paying attention to rank.

Around them, over the city, more shuttles streaked down through the red clouds, heading to other towers, other evacuations. A full-on flight. All these people leaving all their possessions. Sai himself had on a little backpack, filled with the absolute few things he wouldn't leave behind.

Including, unbeknownst to his mother, a small laser pistol he'd bought earlier that year when the rumblings began. When a boy like Sai might find his family's position making him a prime mugging target. Even though he barely knew how to fire the thing, having it made Sai feel a little bit safer.

A roaring noise drew Sai's eyes away from the crowd to another tower across the way, where another rescue shuttle, apparently full and with plenty left behind, withdrew its struts and made to take off. Its engines spun up as the shuttle's front jets pushed the cylinder vertical. Hot fire spewed from the engines, and the cylinder began its climb.

The shuttle's light came so bright that Sai didn't notice it at first, but he caught the millisecond flash as, from another tower, a rocket flared. The shot streaked towards the lifting shuttle, struck the craft just below center. A rippling boom gave way to a crackling, sparking rise as the shuttle continued thrusting.

The rocket, though, had knocked the shuttle off its course, tilting the ship towards . . . them.

Sai's mother reacted first, grabbing Sai's hand and pulling him away from the ledge, back towards the tower's rooftop access, the stairs leading down, even as the crowd surged towards their own shuttle.

Sai didn't have a chance to scream, to ask about his dad, before his mother threw them both to the ground and the stricken shuttle hit their own. Sai couldn't see what happened then, but later, watching historical recordings, he saw the damaged shuttle's nose strike the midpoint of their own. The nose pierced and then pushed their shuttle off its base, turning it over and thrusting it all the way off the side of the tower.

The wounded shuttle's engines began breaking apart as the collision added to the rocket attack's stress, sending the burning nacelles spinning down to the tower's ceiling, directly into the scattering crowd.

"Don't look," Sai's mother said. "Crawl. Keep moving. With me now."

Sai kept down with his mother as they went back towards the stairwell. Heat brushed his back, burned at his clothes, but the tremendous rending, crunching, hissing noises coming from the disaster blocked the screams. Smoke singed Sai's eyes, burned his throat, and the tower's roof scratched his hands as he pulled himself along, after his mother, towards a home no longer his.

"DO you always talk so much in your sleep?" the woman asked Sai, jarring him away from the rooftop into a small, bright and empty room.

A smiling, icy-eyed woman stood over him, one finger on her chin and the other holding a long syringe with something off-white in it.

Sai could feel his arms and legs, could feel the restraints holding them fast. Nothing cloaked his face, and while Sai could feel residual aches from the skiff crash, from the fight with the infected, in general he felt good. Really, really good.

"Where am I?" Sai managed.

"That wasn't my question." The woman reached down, pulled up the thin sleeve on Sai's right arm. Looked and felt like some sort of cheap gown. "One more time. Do you always talk so much in your sleep?"

"What? Why does that matter?" Sai said, straining to sit up, to see what she was going to do. "What's in that? What're you doing?"

The woman stopped, pressed her hand against Sai's forearm, and turned a somehow more rigid smile at him. "Answer the question, please."

"What, do I talk in my sleep?" Sai said. "How should I know? I'm sleeping!"

The woman nodded, her eyes flicking towards the ceiling, "Of course. That makes sense. We'll observe over the next few days and see if the virus makes any changes to that behavior."

"The virus?"

Sai felt the prick as the woman stuck the needle into his

arm, just above his elbow. Felt the strange rush as the foreign liquid entered his body, ran along his veins and vessels.

"Yes," the woman pulled the syringe away. "We've spent the last few hours building you up. Now you are healthy enough for us to see whether a DefenseCorp soldier can handle our latest generation." That icy smile threatened to falter, but the woman hid it behind a look towards what Sai assumed was his cell's entrance, a glass door spreading from wall to wall. "If not, then my job becomes so much more difficult."

Sai wanted to say he didn't understand, wanted to get more from this woman, but he knew what he'd fought against in that room. Knew the strange creatures present in this tower, and he could guess where they'd come from, where he might be going.

And what his children might have just lost.

"Sai," the woman continued. "My name is Dr. Anaskya. I will be watching you, and listening. If you wouldn't mind, after I am gone, please continue to talk. I would love to hear the end of your story, and if we can understand how the virus impacts your dream speak, so much the better."

Sai, though, barely heard her. He lay back on the thin pillow, stared at the ceiling, and felt the infection spread like hot fire.

Shopping Trip

If Gregor calculated his life spent with or without armor, a gut-level estimate suggested it'd be lopsided in armor's favor. Spending his youth mining cold comet rock with potential for vacuum exposure, and his adult life in various combat zones, meant wandering out into city streets with nothing more than a thin active-wear outfit felt very strange.

At least Dynas, with its humid, swampy climate, kept him warm. And Gregor had long since rendered himself, through so many missteps and clunky statements, incapable of blushing, so as faces turned his way, he broadcast a big grin. A confident, strong, half-naked man appearing from a closed tram station—what was so unusual about that?

Apparently, everything.

Emerging from the tram station, especially coming from the marsh and monster-ridden outskirts, put Gregor's faux smile to the test. He'd served on urban planets before, spent his time in obscure backwaters on DefenseCorp assignments, but this place didn't seem to know which it was, or wanted to be.

Coming off the tram, down in the station, the whole group had confirmed how wet everything seemed to be here. The high humidity glazed tiles, walls, rails and stairs. Things were even worse up on the surface; leaving the station meant stepping onto a watery sidewalk, tilted ever so slightly to run the moisture into large, yellowed troughs bordering the narrow street edges.

The blotched black buildings adopted similar philosophies, arranging themselves into slopes and funnels so that the perennial wetness would drip and drop into designed points and keep the people walking by dry. Rather than blocky, flat roofs, everything ended in angles, as if someone had built a city from spears.

The streets, too, sloped from the middle towards the troughs, and at a steep enough angle that Gregor wondered what sort of vehicles might drive here, until he noticed the lines strung between the buildings. Cable cars, then. Dangling above the wet.

The tram station opened onto an intersection, a cable's nest directly above for the cars to somehow navigate. Crosswalks, for the few people Gregor saw, were grated, studded metal laying over the slanted roadways. All in all, a marvel and a mess.

Dynas didn't seem conducive to civilized life, and yet here this place existed. Bending all the rules, just to mess with the galaxy's genetic code.

Gregor held up a hand towards the nearest person, one of a half-dozen in sight. This one had just crossed the intersection and paused when Gregor left. An older man, though Gregor couldn't be sure, given the respirator the man wore over his face. The device connected to a tank on the man's back, linked up to what looked like a wetsuit.

"Going for a dive?" Gregor said, and the man cocked his head, then walked over Gregor's way.

"Are you sick or something?" the man replied, the respirator distorting the voice. "Where's your mask?"

"Lost it," Gregor said. "Down there." He pointed back towards the tram station. "Can you help get it back?"

As compelling stories went, Gregor was well aware he couldn't tell them worth a damn. He wasn't a liar, wasn't a tale-spinner. The man seemed to agree.

"Lost it?" Now the man backed up a step. "What're you doing down there anyway? That station's closed."

"Work. Things went wrong."

"Then get yourself to a hospital," the man swept his mask over Gregor. "Before you get yourself killed."

Well, that didn't go well. The man turned his back on Gregor, started to walk away. Sever needed an outfit, at least one, so Gregor reached out, grabbed the man's arm and pulled him back into the station's entrance.

The man resisted, a slight tug against Gregor's over-whelming force. Warm water splashed as the man tried to back-pedal, tried to slip free, but Gregor knew how to keep hold. Get that grip just right above the elbow, clench down hard and keep moving.

What didn't happen, what Gregor expected but never came, was a cry for help. Other than muttered curses, complaints, the man didn't shout or scream. And as soon as Gregor pulled the man behind the entrance, near the metal door sealing away the tram itself, Aurora blitzed the unlucky citizen with a nerve-stunning bolt from her rifle.

"THAT WASN'T REAL ELEGANT," Rovo said as they went about removing the man's suit, revealing ratty underclothes spotted with mold. "How many people saw you?"

"Some, but I do not think they cared," Gregor replied, prying off the mask and revealing, indeed, a wrinkled and weathered face beneath. "This is a strange place, and I do not like it."

"That makes two of us," Rovo replied. "Look at this mask. It's a full-on respirator. Filtered oxygen, total block on incoming air. Did you see anyone else with these?"

"Masks, yes," Gregor said. "Everyone. Not the full tanks."

"The people we fought at the outpost wore suits too," Aurora replied, peeling off the man's boots. "But our armor said the atmosphere here was safe. So what are we missing?"

"Safe based on our garbage intel," Rovo said. "New planet, new rules. We don't know what's in the air here, but apparently it's worth avoiding."

The man's wetsuit could have fit either Gregor or Rovo. They obviously needed two more outfits, and after the joy spent smuggling one hapless citizen off the streets, the trio agreed on a softer approach: two would wait at the tram station with their armor on, filtering away, while the third would go in search of a place to buy outfits for the others.

"You are smaller," Gregor said to Rovo. "Less threatening, it should be you. Nobody notices a mouse."

"Yeah, except I'm busy," Rovo replied. "I've been cracking into the communications buzzing around here, and I'm getting close." He tapped the man's respirator. "Unless you can do that, I think I'm better used that way."

"Are you calling me useless, rookie?"

"No, I'm saying I trust you to buy clothes from a store."

"Ah."

"Let's go," Aurora stepped in. "Rovo, help me drag this

guy to the utility closet. We'll lock him in there. Gregor, suit up and get going. I'm sick of being down here, and we're losing time."

MINUTES LATER, feeling squeezed tight with a too-small wetsuit on and the respirator over his face, Gregor went back to the streets. They'd found other things on the man, including, in a thin, sealable pocket in the wetsuit's chest, what looked like a corporatized ID card. The man's picture and various account numbers etched across it, along with contact information if the card happened to be found.

Gregor had seen cards like this before—the comet company had issued them. Meant to hold your whole identity, including your cash. The people holding these were meant to spend whatever they earned at company stores, a closed economy. The card answered another question about the city: it wasn't a free society, but a working one, captive to their corporate masters.

Back on the surface, Gregor tromped along the street, making a straight line away from the tram station to keep any route-finding easy. Now that he wasn't just searching for victims, Gregor saw the city coming to a sort of life.

Stores were opening as the morning rolled into serviceable hours. Those cable cars, built like ovals but with dripping guides funneling the wet away, trundled by Gregor as he walked, loaded with people in various wetsuits and rain coats.

The stores all had their own names, but every single one also happened to have the same logo just behind their labels, an infinity symbol drawn with DNA's double-helix. Inside, goods ran the gamut, though inventory seemed sparse. Prices high.

A secret planet, a secret society equaled high shipping costs.

The first shop he found that sold wetsuits and rain coats offered, more prominently, repairs. Another sensible move with limited supply; keep your gear in good shape rather than buy new. Back on Snowball, you kept your same armor until you outgrew it or you died.

Gregor passed through a double door to get into the store, a simple glass chamber between them serving to blow away the moisture. Inside, cool, filtered air blasted Gregor's face as he pulled off the mask and stared at rain coat racks to the right, wet suits to the left.

"You're early," said a voice, that, when she rose from behind a counter covered with stitching and sealing equipment, belonged to a younger girl. "Aren't you supposed to be at work?"

"I am a customer?" Gregor said. Supposed to be at work? He didn't know this girl.

The clerk pointed at Gregor's wetsuit. "Your shift started an hour ago."

"It did?"

Now the girl's face changed, from curiosity to an eyes-widening fear. She turned, reached for something beneath the desk, but before she got there, Gregor lunged through the store and, for the second time in as many hours, gripped an arm and held it still.

"Don't touch anything," Gregor whispered, then snuck a quick glance towards the back of the store. A door there, but nobody else in sight. "This does not need to be difficult."

Gregor felt the girl shiver, felt her try to pull away from him.

"You're one of them, aren't you?" she said. "They said some had escaped the quarantine."

"What quarantine?" Gregor said. "I only want some clothes."

"You mean, you're not infected?"

Ah. That would make sense. If this city knew about Felix and his diseased hovel out there in the swamp, no wonder they would be afraid. Who would want to end up like that?

"I am a visitor, that is all," Gregor said. "I mean no harm."

"Then let go of my wrist?"

"You will not make me regret it?"

The girl shook her head, looked at Gregor's hand, and huffed a half-sob. "You're here. That's punishment enough."

FOUR

Traitor's Mark

THE TRAITOR SLEPT in the tower. In a muddy yellow room appointed with galaxy-spanning art, with line lights curling across the ceiling in patterns that suggested a brighter, more whimsical present than the one Eponi lived in. Dreamed in.

Despaired in.

She didn't think it would be this bad. Sever hadn't ever been a family, not really, not formally. Their missions were too edged, their members too busted up and broken to get along outside the tight briefings and battle lines. At least, Eponi had always thought so: she flew the other four in, let'em raise hell, then picked them up and soared back to the stars.

Until she'd seen Sai, with all those weapons pointed at him, and his armored face looking right at her. Through that metal, that glass, Sai's disappointment had seared her, and Eponi had spent the rest of the night drinking herself into a stupor, sealed away in this room with a bottle of raw sewage that nonetheless did the job. Dynas's own distilled sludge, a brownish bourbon variant, leered at Eponi from the nightstand, a half-filled tumbler resting on the yellowed, metal table.

Without her armor, with her other gadgets long taken from her, Eponi resorted to the room's actual clock on a tiny screen bolted to the wall that also told her the temp (hot), humidity (drenching), and weather (foggy). The time, past eight in the morning now, said that Eponi needed to get up. Needed to figure out what she could do with her life.

As a racer, spinning through the galaxy's circuits, she'd made countless split second decisions. Not just whether to go left or right, over or under, but which brand to support, who to sign on with, whether you could trust a race course to actually deliver the winner's purse when Eponi crossed that line.

Eponi looked through the closet, filled with stock-standard uniforms in the company's black-and-gray color scheme, and chose one at random. She could put on this uniform, embrace her new role as insider informant and help the people running this planet round up Sever, or she could . . .

What? What else could she do? Eponi didn't have any weapons, didn't have any secret knowledge of a super bomb she could turn on its creators. No contacts she could radio for support—given what she'd seen here, Eponi already thought DefenseCorp's no knowledge briefing stank like bullshit.

The uniform proved floppy, but workable enough. Cleaning up in the bathroom distracted Eponi for a few minutes, though she kept avoiding her own eyes in the wall-spanning mirror. No shampoo, no hair brush, or anything beyond a faucet and some towels for the shower made the ritual a short one.

Sever's mission had them rescuing a VIP, then getting

the whole squad off planet and to . . . somewhere. From what Eponi had seen when she and Sai had rammed a skiff into this gigantic building, the one thing this place might have that she could use would be a ship. She could pull some gambit like in a movie, steal the craft from under the evil-doer's noses and race to the rescue.

More likely, she'd make it to the controls, some security would disable the ship, and then Eponi would get summarily executed with a shot to the head seconds later. Hardly a heroic death, and Eponi didn't want death of any kind.

Her room had one main door, a single affair that, from Eponi's recollection, led out into an apartment-style hallway filled with other doors. Eponi couldn't test that recollection because, when she tried it, the door didn't open. The push-button meant to release the thing didn't respond. After trying it a couple times, Eponi wandered over towards the window, which only showed Dynas's endless yellow mist.

Trapped. Alone with her thoughts. Not ideal, because being alone with her turmoil would drive Eponi to—

The door shot open. A man she'd never seen stood there, uniformed like her—though his fit better—and holding two small branded cups.

"Coffee?" the man said, holding one cup out to her.

Eponi tried to read the branding, but the logo obscured any words. A spiral of sorts, with twinning, swirling lines that looped across each other. Like DNA, maybe?

Her eyes flicked to the ceiling, confirmed that the lights matched. Okay. So there was some method to the design here, even if Eponi didn't know what the shapes meant.

"Thanks," Eponi offered as she raised the cup to her nose, smelled it. Definitely coffee. Warm, but not too hot.

Could be poison, but Eponi laughed that idea away, drawing a quizzical look from the man. Why would they poison her when they could've shot her already? Why put Eponi up in a room at all when they could've tossed her off the balcony, locked her in with Sai?

She took a long drink. Enjoyed, for the first time in a long while, coffee that came from something better than DefenseCorp's mass produced product. In fact, the earthy, nutty coffee seemed way too good for Dynas. More evidence that this place had backers beyond its backwater status.

"Like it?" the man said.

"Sure," Eponi replied. "So what're you supposed to be? My caretaker?"

"Not really," the man replied, then stuck out his coffee cup, tapped it against hers. "The name's Ben Taigo, and I volunteered for this."

"And what is 'this'?"

"That's what I'm trying to figure out," Ben said. Eponi noticed Ben had been very careful to not come more than a step into her room, as if following some strict code. "Most of us know that a group attacked us yesterday at a fringe site. There's a lot of hurt, angry people right now."

Eponi drank her coffee. Watched Ben. He didn't have any visible weapons. The door had stayed open. If she wanted to, Eponi could launch the coffee into his face, lead in with a strike and then break for freedom. Maybe take Ben's ID card with her, use it to get up—

"You hearing me?" Ben said, sharper. "I'm saying it's not real safe for you here, even with the tops offering protection."

"Is that supposed to scare me?" Eponi folded her arms.

"A racer like you? Guess not?"

"Wait, you know I'm a racer?"

"Of course I know! That's why I'm here!" Ben broke his code, wandered into the room, arms going all over the place. "I remember you, this hot shot going places, burning up the charts and then nothing! Rumors hit the waves for a long time, everyone assumed you'd crashed, or just decided you didn't want to do it anymore, and suddenly you're here?"

"Don't think it was that sudden."

Eponi looked at her coffee to keep from blushing. She hadn't been around fans for a while, was a little out of practice.

"Maybe not for you," Ben whirled back her way. "Here's the thing, Eponi, when you're on a planet like this, where they keep the waves restricted, everything's a surprise. So here you are, coming in as a . . . mercenary or something?"

"A pilot. The pay's more regular."

"But way less exciting, right?"

"Don't know about that," Eponi said. "So, Ben, thanks for the coffee, but you think there might be some food somewhere to go with this?"

"Sure, right," Ben laughed. "Going to warn you, though. Food's not that great here right now. Been a lid on most shipments, so we're hitting the cheap rations."

"A lid? Why?"

"Isn't that why you're here? Whatever gang you flew in with?" Ben said, leading Eponi out of the room, into the hallway, as if they were the chummiest pals to ever live. "We're having issues with some of our treatments. They're not staying contained, so the tops don't want a lot of traffic right now."

"And you think I'm related to this?"

"Why wouldn't you be? Some sort of inspection team coming to see what's cooking on Dynas? Get out with the evidence and then we get burned to ash from orbit. That's the plan, right?"

Eponi tried to keep up with Ben's verve. The man had swerved from fan to feisty real quick. So far as Eponi knew, as Aurora had said, the briefing began and ended with the VIP and getting him off world. Nothing about a bombardment. Then again, from what she'd seen with the diseased things Sai had fought, maybe Dynas deserved a good laser scrubbing.

"Look, Ben, maybe I need more coffee to keep up with you," Eponi said as they reached the elevators. "I fly ships and I do it well. I'm not in some scheme, and don't want to be."

The lift's circular doors swooshed open seconds later and Ben led Eponi inside. Tapped his card against a panel next to the door. The screen pulled up a list of his common destinations, denoted by a blaze-orange title at the screen's top, and Ben tapped the one showing a fork and knife.

"Right, just a pilot," Ben said. "Here's the thing, Eponi, and it's a big one, so listen close. This place has a lot of problems, and they're only getting worse. We need help. I need help. And I think, I hope, and man, Eponi, I *believe* that you are the one to provide."

"Is there something wrong with you?" Eponi backed away from him, towards the lift's opposite side.

"What do you mean? That maybe we're all a little nuts, being stuck on this world for years with diseases that get deadlier by the day? How would that mess with anyone?" Ben delved deep into a shuddering laugh, then shook his head. Took a big breath. "Sorry, sorry. Sometimes it all just gets to me, you know?"

"Sure." Eponi did not know. Did not care to know. "How am I supposed to help?"

"You're a pilot, Eponi. I need you to get me outta here, before Dynas kills us both."

FIVE

Cutting Across Town

THERE WERE jobs and there were careers and there were smart decisions and there were stupid decisions. Rovo, his father said, had picked none of those options by deciding to move into DefenseCorp's more active arm. A desk junky who had a stable life floating over his homeward transferring interstellar communications to their proper parties, Rovo had done the unthinkable:

Rovo had given up a safe, decent life in a galaxy that didn't offer many.

Walking in a wetsuit through a diseased city on a backwater world with few friends and many enemies had Rovo giving his father points. While excitement had been the goal, Rovo had found getting close to death didn't really add much to life.

Things weren't brighter, more fulfilling just because lasers had scored metal close to Rovo's skull. Instead, Rovo found himself twitching more, looking around all the time, sure some hidden sniper or diseased figure loomed behind the next shadow waiting to pounce.

Gregor had returned with two wetsuits and a disturbed

look on his face, a menacing visage for such a big man. He'd talked about the shopkeeper, how she'd pulled herself together enough to sell him the clothes before asking, at the end, for Sever to take her off world with them when they left.

"I told her we would," Gregor said, "but it felt bad to lie to someone so desperate."

"If we get the VIP off world, she might get her wish anyway," Aurora said. "There's enough illegal garbage here to get some cleansing intervention."

Rovo kept quiet during that conversation. He'd seen those orders come across his terminal; when planets grew too unruly, when populations presented too large a danger to the established galactic order, neighboring systems would pay DefenseCorp to solve the problem. Defense-Corp would show up with an angry fleet, demand ridiculous concessions with bristling weapons to back them up.

Half the time the people would come to their senses, take the hit and crawl back to their hideaways, usually with DefenseCorp securing another big contract to bring in a brutal police force until the planet's old owners put everyone back in their economic chains.

The other half . . . DefenseCorp billed a lot of cash for population wipes, but the profits looked good on the balance sheet. Rovo wouldn't mind repressing those documents from his memory.

Maybe he'd replace them with what he saw now, a soaked city with shadowed people huddling through the streets, looking defeated, haunted, or, rarely, resolute. Like Fate had come and everyone had accepted it.

Aurora led them along the sidewalks, heading towards the VIP's signal position. She'd popped the wristlet computer free from her armor, cut a slit along her wetsuit so she could peel the cover up and look at the directions every few blocks. Not that the thing had a true map, but Sever had north, south, east and west. In a gridded-out, rigid city like this, that was enough.

Rovo trailed, giving space between him and Gregor, and Gregor did the same with Aurora to keep it plausible they were separate citizens trudging along towards whatever end. After the first blocks proved dull—Rovo couldn't stay interested in the dark buildings, their endless gutters and dripping spouts—he went back to the pet project: break the city's encryption.

Transmissions flew around at a frenetic pace, each one buzzing in his ear, as Rovo's Bug, a tiny transmitter in his ear that synced to Rovo's own wristlet computer, picked them up and tried to parse their encoding. Sometimes one would use the same scheme as the skiff guards at the outpost and Rovo would get a clear burst, some comment about an ongoing patrol or a potential problem here or there.

Too many others, though, played along a different band, at a higher frequency beyond most traditional receiver ranges. DefenseCorp used this level for more sensitive communications, for operations in progress. Sever's own signals went out up here, though Aurora had cut those after they left the tram station.

If Sai or Eponi had finally decided to call out, they'd get silence now.

Rovo, rubbing away on the Bug's program, adjusted the machine's parameters as he walked. Meant to be used without sight, in stealth situations, the Bug relied on a direct interface through his armor or through a more manual, but more fun, process. Using his fingers, Rovo could adjust the specific frequencies the Bug heard, and the cypher the device used to break the encryption on any messages it caught.

Like solving a puzzle by turning a marble, trying to find the rough spot on a smooth sphere.

Solving this one took the entire morning plus six blocks walking in wetsuits, but when Rovo caught the first clear burst, a sharp instruction to get more players in the field, the endorphin rush made all the effort worth it. He wanted to run up to Aurora, to Gregor, tell them they could hear everything now.

Instead, he used the signal they'd discussed, and splashed into a street side puddle, like someone who'd tripped and lost their footing.

Aurora didn't turn back, but took a hard right, heading into a small restaurant on the corner. Gregor, glancing back at Rovo, followed her. And Rovo followed him. Not exactly high level spy craft—anyone watching would, no doubt, find it strange that three people in a row had gone into the same place. The restaurant staff, going by their looks, sure didn't expect them.

When he came through the door, a glass thing beneath a scooped overhang diverting water to the sides, Rovo saw Aurora and Gregor sharing a table with room for more. A bit surprising, but Aurora caught his eyes and nodded next to her.

Breaking the stealth game entirely, then.

"You cracked the code?" Aurora said, without even a hint of thanks.

"Yeah," Rovo said, sliding the metal chair against the sealed tile and taking his seat. "Something's got them riled up."

"Us." Gregor picked up the menu.

An actual printed menu. Rovo hadn't seen one outside of movies. Everywhere he'd been, DefenseCorp ships included, just projected things on tables or tablets. Easier to change, less manufacturing. Except, he supposed, on a planet so divorced from supply chains that paper and laminating plastic were easier to come by.

"Anything coming through?" Aurora asked.

In fact, there had been. During the short time from stumble to entering the restaurant, Rovo had heard more quips across the waves. After the call for more players, there'd been a general warning to keep things tight, that the people responsible for the accident out on outpost twenty-three hadn't been found.

"Not a big leap to guess that's where we were," Rovo said.

"We expected this," Aurora said. "We're close to the VIP's signal now. We move fast, they won't have time to catch us."

So fast, they didn't bother eating. Stood up on Aurora's signal, broke from the restaurant, out across the soaking sidewalk and right onto one of the cable cars that'd pulled up, stopping to let a couple sopping people off.

Nobody bothered collecting any payment for hopping on, and Rovo didn't see a driver. All automated. The cable car's inside had crowds, and ceiling fans blowing across them all. The day's heat had come on strong, and the open windows meant the fans didn't do a whole lot to cool things down. But Sever was moving.

And they'd been noticed.

Rovo's Bug picked up more transmissions. A cafe reporting a strange trio that came in apart and left rapidly together. Boarded a cable car, all in cheap wetsuits.

Cheap? Rovo glanced down at himself, compared his to the others on the tram. Sure, some suits had casings for wristlets and other computers, had emblems or insignias blazing along chests and sleeves, or fit better than his squelchy, tight thing, but cheap?

"They're onto us," Rovo whispered to Aurora, who

didn't look quite so intimidating in her own suit, until she looked his way.

"I know," Aurora replied. "There's one in this car. Three people back."

"Can I look?"

"No."

Rovo kept his eyes forward. The crowd kept the Sever trio towards the cable car's front, and at the very next stop, two blocks away from the restaurant, Aurora dragged them off again. She kept them moving as they hit the sidewalk, muttering again to Rovo to keep his eyes forward.

When the cable car pulled away, its splashes were replaced by smaller ones, following theirs. Could be a normal pedestrian. A citizen going about their day, maybe to grab an early lunch. Or . . .

"Cutting," Gregor, to Rovo's right, said, and the man crouched, as if he'd stumbled.

Rovo looked over, wondering, in time to see a following, uniformed man stop dead in the sidewalk. Unlike the guards back at the outpost, whose military-grade gear didn't bother with corporate logos, this guy had a thick, black-blue raincoat and matching pants. A big, weird helix shown in white on his chest.

"Rovo, run," Aurora hissed, and she took off as Gregor erupted from his kneel, twisting back and delivering a long jab right into the tailing man's face.

Rovo gaped as the man hit the ground, limbs akimbo and so very unconscious. Then Aurora grabbed Rovo's arm and pulled him along, sprinting through puddles as the Bug intercepted one coming disaster after another.

SIX

The VIP

Aurora's first mission with Sever, as the squad's newest rookie, had been on Pledea Four's scorched surface. She'd landed along with a whole DefenseCorp contingent, paid for by corporate mining interests that wanted Pledea Four cleared out for their machines.

And what did they want cleared away?

The prospectors, the species and humans that'd come before and found the diamonds and harder gems beneath the blue lava floes. The ones that'd declared the claims for their own and that, legally speaking, had every right to keep them. What that same rabble didn't have, though, was the right to declare the whole planet off limits to corporate interests. Once the prospectors started sabotaging the big machines and poisoning any representatives that came to visit, their days were numbered.

Aurora had heard the prospectors had offered Defense-Corp a cut from the metals they mined, said to be worth more than what DefenseCorp would make from this cleansing. But not worth more than the relationships, than a galaxy filled with contracts.

So Aurora, Sever, and other squads had stormed into prospector villages and, threatening deadly force, asked the prospectors to leave. Except they found nobody. Aurora, assault rifle raised and ready, heat shields up as she wandered through Sever's designated, makeshift mechanical camp, only saw remnants. Abandoned terminals, some supplies, but not panic.

The prospectors hadn't run. Or, they had, but not in a hurry. Meals hadn't been left half-eaten to bake in Pledea Four's black-rock surface, under its ashen sky, glowing an eerie blue from the lava lines marking its surface.

Word went around that all the camps were empty. DefenseCorp had the planet blockaded, so the prospectors could only have gone down. Underground, into all that heat, to their conflict's source. Aurora's commander hadn't hesitated: with their armor, Sever could take the heat, so away they marched, into the mine and down.

With thick rock on all sides supported by fabricated steel cross-beams and yellow, geothermal-powered lights, the mine tunnels weren't all that unpleasant. While, compared with corporate efforts, Aurora found the occasional loose wires and smudged supports unsettling, the overall effort seemed to discredit the idea that these miners were haphazard, dirty and unorganized.

As they went deeper, Sever passed organized break points, hollowed chambers packed with supplies and ready to protect miners in case lava leaked or some gas ruptured. Professional, quality. The sight had Aurora feeling a little sick, a little scared.

But rookies, so her commander had said, needed to keep quiet and learn. So Aurora said nothing, followed the pack with her rifle raised, looking for someone to shoot.

Communications across the surface fizzled and vanished as Sever went deeper, as the other squads descended into their own mines. Cut off and out of touch, Sever's commander finally acknowledged, deep and surrounded by rock, that the mission hadn't been going according to plan.

Keep cautious, stay alive.

The objective stayed the same.

Six meters split Aurora and Sever's leading man, a big guy like Gregor who preferred explosive launchers. They approached another widening in the tunnel when the lead stopped, held up his hand for the squad to follow suit. Aurora performed her rear-guard role and turned back around, shining her rifle's light back up the tunnel.

The prospector's mounted lights went out, and Sever's suits compensated, shoulder and knee lights flaring on to give a clear, refined white view. Just in time to see, hear rumbles go off from above. Pocket explosions, detonating rock and collapsing tunnels.

Aurora dove to the floor as the booms and bangs continued, as her squad shouted over their comm channel and rocks pounded them. A billion tons were going to fall on their backs.

Run.

The command came clear, though later Aurora wouldn't, couldn't be sure anyone in Sever had actually said it. Maybe it'd been her body, her mind telling her that sitting in the collapsing mine would lead to a quick death. That she had to move.

She jammed her feet against the shifting floor and pushed, picked herself up and ran upwards as rocks slammed and fell against her, shoved her to the side or tripped her. Somewhere along the way she dropped her rifle so she could use both hands, scrambling her way through the dark falling rock.

Ahead, at what had once been a boring stretch, the

tunnel looked like it had disappeared. A bright, blue glow rose up, shimmering with heat. Aurora clambered to the edge, looked down into a wide blue lava river. Beautiful, instant death.

Looking at the gap, Aurora's helmet calculated three meters. Her boosters took the appropriate kinetic energy from her suit's batteries, and Aurora jumped off as her ledge crumbled away. A suited up soldier like her wasn't meant to fly, but here, deep beneath the surface, she flew. High and far enough to smash against the tunnel's roof, scraping against it and bouncing back to the floor.

Aurora dug out the last meters to the surface, following the ramshackle trail of collapsed beams and her helmet's depth calculation to get back, to escape. She'd thought she was alone, but moments later, from her same hole, two other Sever members made it, the three of them standing alone around the collapsed mine, blue lava rising up around them.

DefenseCorp cleansed the planet from orbit after that. Erased the settlements, burned down the mines, and handed Pledea Four to the corporations clean and ready.

AURORA WAS STARTING to hope the same thing would happen here. She slipped and slid along the slick sidewalk as she sprinted with Rovo behind her. At the next intersection, Aurora took a hard right, every breath feeling like inhaling a swamp in Dynas's infernal humidity. Again, water flowed away from her feet and splashed around.

How Dynas could be so wet with zero rain—the day seemed foggy, though far from the choking mist that'd cloaked Dynas outside the city—left Aurora incredulous. She understood, now, why everyone they passed on these streets seemed depressed; even without runaway bioweapons like Felix, Dynas was miserable.

A path away from that misery loomed on Aurora's right as she continued running down the block. A lit sign showcased a bottle, a plate and something like a burger on it. With a quick glance back to confirm Rovo still followed, and that nobody followed him, Aurora ducked through the cooling, anti-humidity entrance and then inside the bar proper.

"Why here?" Rovo asked as soon as he caught up with Aurora, who'd stopped just inside the entrance, catching her breath. "This can't be the best hiding spot."

"It's where we need to be," Aurora said.

A few others shared that idea, taking up tables or bar spots in a joint that embraced Dynas's far flung locale with approximately zero decorations. Screens by the dozen littered every wall, tuned into everything. Enough to make someone unused to the chaos go insane. At least they were all muted, so the only noise came from conversations, from the kitchen calls saying this or that was ready. Late breakfast in full swing.

Aurora focused on a single man at the bar's far end. A short, thin guy, wearing a poncho and sipping on what looked like fruit juice and something stronger, the man hadn't turned his head their way yet.

"That's him?" Rovo followed Aurora's look.

"That's our guy," Aurora replied. "Looks real desperate, doesn't he?"

"Not really."

Exactly, and Aurora hated pointless missions. If this guy had called in Sever just because he'd become bored with his life choices, if he'd decided Dynas wasn't where he wanted to be and, because he had the cash, wanted a fiery ticket out, then Aurora would be sharing some harsh words. Some harsh fists, too.

"You're them, aren't you?" the man said, looking over as Aurora and Rovo took seats next to him. "I received the confirmation that you were coming. When everyone started freaking out, I assumed you'd arrived."

"They're after us already," Aurora said, "and they know we're here."

"Of course they do," the man replied. "The whole city heard about your entrance."

"We don't do quiet," Aurora said. "DefenseCorp sent us because you called for an extraction, and that there'd be resistance."

"And there's been resistance," Rovo added.

"Hey," the man called past Aurora and Rovo, to the bartender. "Can we get another round? Three more of what I'm having."

The bartender gave a nod back that he'd heard.

"What are you having, and can we have it somewhere safer?" Aurora said. "They're going to find us here."

"Of course," the man replied. "Perhaps your ship? On our way off world?"

"Don't have a ship," Aurora said. "We need to steal one."

The man laughed, a bitter, hopeless sound, then guzzled his first drink empty.

"If you don't have a ship, then we're all dead." The man reached down, patted a cloth-covered case Aurora hadn't noticed he was sitting on. "See, the people that run this place want this, and they'll kill you to get it. Kill me too, once they find out I have it."

"I don't care about the why," Aurora said. "Our job is to get you out. To do that, I need to know two things: do you have a safer place we can go, and do you have a name?"

"A name? Sure, it's Kashmal." The bartender dropped the three drinks next to them, and Kashmal grabbed his. "As for a safe place, my apartment works. Nobody gives a damn about me."

"Then let's go," Aurora said, standing up.

"Whoa, wait." Kashmal gestured towards the drinks. "Drink up. Then I'll let you in before I get going."

"Going where?" Rovo asked.

"To work, obviously." Kashmal's teeth glittered as he grinned. "Gotta keep up appearances when you're stealing from the bosses."

Aurora tried to think of what to say. Tried to reconcile why Sever had been sent to this hellish planet, put in danger, all to help a drunk thief. What had Deepak, DefenseCorp been thinking to take this on?

Instead, Aurora grabbed her drink, raised it to her lips and sent it down.

SEVEN

Captain Happy

SAI HAD RUN up these stairs countless times growing up, always aiming for the rooftop and its view over his home city, the green mountains in the distance, and the broad sky above. Now he ran down them, his mother close behind, beating a desperate crowd and the hungry flames that followed.

The stairs themselves, heavy emerald-green steps, shook as explosions continued above and distant attacks struck down below. A riot and rebellion in full force, dragging civilization into the depths with it.

Not that Sai cared overmuch about those things when putting one foot in front of the other meant survival. He jumped several steps at a time, hit the next landing and rebounded off the wall, zipping down the next stair with panic-driven alacrity.

"Sai!" His mother's voice pierced that focus veil, stripping away his zen acrobatics and causing a stumble as Sai hit the next landing.

Back against the wall, looking upward and breathing hard, Sai saw his mother, still carrying that damn katana, round the landing above him, her cropped black hair flying out as orange light cast down. Ash sprinkled around them, punctuated by the occasional larger, falling piece. Other families pushed and shoved behind Sai's mom, faltering and falling or keeping upright and desperate. Screams, shouts, it all blended together.

As his mom descended the next stair, the crowd reached her. Faster and more frantic people pushed her aside, and Sai watched as his mother lifted the katana, holding it up like a beacon to keep people from banging into it.

"Take it!" Sai's mother shouted, a voice that wasn't louder than the rest but that Sai heard anyway, clear and strong.

And even if he hadn't, when she threw the katana to the side, down another stair ahead of the people, Sai would have understood: Get the sword and get going.

He took the steps fast, scooped up the sheathed sword and kept running, using his mother's training to keep his feet fleet while people behind him crashed and toppled into each other.

Sai would wait for his mother another dozen floors down, back at their apartment. The one he'd already said goodbye to an hour earlier, back when the universe only seemed mostly insane. Before his father had been blown apart in a rocket attack on their ride to safety.

No time for memories now.

Sai kept going, sucking in air, keeping the sword balanced, and jumping from one step to the next. When he reached their floor, Sai barged through into the hall leading to their apartment. Behind him, the crowd surged past, continuing to ramble towards the bottom and the war waiting for them there.

Sai stopped in the hall and stared at the people

streaming by, sword in his arms. Waiting, watching for his mother to arrive. Fear, excitement, and grief's first touches flooding every nerve.

His mother would survive that crowd. She had to.

TIME PASSED SLOW when you had fire burning you up from the inside. Sai didn't move, barely breathed as the virus Anaskya injected spread. On a flat cot, without sheets and a pillow's barest fraction, Sai alternated between closing his eyes and opening them when terrible dreams, despair, and all that went with both threatened to steal away with his mind.

Sai gazed at the gray steel tile and pushed away the falling tower, the crowd, the katana and everything that went with it. Now was no time for memories, for falling back into them. He needed to focus, to understand what this thing was doing to his body and try to find some way to counteract it, or, at least, see what he could do with it. Whether he could get out.

"Time to get moving," a cheery voice said, and a moon-shaped man's face appeared over Sai's head. "Are you feeling it all over yet?"

"It hurts."

"Good, it'll do that. For a while. Then maybe it won't!" The man smiled, then frowned. "C'mon, get up. Time to go."

"Where?" Sai pushed through a test to his legs, his abs, his arms. The muscles weren't thrilled, but they could move. Could twitch. "Why?"

"We ask the questions, you provide the answers," the man replied, as if Sai had asked what he'd be getting for his birthday. "Move, please. Or I will move you, and you won't like that."

"I'm going," Sai grunted, then pushed himself to the cot's side, the big man making room.

Moving felt like sliding a solid around a pool, with the solid being the virus and Sai's body the water sloshing around it. Not in a nauseous way, but more like a great, hot radius sliding throughout Sai's blood. Standing up sent the effect towards his legs and below, while his chest and arms trembled, sweat with the heat's sudden absence.

"What's happening to me?" Sai said. "The woman didn't explain."

The moon man slapped Sai before he could react, a hard blow across the face, followed by a pat on Sai's cheek, a lesson delivered to a child.

"No questions!" the moon man chirped. "Now let's go. Outta the cell."

Leaving his cell meant stepping into a wide hallway with circular bends in the distance. All along, every few meters, the wall would shift to solid glass with icons projected on it showing the captive's vital signs, the cell's temperature and oxygen percentage, and other acronyms and abbreviations with red and green graphs that Sai didn't understand.

The cells were also staggered, so Sai couldn't see straight across into another one. As he walked along behind the moon man, every step blending weirdness around his body, Sai started to understand why: this whole process might be easier to take if you didn't have to see someone else degrade.

Some cells they passed were empty, others not so much. Sai saw women and men, adults, looking like him, lying on their cots staring at the ceiling in obvious pain. Others paced, with halting movements as they looked at the ground. These were worse; they often had skin patches in different colors, or strange growths hidden by large gowns.

None looked up as they passed.

Sai started to ask another question, then stopped himself. The moon man hummed a tune, something light that looped back on itself like an advertising jingle. Beyond that, the only noises in the hall came from far-off machines rumbling away.

No windows. No artwork. No emotion in the dark stone and steel.

After two rounded turns, the moon man led Sai into an elevator, one larger than Sai's cell. His guide pointed to a brighter spot on the floor, where the tile had been painted over with a rough white.

"Stick yourself right there and don't move a muscle," the moon man said. "We're going for a ride and I don't want you to get hurt."

Sai managed a quirked eyebrow, but stayed quiet and listened to his captor. His hands itched for the katana. Something to hold, give him purchase in this surreal hell that he'd entered into.

His guide keyed something on a handheld computer, and the floor under Sai vibrated ever-so-slightly. As if falling into the lightest sand, Sai sank a centimeter or two, before the white—apparently not just paint—reformed. Sai tried to lift his feet, just to see, and found them locked in.

"Just for safety," Captain Happy said. Sai decided he needed to give the man a name or he'd go insane, and the moon man's voice reminded him of a show his kids had watched when they were younger, before Sai had started this planet-hopping life. "Hold on!"

The elevator lurched and they descended, smooth and quick. Captain Happy resumed his song during the trip, which may have taken five minutes or five hours for all Sai knew. The viral heat spread to his face, and he found himself in a battle to keep his suddenly heavy eyelids from falling shut, his mouth from hanging open.

The elevator stopped and Captain Happy led Sai out and into a wide room, an antechamber with other glass doors leading away to who knew where. Spread across the floor, at regular intervals, were more white tiles like the one Sai had been trapped by, and, with Captain Happy's efforts, released from in the elevator.

People already stood in several of these, looking as delirious as Sai felt. Their hands rested on small stands, wrapped up in wires and cuffs. The stands, pure glass minus an embedded column, projected vital signs across the top for every subject.

"Thank you," Anaskya, sweeping over from a captive, said to Captain Happy. "Bring the rest, please. It's going well."

"One at a time?"

"One at a time." Anaskya gave Sai her practiced patient smile. "We'll need to get each one set up, and it's safer this way. For all of us."

Captain Happy didn't object, wheeled around and wandered back into his elevator. Sai watched the big man go until he felt Anaskya's hand on his shoulder steering him around towards the white patches, the stands, the next step.

"You're looking quite well," Anaskya said.

"Don't feel it."

"I'm sure, but be confident," Anaskya guided Sai forward. "You're in far better shape than most of our subjects. Consider this one here." Anaskya, holding Sai's arm now, nodded towards an older man, covered in sweat, who seemed lost to the world. "He worked with us for years. Desk duties, nothing like the hard training you're used to. His body can't accept the change."

"What," Sai focused on the words he wanted to say, like talking through glue, "is wrong with you?"

Anaskya nodded, resumed the movement, "You should have been told that there are no questions allowed. It disrupts the mood. My mood, their mood. The whole experiment is at risk if the subjects question the motives. Please, take your place."

They'd stopped near an empty spot, though a glass stand had been placed in front already, waiting for someone to don its cuffs, stick their fingers into its measuring slots. If Sai stepped up to that podium, he'd be trapped. Slotted into the next phase without any answers.

He tried. Sai put all the effort he had into his hands, his legs to turn and reach for Anaskya, to tackle her and maybe wrest away a badge, something that could get him away from here.

Except his muscles didn't respond like they used to. Sai didn't snap into action, as he had hundreds, thousands of times before. He half-turned instead, and did that with such slowness that Anaskya had time to laugh and take a step back. She let Sai complete his rotation, then reached out and guided him, as Sai tried and tried and fought to resist, into position.

"Don't worry," Anaskya said as she pulled out her little computer. "Your strength will come back. The virus has to work its magic first."

Sai felt Anaskya clip his fingers, his arms into the cuffs. She did each motion gently, as if Sai were some porcelain sculpture prone to shattering. And by the time she finished, with fever burning him up, Sai could do nothing more than fall away into his roiling nightmares.

Not Alone

AURORA GAVE the signal on their way out from the cable car. Three single-finger taps against her wetsuit thigh and Gregor knew what to do. Sever had these silent signals ready for ambushes, for missions where vocals could be intercepted. This one, cutting, had been designed for use with their armor on, for a quick turn and smash with the hammer or blast with a rifle.

Without either, damp inside the tight wetsuit, Gregor used the weapons he always had available. While he slipped a bit spinning on the wet sidewalk, his trailing target couldn't get any traction to dodge, so Gregor had laid the poor man out with his heavy haymaker.

And now Gregor ran. Across the slanted street—a challenge all its own with the slick surface—to the left and away from Rovo and Aurora. Cutting's whole purpose lay in drawing attention from Sever's other members, letting them set up a reverse ambush. At least, that's what Gregor hoped was happening; without their armor, Gregor, Aurora, and Rovo had no way to talk to each other from a distance.

As he rounded the intersection, the same one where they'd ditched the cable car, Gregor went right and kept at it, breaking around people and noticing the gradual change in buildings from concentrated residential, restaurant and recreation to corporate-labeled entities. Unlike most cities, though, all these windows held the same corner logo, that spinning helix.

Sprinting through the enemy's core didn't seem smart, so Gregor slowed down, drawing glances from passing people but no follow-up. Typical for a fearful, desperate place; everyone had too many problems to take on another. Walking and brushing the sweat away, Gregor tried to keep going in a straight direction. Ideally, any pursuit would fall in behind him, then Rovo and Aurora would fall in behind *them* and handle the enemy.

Only Gregor didn't see his squad mates. Didn't see any enemies either. The wet streets weren't crawling with crowds, but the hour must have been creeping close to lunch, because all these office doors were sliding open and disgorging chattering, grim people.

Two options, then. Either go back, try to retrace Aurora's steps and find out where'd she'd gone, or keep going and hope they turned up sooner or later. Going back risked being found again, but going forward would put him in the same situation as Sai and Eponi: isolated and alone in enemy territory.

"Don't stop walking," the whispered words hit Gregor's ears from behind, and in the window to his left, he caught a woman who'd just left her building.

Wearing a clear plastic poncho, she looked as ridiculous as everyone else on the street, and seemed about half Gregor's size, but she kept close on his heels, one hand disappearing into a pocket.

Could be a bluff. Without armor, though, calling the woman on it would be risky, and who knew how many allies she had in the sopping people stepping past. Gregor could throw down with the best, but even he might have a hard time punching out a few dozen in the slick street.

So he walked. One foot in front of the other. Didn't say a word, because he doubted the woman would hear him without Gregor speaking loud enough to carry in the crowd.

After a block, she told Gregor to turn left. After another, right. Then straight for two more, before they wound up somewhere Gregor didn't expect to see, didn't expect to exist.

A DefenseCorp building. Right here, the DC logo paired with the helix one in a united effort. The woman guided Gregor right to the entrance, locked from the outside.

"Don't make any moves," the woman said, then stepped around Gregor and swiped her handheld against the door. "Go in."

Thoroughly confused, Gregor followed the directions. For all he knew now, this woman might be his boss. Might be farther up the ladder than Aurora, able to fire him right then and there. Not that being employed was doing Gregor much good on this planet, but adding career anxiety to what had become a disastrous mission wouldn't help anything.

Inside, Gregor realized this wasn't a business office. Not a liaison space, where DefenseCorp could sign deals and conduct administrative work.

Stacked cases, all locked, lay around the wide entry space. Cheap, grey plastic tables filled in elsewhere, laid over with active gear. Doors, locked with those black scanners, split the walls, no doubt leading to further storage rooms. Several dots stuck down from the ceiling, devices that could track Gregor's movements and, on command, shoot out little, lethal energy beams.

Gregor had seen arsenals like this before. Dropped into places where DefenseCorp saw a profit advantage to having supplies ready for use. If, for example, missions were going to be commonplace. If a planet was a violent mess.

Like Dynas.

"You're not supposed to be here," the woman said, stepping around Gregor. Before slipping off her poncho, she pressed something on her handheld that sent the windows dark, that locked the front door. "Who sent you?"

"Who sent me?" Gregor said, still running his eyes over the supplies. No armor. Either that justified its own room, or this arsenal belonged to a different DefenseCorp division. "Why are you here?"

"Business," the woman replied, folding up her poncho and setting it on a nearby table.

Without the poncho, the woman revealed what it must be like to live and work on Dynas long term. She kept her dark hair cut close, her darker skin soft and wrinkled, though Gregor wouldn't put her all that old. The heavy humidity, most likely. Beneath the poncho, she wore aggressive athletic gear, like what Gregor and the others wore between missions back in space, except this set bore frays and stains from heavy use.

"Me too," Gregor replied.

"Really?" the woman said, crossing her arms. "Because I thought you were just here to make noise. Rile people up. Get me in trouble."

Gregor matched her stance. If she wanted confrontation, Gregor could deliver.

"We came because we were asked to come," Gregor said. "What were we supposed to do when these people tried to kill us? We were not warned."

"Because I didn't know you were coming."

"Not my fault."

The woman shook her head, turned and, waving for Gregor to follow, went past the arms cases towards the middle-back door and scanned her way through. Behind the imposing barrier was . . . a home?

Spending so long on the *Nautilus*, surfing the stars between brief planetoid deployments filled with action, Gregor had almost forgotten what it looked like to have a long-term place larger than a bedroom.

Here, with a white stair leading up to a loft, was a small apartment. A kitchenette sat to one side, with a tiny table for two beneath the stairs and, further back, a rather cozy living room dominated by a thrumming dehumidifier. One that, by its colorful exterior, had been painted.

Paint, in fact, was everywhere; on canvases framed on the walls, on the walls themselves, the tiled floor and the ceiling. Some patches looked like they were still in progress, others looked like they were being painted over, and not for the first time.

"Get in here," the woman said. "I don't want anyone else coming in and seeing you. Not till I know whether you should be dead or alive."

"If I am coming into your home, I should know your name," Gregor said. "I am Gregor, and you are?"

"Lani works," the woman said. "And I'm not fooling. Get inside."

Gregor risked a look back, wondering if some enemy had pushed Lani's urgency. Nothing had come into the lobby, nobody was trying the door, but Lani had fight on her face all the same, so Gregor complied and walked, wet boots and all, into her apartment.

After shutting, and locking the door with both digital and manual bolts, Lani ordered Gregor to take off those boots, then make his way to the couch, keeping his hands where she could see them the entire time.

Then she offered him some water.

"I feel I will never be thirsty here," Gregor said.

"Yeah, all that's on the outside. You still gotta stay hydrated." Lani pulled two glasses from a cabinet, filled them up from the same spout, handed one to Gregor and took a long swig from the other. "There's a million ways to die on this damn world. Would be pretty stupid if you let water be the one."

"You are not wrong."

"So tell me your story," Lani said. "And make it a good one, because I don't wanna kill you while you're on my couch. Those are good cushions."

The cushions, tanned and soft, were definitely high quality, and Gregor respected solid craftsmanship, so he told Lani the bare bones about why Sever had come to Dynas. The call, the landing interception, and the tramway to town. No Felix, nothing about Sai and Eponi going missing.

Lani didn't seem like the enemy, but trusting anyone outside of Sever was a poor play.

"Have you seen it, then?" Lani asked when Gregor wrapped.

"Seen what?"

"What they're doin' here. With the viruses."

Felix, mostly molded over, and his thralls came crashing back. Gregor's dive into the biomass to save Rovo. The lingering feeling that leaving the outpost un-torched had been a bad choice.

"I saw."

"Then you know why we're here," Lani said.

"To destroy it?"

"To watch it," Lani replied. "Lotta companies are interested in Dynas, what they have going here. Get it right, they say humans won't have to terraform a planet before taking it. Just pick the right people to send in. What a perfect future."

Gregor took that in stride. Dynas hadn't been the first DefenseCorp mission he'd undertaken with genetic engineering undertones. Those had all wound up in fiery demolitions, and given what Gregor had seen already, he bet DefenseCorp would be sending a cleansing fleet to Dynas soon after this mission ended.

"They are failing," Gregor said. "What we saw was a disease, not an enhancement."

"Like all the others," Lani said, frowning. "Used to be, Helix would let us know when things failed. Let us clean up. Now they're not being so nice. Think they know time's running out."

"Because of our mission?"

"Are you blind, man?" Lani gestured towards her door. "You see those people out there? Nobody believes in this anymore. Nobody wants to be on this wet rock. Helix needs a breakthrough, or everyone's going to quit, and you can't force this many people to keep quiet."

"If all this is true, and you are supposed to be watching them, then why did you find me?" Gregor asked.

He hadn't thought Lani could frown further, could get her eyes to go even angrier, but Gregor had thought wrong.

"Because we're getting left behind," Lani said. "Helix isn't getting us info, and they've been bulking up security.

DefenseCorp just gave us new orders, and you're going to help me carry them out."

"Why would I do that?"

"Because, if you do, I'll make sure your squad gets its ship off this blasted rock."

Drafted

THE HOSTAGE BREAKFAST turned out to be pretty good—while later than her usual jaunt through eggs and toast, Eponi decided that time had no meaning as she had no control over how to spend it. Ben spent the whole meal jabbering to her face, asking the occasional question about the race courses before descending into another long monologue about how, if he'd been allowed to design the racing craft, Eponi would never have crashed. Nobody would, and things would be so much better.

While Ben dove deep into his own ego, Eponi wandered her eyes around the cafeteria, a space big enough for several hundred and holding that many, but far too quiet for that number. The DefenseCorp messes Eponi had experienced were filled with bragging soldiers, chattering executives and bantering accountants. People would be playing games on the tables, or laying out strategies for the next simulator run. Here, even as people sat across from one another, the default expression seemed to be the vacant stare, the lost look into nowhere.

Along the cafeteria's walls and splattered across the

tower's corridors were posters drawn up in vintage art styles depicting miracles yet to be worked by Helix. Most showed planets or asteroids getting a human makeover, but without the cumbersome suits and supporting ships required for colonization. Soft, ambient tones played over a speaker system, interrupted by announcements directing so and so to such and such. Low tech systems—DefenseCorp would send any orders direct to your device—but given the strange status here, maybe that's what Helix had to work with.

After the meal, Eponi didn't know what to expect. Did Ben have a traitor's itinerary? A list to run through before he left his friends behind?

Assuming Ben had any.

"We're going to the bays," Ben said when Eponi asked. "You've already seen one."

He delivered that last with a wink that made Eponi want to throw up.

"What're we going there for?" Eponi tried as they went back to the elevators.

"Why would we bring a pilot to the ships?" Ben replied. "No idea, Eponi. No idea."

She wanted to slap back at the sarcasm, say she understood what the hell was in the bays, you piece of garbage, but that it made no sense to put an enemy into a craft that could hurt so many. Eponi had already crashed one skiff to make a mark, a big shuttle would only do worse.

"So when did you first decide to be a racer?" Ben asked while they waited for the elevator. He sucked on something that looked like a lollipop, but Eponi suspected the frizzy white, decidedly non-candy look meant the treat did something else entirely.

"When does anyone pick a passion?" Eponi said. "When I was a kid."

"Right, right, but I mean, when did you actually go for it?"

"When I had the chance," Eponi said.

There were people she wouldn't mind giving her life story to. Like, say, any of the news outlets covering the racing circuit and its drivers. She did not want to give anything to Ben, who continued to fill her every sense with creepy alarms. Not a soul in the cafeteria had come to talk to him, none had given Ben a hello as they'd walked, and the man had kept up his goofy smile the whole time.

Eponi had seen movies. This guy matched every flag.

At least he took the hint and kept quiet till the elevator brought them to the landing bay. Unlike the one Eponi had blasted the skiff into, this floor looked undamaged. It also looked skiff-less, meant for bigger transports. The ships that'd run goods up to the stars and back.

Several filled the bay right now, all the same twin-engined, oval shaped freighters built for short system hops and limited longer journeys. Given Helix's apparent desire to keep itself secret, Eponi wasn't surprised to see this sort of ship here: hard to escape if there's nothing capable of it around.

If the cafeteria had been dismal and lethargic, here, at least, people moved with purpose. They guided cargo drones across the black-painted floor beneath broad, white lights between giant openings on the tower's sides, kept somewhat protected thanks to that same microscopic nano-net that cloaked the city itself. One ship had cargo getting loaded, each crate shuttled on with care in high-quality silver-lined boxes.

"You're sending sensitive stuff," Eponi said as they came off the elevator.

"Don't you know what we're doing here?" Ben replied. "All medical, all genetic. Of course it's sensitive."

"Sorry, I forgot to mention I don't care."

She did, but feigning disinterest to keep Ben from talking was about the only card Eponi could still play. Not that it worked.

"Don't worry, I'll tell you all about it anyway." Ben pointed towards the shuttle being loaded. "That's ours."

"Ours?"

"Yep. We're running a delivery today. Customers picking up an order."

An order of what? A virus that's causing people to turn into those monsters that Sai had to fight? That caused its own scientists to freak out in bathrooms? Who would buy that?

Too many questions, too few answers, and Eponi suspected Ben wouldn't give the latter. Still, she followed him to the shuttle, up the ramp and inside the cramped habitable quarters.

Unlike the drop ship, meant for heavy armor transport, this shuttle had cargo in mind. A little room for crew, maximum for freight, the living space on the ship condensed into three cot-filled rooms, a single circular rec space with a pre-fab meal maker, and then the quick hallway to the cockpit. No frills, no fancy, just focus.

Ben didn't bother with a tour and Eponi didn't ask for one. She'd seen these models before, though DefenseCorp generally dispensed with pacified sissy ships. Not aggressive enough, not diverse enough in their applications. If it couldn't have a dozen turrets attached, DefenseCorp said, then why bother?

The cockpit, though, mirrored the one in the drop ship. Standard twin pilot layout, with flight sticks and screens littering every surface minus the ceiling, where manual levers for every system backed up the on-screen counterparts. Redundancy meant survival in space and when Ben took the co-pilots seat, gesturing for Eponi to slip into the chief spot, she wondered whether he actually intended to back her up. Whether he really intended for Eponi to fly.

"What're we doing here?" Eponi said. "Why am I in this seat?"

"Because, and here's the truth Eponi," Ben shook his head so wide that any sincerity flew right off. "There's not enough pilots left here. We've lost a bunch. They either take one of these ships and just flee, or, well, accidents."

"What kind of accidents?"

"The ones we're not going to have," Ben nodded out the front window, to where another cargo caseload made its way towards the shuttle's back bay. "We've learned a lot about transporting this stuff, making sure it doesn't break free in vacuum. It's all totally fine now."

"Are you trying to reassure me or yourself?"

Ben laughed, which did nothing for Eponi. Not that it mattered what Ben said. The man seemed like he really was going to ask her to fly a shuttle, which meant that Eponi would have her hands on a ship. A way to get off this planet, away from it forever.

She'd abandoned Sever. Saved Sai and turned him over. For all she knew, Aurora and the others might already be dead. That base had been crawling with Helix guards. Aurora, Gregor, and a rookie? Not good odds.

"So that's the story," Ben said. "We're going to head up, meet with a partner, and deliver the containers. You do well on this one, guess what, we trust you a little more. I know it seems desperate, given that you worked for the enemy a day ago, but hey, we're all desperate around here."

"Still seems crazy."

Ben smiled, then shifted himself a bit, untucked his

shirt with his hand, raising the hem just enough to show a micro laser's protruding hilt.

"Eponi, we live in crazy times. You're going to do what I say, or I'm going to shoot you and try again another day," Ben said. "They're going to finish loading, we'll get the go-ahead, and then you're going to make a great delivery. Nice and easy."

Eponi rolled her eyes, a move that, for once, seemed to throw Ben.

"If you knew how many times I've had guns shoved in my face," Eponi replied. "You want me to fly this ship, fine. You want to deliver your disease to someone, cool. Whatever. I'm not in this to be a hero. I'm here for the cash. I'm here to live. So put your laser away and let's get this done."

TEN

Dirty Secrets

By the time Kashmal finished his introductions over the second round, by the time he'd finished explaining what disasters were at work on Dynas, Rovo started to feel like they'd entered a joke; what do you get when two soldiers and a genetic engineer walk into a bar?

An interstellar crisis.

So the punchline needed some work. Rovo played with it as Kashmal led them from the bar and, with a slight wobble to his walk, back to his apartment in a tall building two blocks away. Though Rovo couldn't tell it by the constant ochre overtones across the sky and the damp city, his wristlet computer's clock told him time had slipped into the afternoon.

While DefenseCorp hadn't given Sever any timetable for this mission—easy to do when Sever had to find their own ride off planet—a successful conclusion tended to be less likely the longer things took. Especially since the enemy knew Sever had made it into the city.

Though Gregor's trick had done its job. The Bug kept Rovo apprised of the city's policing, and the various snippets sent by more secretive forces, and none had good pins on Sever's locations. It seemed there were enough other issues in the city, like a large protest at the tower's main entrance. Eyes were watching, but amid the shuffling wetsuit crowds, Sever went unseen.

Kashmal's building lacked the finery Rovo might have expected from someone involved in crafting humanity's next version. Black brick flowed up for ten stories before ending in a metal overhang that shot the dampness down the sides in a continual, slim waterfall. Kashmal, his suitcase in one hand and an ID card like the one Rovo had stolen—and still had in his wetsuit pocket—in his other beeped them in.

"Don't act like you're not impressed," Kashmal said as they went inside to a lobby filled with mailboxes, grody green tile, and nothing else.

"That won't be a problem," Aurora replied.

A dripping elevator took the trio up to the eighth floor, and Kashmal led them to his apartment, a corner one. Whether a corner apartment meant anything on Dynas, Rovo had no idea.

Though, upon opening his apartment door, Kashmal proved he could not afford basic sanitation. Leftover food of unknown, multiple, origins made itself known in a stultifying wash that had Rovo back out to the hallway to get one more humid breath before descending into Kashmal's brutal hotbox.

"Ah, last night," Kashmal said as he wandered through his own place, shuffling off random garbage into a bin he'd picked up from beside the door. "Things weren't too good, and everything decays so fast on this damn planet."

"Things weren't so good?" Rovo said, taking in the desperate straits of someone who'd long ago given up on the sanitary things in life. "What happened?"

Beyond the scattered wrappers and food bits, the apartment flickered its way to daylight as Aurora, stepping around Kashmal, began pulling heavy blinds up and cracking open windows. A bad move for secrecy, but a necessary one for survival.

A living room, a kitchen, a short hallway to a bathroom and, according to Kashmal, two bedrooms sufficed for the layout. Nothing had made it to the walls, except odd-colored splotches here and there. Rovo touched one, his finger coming away damp, and frowned. Mold, on a planet like Dynas, seemed like an inevitability, but that didn't mean Rovo had to like it.

As Aurora set about debriefing Kashmal, she flashed a signal to Rovo behind Kashmal's back, a simple two fingers pointing to the ground. Take a walk around, Aurora said, and do it quietly. A single finger would've had Rovo breaking down doors and prepping for a fight.

From the kitchen, a dismal affair with a small fridge and two food prep machines atop a grimed gray counter, Rovo went on back to the hallway. Took a peek inside the bathroom, which looked serviceable. Rovo took a long look at the cabinet above the bathroom's vanity, wondering how many pills he might find in there. His reluctance to touch anything in the damn dirty apartment, though, kept his hands at his sides.

Towards the back, the hallway ended with two doors. One open to what looked like Kashmal's messed over bedroom. At least that window had its blinds up, giving the sheet-covered bed some light. The other room's door was shut, an old-style knob with physical key combo looking back at Rovo.

How long had it been since Rovo had seen a lock like that? Everyone ran on electronic ones now, the slight decrease in security conquered by the convenience gained by always having the 'right' key in your pocket, in your computer, ready to go.

Rovo glanced back down the hallway, saw nobody coming to check on him, then reached out and touched the door's knob. Tried to turn it, ever-so-slightly, and the motion stopped hard. Locked, then. Rovo tried turning the knob back the other way, just to be sure.

Stuck there too.

Wait.

Rovo turned the knob back along its locked range. Felt the jiggle again. This time, when he twisted the knob back left, the jiggling began immediately. Not frantic, but like someone, something saying hello. Communicating through the metal.

Rovo stepped back, let go of the knob. Stared at the door. He could talk, ask if there was something in there, but that would break Aurora's quiet look-around rules. Curiosity could carry Rovo a long ways, but crossing his commander on a mission that'd already gone so far sideways went out of bounds for the rookie, so he turned and went back to the living room.

"So if I'm understanding you right," Aurora was saying as Rovo came back. "You want to go to work, even though we're here to rescue you?"

"I don't see a rescue here," Kashmal leaned against his counter while Aurora had stayed standing. "I see two mercenaries in wetsuits, without weapons or ships. I have what I need in this suitcase, but you don't have your end ready. Until that happens, I've got appearances to keep up. Work to do."

"And we're supposed to do what, then?"

"Your job, maybe?" Kashmal said. "I'm paying DefenseCorp for a rescue, not for a chance to babysit. It's just after lunch. I'll be back here tonight. You get your ship, meet me here or send me a message."

Aurora rolled her eyes towards Rovo as Kashmal set about putting his own poncho back on. Rovo flashed her three fingers, indicating a successful search that found something interesting. Four would've meant mission critical, five; dangerous.

"Kashmal," Aurora said, keeping her eyes on Rovo. "Where do you work?"

"Over at Helix's tower," Kashmal replied, pulling on his boots. "It's where anyone working on the genetic piece goes. So they can keep eyes on us."

"Then I'm coming with you."

"Oh, is that your grand plan?" Kashmal laughed. "Come walking right up to the enemy and waltz inside? They'll kill you, and then they'll torture me."

"That won't happen," Aurora replied. "We'll be fine. I won't go in with you, you'll just get me close enough to handle the rest."

"What about your friend here? Is he going to join us in our mutual destruction?"

"I'm staying," Rovo said, guessing Aurora's play. "You said your material is in that suitcase? Then it makes sense to protect it."

Kashmal, for the first time, seemed unsure. No ready comeback kissed his lips, and instead he shot a nervous look Aurora's way, as if hoping the commander might overrule her comrade and keep the trio together. When Aurora nodded, Kashmal frowned hard.

"Are you sure that's the best course?" Kashmal found his words. "My apartment is very safe. Nobody suspects it."

"Because it's too disgusting to bother searching?" Rovo said.

"Maybe!" Kashmal said. "But you try keeping a place clean on Dynas. This whole world is rot."

Seeing no budge from either Sever, Kashmal deflated, relented, and with some sputtering about not digging through his stuff, the VIP led Aurora out of the apartment and away.

Rovo counted to fifty, waited for Kashmal to come barging back in claiming a forgotten something, but the man never appeared. Aurora didn't either. Rovo, the rookie, was all alone on a hostile world, in a hostile city, with a, frankly, hostile apartment all around him.

"Time to figure out how hostile," Rovo muttered.

First thing, he took Kashmal's suitcase and, gently, slid the silver metal thing—about the only clean object in the space—beneath the apartment's lone couch. Not the best hiding place, but it would be safe from cursory looks.

Rovo went digging through Kashmal's kitchen drawers next. Sever had managed to take their small weapons with them from their armor, but Rovo didn't want to give off a telltale laser flash unless he had to. Kashmal's knives, sharp enough given their lack of use, would be better. He took a larger one, then went back to the locked door.

"Hello?" Rovo tried. "Is someone in there?"

Silence. Which could mean anything. Someone not capable of speaking, an imaginary jiggle, someone who didn't understand Common—as hard as that thought was to comprehend.

"Jiggle the knob if you can hear me."

Still nothing.

Guess he'd have to try this the hard way. Rovo went back to the kitchen, dug around until he found the small toolset so required of any home. Screwdrivers and the like, those things that were so ubiquitous throughout a galaxy that had moved on in so many other ways. Some tech just never went out of style.

Rovo went back to the door, crouched in front of the knob, and took out a flathead screwdriver and a hammer. Nothing about the knob and the lock looked sturdy, and nothing about Rovo gave a damn about Kashmal's apartment staying put together. The man would be leaving soon anyway.

Sever's rookie put the flathead's edge against the keyhole, pushed it in as far as it could go, then took the hammer and began to pound, pushing the screwdriver in a little bit further every time. Not too subtle, but as sounds went, rhythmic hammer blows had to be less suspicious than kicking open a door or burning holes with a laser.

Once the screwdriver had wedged its way in, driving itself through the key's slots, Rovo leaned on the tool, forced its turn, and snapped the lock free from the door jam. Rovo planted his right hand against the loose fiber door, keeping it closed until he let go of the screwdriver, until he stepped back and drew the knife, leveling it at the opening, ready to stab whatever sat on the other side.

"I'm going to open the door in five seconds," Rovo said. "Stay away from it, and stay still. If you have hands, raise'em high."

He counted to three, out loud, then swung the door open.

Standing there, amid a huge and dirty clothing pile, a couple of ratty books by her feet, stood a little, dark-haired girl, eyes wide and scared beneath a sole soft-white light.

ELEVEN

Security Breach

If you give a merc a mission went the saying, a common one among DefenseCorp members who could conclude the statement to match whatever insane task they'd currently been assigned. Like, say, trying to get a VIP off a planet when that VIP wanted to clock in and work another shift.

Not that Aurora had a good way to get Kashmal off Dynas at the moment, but him rotating hours in a Helix lab wouldn't help them find a solution.

Unless Kashmal could get her inside that looming tower.

The ugly building, all sloping edges and spiked sections, as if designed by some modern fairy tale villain, held sway over the city's skyline, regardless of where Aurora and the others went. A menacing shadow, always lurking behind the nearest rooftop.

Skiffs and larger ships buzzed the tower in swift swarms as Kashmal and Aurora rode a cable car down a main road that had the tower sitting center stage. The car's roof, a glass affair smudged with moisture, nonetheless provided a clear view of Dynas's dreary business. Riding gave a clear look at the groups shuffling along the street, splashing their way from lunch and back towards offices, homes, or, maybe, bars. Like any other city, except—

"Miserable, isn't it?" Kashmal, sitting next to her near the car's front, said. "This whole place? Just awful one minute to the next."

"I've seen better planets," Aurora replied, sweeping her eyes around the car as it picked up new passengers. Gregor had done a nice job pulling off pursuit, but Sever missions taught you quick that you couldn't be too careful. "I've seen worse."

"Worse? Like what?"

"Fantares. During the first settlement. People with no options making homes out of bombed rock." Aurora and Sever had played guard duty during that one, though most Fantares migrants had bigger worries than getting in fights. "You have homes here. Lights. Hell, cable cars."

"Oh yes, when humanity sails the stars, such technological marvels like cable cars ought to be appreciated."

Aurora *did* appreciate the cable car. After spending the morning hiking around the city and yesterday in pitched combat with soldiers and strange mutants, sitting down and watching the blocks go by felt pretty good. Kashmal, though, continued running through complaints, as if entering Dynas in a competition for the galaxy's most decrepit planet, with Aurora as the judge.

Learning to tune out ramblings from various mission targets, senior and junior officers, and crowds was a skill Aurora had developed with strict intensity. She focused on the car, on the sidewalks and the sky, anything to blot out Kashmal's continued commentary. She didn't care.

At all.

Because at the end of this, Aurora would either be dead or sent along to the next mission, with another complaining, panicking person to save or shoot until she finally amassed enough cash to never need to listen to this garbage again.

"But you see, they can't give us the conveniences because they don't want those ships coming here," Kashmal said as the car slowed to an announced final stop and Aurora tuned herself back in. "Secrecy doesn't help you if the people keeping those secrets decide it's not worth it."

"Or if they decide to sell those secrets for cash?"

"Exactly. Now get up, go." Kashmal nudged Aurora out from her seat, into the aisle, cutting off others making their way off.

Aurora preferred to go last, to help rule out potential tails and account for everyone on the car, but once Kashmal had her in the flow, there wasn't any stopping and she stomped off into a crowd heading towards the tower. Kashmal went behind, and then in front of her, smelling his own breath, as if realizing spending the first half of his day lounging in a bar wasn't the best call.

"Kashmal," Aurora said, catching up to the VIP as they weaved through the walkers. "Ever push me again and I'll make sure you spend the rest of this mission unconscious."

Kashmal laughed, "Please do. The sooner I can leave this place, physically or mentally, the better."

The back-from-lunch crowd congested as they entered a broad courtyard, at least several blocks wide, at the tower's base. People shifted in and out from several streets, going past corroded statues displaying Helix logos, with stone bases etched in with names Aurora didn't recognize. Company founders? Employees? Victims? Who knew, who cared.

More interesting, by far, were the chants ringing out as

they came closer to the tower. The coming-and-going crowd funneled into a chained off entryway, and on either side, dozens more stood behind those chains carrying signs and shouting . . . things?

Rather than truth to power, it seemed like Dynas's protest movement took its cues from Kashmal, or maybe vice versa. The signs demanded more modern food, links to galactic entertainment networks, better medical care. Several suggested conspiracies around missing persons, and Aurora couldn't help wonder if some of those had become Felix's virus-mutated playthings.

"A hodgepodge," Kashmal said as the incoming line became a strict two-by-two affair. "People that don't understand the work being done here, that are trapped here anyway by spouses or circumstance. Hopeless."

Aurora stayed quiet. Studied. Up ahead, it looked like they'd reach a security checkpoint where her lack of corporate ID would go from minor nuisance to critical issue.

"How will you get in?" Kashmal said as the line moved forward. "You can't threaten them all."

"I could, but I won't. Keep your beacon on. When we call, it'll be time to leave."

Aurora stopped walking, turned to her side to let the other workers drift by her. Kashmal had the sense to keep going without looking back. It wouldn't look good if Aurora started a fight next to the person she was supposed to protect.

Right now, Sever Squad had lost its squad name. Every member was on their own, and while seeing the skiffs all head towards the tower's upper levels gave Aurora some hope Eponi and Sai were inside, she had no idea where. Gregor, too, hadn't shown up at Kashmal's place nor tried to contact them via Sever's secure line. He might be dead, a prisoner, or, like Felix, something worse.

Rovo, at least, had a safe spot. Aurora wouldn't have to worry about the rookie for a minute or two. Best case scenario, Aurora would swoop down in a shuttle—with Eponi piloting—and they'd pick Rovo and Kashmal's case off his building's roof, rocket towards space and never, ever set foot on Dynas again.

After giving Kashmal twenty paces, Aurora rejoined the flow. As she neared the check-in gates—large gray arches that scanned for metal and many other things— Aurora counted four security guards. All human, with the glassy-eyed look that comes from leaning too hard on tech to do their job for them.

Aurora, too, wasn't the only one having ID issues at the moment. Another man had already left the line and seemed to be beseeching one of the security personal, all wearing thick black uniforms with that double-helix on the chest in white, to no avail.

"Do you even know how long it'll take me to get back home?" the man said. "I might as well take the day off!"

"Fine with me," the guard replied, a brick monotone that matched his broad shoulders.

"Is it? Is it really fine with you?" the man said. "Is it fine with you that, when I'm not getting my work done, you won't have a job because this whole place is going to fall apart?"

"Not my problem."

Aurora had to give the security guard some points for that response. The sheer don't-give-a-crap attitude. Which made what came next harder. Slightly.

Coming up behind the complaining man, as he spun up his arms for another exaggerated display of highfalutin' fury, Aurora shoved him right into the guard. The man's upswing hit the guard's face, and Aurora stepped past, stuck out her left foot and snaked the back-pedaling guard's ankle, sending both him and the protesting, fumbling man crashing to the ground.

As eyes homed in on the mess, Aurora pushed and wove her way through the arches, which immediately turned red and broadcast a loud, clanging alarm. Everyone near Aurora wheeled around, while the fallen guard cursed out the man, and nobody caught a clean look at the Sever leader quick-stepping through.

For the moment, Aurora had made it inside the tower. Any competent security force would play back the seconds around the alarm and spot her out, which meant speed now took precedence. The only problem, though, was where to go?

Beyond the tower's entrance, four elevator banks drew cleared personnel, and Aurora picked one at random. Without a firm destination, anywhere-but-here took precedence. When she made it close to the elevators, Aurora simply followed a poncho-sporting man in front of her as he stepped into one of the boxes, as he entered a floor by scanning his corporate badge and speaking the number.

"Same," Aurora said, when he looked her way.

The elevator doors slid shut, sealing them inside.

"Same?" the man replied. "I don't recognize you."

The elevator moved, dropping fast.

"New here."

A floor counter, hot red numbers over the door, vanished into the negatives.

"New? What's your ID code?"

Aurora hit the man once in the stomach to double him over, a second time in the skull to knock him unconscious. She stripped off the ID tag as the elevator settled on its chosen floor. The doors opened as Aurora pushed the limp body to the side, doing what she could to keep the man out of immediate sight, ready to fight whomever stood on the door's other side.

Except the hallway stood empty, the elevator opening into a corner foyer coated in blue-black tile. Aurora took a cautious step out, looked either way. She could see glass sections breaking up the tile every so often, and someone, somewhere, screamed.

Behind her, the elevator shut and streamed away, carrying the unconscious man with it.

Scientific Method

Sai found his mother back up the steps. Three stories above their apartment, left battered and trampled on the stairs, but still alive. He threw her over his shoulder as the tower continued to shake, as alarms continued to ring, and carried her back to their apartment. Laid her on the bed none of them had thought would see another minute's use and began a new life.

With the katana and, eventually, other weapons he took from people raiding the building who thought Sai and his sword would be easy pickings, the son became like everyone else still on his home planet: a raiding refugee. He broke into his neighbor's places, friend's former homes, and took whatever provisions he could find. Made his family's apartment into a sanctuary, a fortress.

And waited for his mother to heal while buildings burned outside. After some days, DefenseCorp started its purge, and the company filled the skies with different ships than the evacuation shuttles. These were heavily armed craft, dumping soldiers who cleansed any who wouldn't surrender with extreme, lethal prejudice.

Some time more than a week in, the soldiers reached Sai's floor. They'd climbed the tower—the roof was an unstable ruin—and they didn't bother knocking when they came to Sai's door. Beating raiders, starving and desperate people, was one thing. Going up against armed and armored professionals . . . Sai would have tried, but his mother said no. Begged him not too.

"After all you've done, don't let your friends kill you," his mother said from the bed.

"They're not my friends."

He stood at the foot of the bed, holding the katana in one hand and a rickety handgun in the other, its battery barely charged enough to fire a shot.

"You must make them, Sai, or we are lost," his mother said. "You can't fight everyone."

If Sai had a weak spot, his mother was it. What she asked for, Sai would do. He might argue, might hesitate, but he would do it, and for one reason: she had brought Sai into the universe, and that gave her every right to command him.

Sai greeted the mercenaries, when they crashed through the door, on his knees, with the katana on the floor beside him, hands folded and eyes downcast. When the soldiers asked his name, he gave it, said his mother lay wounded in the next room. The leader, gruff and invisible behind his blast-scarred, blue-gray armor, asked Sai whether he lived here.

Sai replied that this had been his home, but it wasn't any longer.

FIGHTERS DID NOT COME BUSTING from the elevator door into Anaskya's experimenting room. Sai leaned, chasing memories, on the podium, a second viral strain racing through his body. Where the first one had made him feel warm, like an aggressive fever had taken hold, this one mingled with its earlier brother to tear Sai apart.

Sai had never been conscious of his own cells, those little building blocks making his body work. Now he could feel every single one as they churned with the virus, as they ran and fought and lost and won, patches flaring along his body and moving as the infection sought its foothold.

Around him, Sai could see others going through the same experience. People older, younger than him tied to their own podiums, growing by one every time Captain Happy brought down another victim to add to Anaskya's subjects.

The doctor would guide the new test to their place, just as she had with Sai, lock in their wrists, and begin the injections. At first, Sai could barely keep up with anything going on around him; the first virus had his body so warped. The new injections, though, woke Sai up even as they tore him down. Like a bomb with a burning fuse, Sai was alert, Sai was ready, and Sai figured he was going to die.

Apparently, he wasn't the only one.

The testing room had four rows, each one with five podiums. About half, now, had patients at them that Sai could see, with at least two people in each row. Anaskya kept things spread out, and she'd placed Sai close to the center. Twisting his head around as the tubes tied to his fingers, injecting into his arms, pulsed fluids ranging from clear to yellow and green, Sai saw most were beating him out; either losing or 'winning' the infection battle ahead of him.

Their expressions made it clear: twisted in pain, or relaxed in that numb way that Sai had seen on too many enemies before they succumbed to their wounds. A few shook, either from chills or knowledge of what was to come. Some others cried, one shouted. No music played, except the soft, constant ventilation whir.

Why had Sai come to this planet again? Found himself in this place? That answer lay inside a part of him that Sai was steadily sealing away, memories and thoughts and goals shunted aside as the viruses gobbled away at his being. Instead, he clung to his family, his children and his wife and his mother and tried, tried, tried to forget about this awful room and the fact that he would die here.

The reality brought tears, eye-filling drops that grew for the first time in forever and dripped down his cheeks, splashing against the podium.

What soldier cried like this in the middle of a mission?

One thinking about birthdays he would miss, stories he wouldn't be able to tell nor hear.

Stop it.

He wouldn't take his wife to the frozen beaches and watch the salted water lap away the ice crystals.

No. Don't.

They would wake up, on those early days when Sai worked DefenseCorp contracts on his home planet, and his family, all five—mom, wife, daughter, son and himself— would go out and greet the dawn star as its shock-white form rose over the southern sky.

The rending crack drew Sai back from his tears, from his memories, and he looked down to see he'd broken the podium. Torn it in half and tossed it aside, his hands hooked to the tubes, still feeding the viral solution.

Sai looked at his left hand, those dangling cords, and pulled. Felt pain and saw bloody spurts as the wires flew away from his hand, his forearm. The solution leaking, now, onto the floor.

"Sai, stop!" Anaskya shouted from across the room, where she was helping another victim into her slot.

Instead, Sai yanked his right hand free. Where before he'd been shaky, barely able to retain his consciousness, now Sai had an exponential clarity. Everything shone hyper-real; he could hear his neighbor's breathing, could smell the days-old sweat coming from their bodies and his own. Sai could feel the vibration as Captain Happy's elevator came descended towards the floor yet again.

And, in all this, Sai could feel his chances slipping away.

Nobody in this room had come here of their own free will, Sai could bet on that. Unwilling subjects could make allies, and Sai needed them fast before Anaskya managed to get whatever security she had in here. So Sai went to the closest person next to him, a fit older woman, and yanked her free.

She blinked at him, not understanding the moment. The reason to go.

"Save them," Sai said, the words coming scratched and mushed, before he turned around to the next one.

Anaskya shouted at Sai again, closer this time. Not close enough to keep Sai from yanking out another man's cords. Not close enough to keep Sai from stumbling up another row, fumbling now as the elevator opened and Captain Happy entered the room. He had to free as many people as he could.

Some didn't help, some simply fell over, vomited, or sat on the ground. But a few responded to Sai's urgent rescue attempts, to their sudden, bloody freedom as Sai pulled them off their podiums.

Two rows down and Sai went for the front, the only row fully filled up. He lunged for the first target, a young woman who looked somewhat coherent, only for a much larger force to shunt Sai aside into an unoccupied podium. The glass thing shattered as Sai fell through it, sprawling on the floor with who knew how many scratches slicing up his prisoner's clothing.

"I thought we talked about the rules?" Captain Happy said, trundling over to stand above Sai. "You're not being very nice. You shouldn't mess up the doctor's experiments."

"Sorry," Sai muttered, then delivered a kick to the Captain Happy's ankle.

The thing was harder than rock, but Sai managed to pack enough force into the strike to move Captain Happy back a step. Sai used the room to scramble away, hands digging into glass bits in the process, before rising up in time to see Captain Happy readying a punch.

The hit didn't land. Before Captain Happy could swing, the older woman Sai had freed earlier ran into the man's back, scratching at him with her wounded hands. Captain Happy grunted, swung around and threw her off, exposing his knees to another swift Sai kick.

When fighting people much larger than you, the first job was to bring them down to your level.

Captain Happy's knees blew out with satisfying pops, and, with a high-pitched squeal, Sai's tormentor fell to the floor. Sai would have finished the job, but before he could, the older woman and several others dove on the man, rending, tearing and biting with frenetic, desperate abandon.

Sai backed away as the cheery man struggled, as he was overwhelmed. Other subjects freed the remaining experiments in the room. Anaskya had vanished, and red lights glowing over the remaining doors, including the elevator, said the obvious.

Captain Happy had been sacrificed, and the rest of

them were trapped. Sai looked around, along with those who didn't join in the vengeance frenzy, and wondered how long they had till the virus claimed each and every one of them, until they went mad and devoured each other or simply died, alone, on the glass-ridden floor.

THIRTEEN

Motives

AN OUTPOST not too far from the Black City, connected by a tram line no longer active. It'd been closed down, and Helix had said to DefenseCorp and other curious parties on Dynas that there was nothing there. Just an outdated facility being shuttered for cost-saving reasons.

"And then, just yesterday, we see a whole bunch of skiffs head that way," Lani said.

They were back in the lobby and no longer alone. Lani had Gregor wait until the other two agents returned from their lunchtime activities, and now the quartet stood amid all those crates filled with active-duty gear.

"You could not receive a new mission so quickly," Gregor said.

Galactic transmission times, limited by light speed and quantum links, could take forever. DefenseCorp had split itself into numerous regional groups for that reason. The galaxy's left side might not know about disaster on the right for years.

"Our directives are broad," Lani replied. "Keep Helix in-bounds, at all costs. Everyone knows what they're doing here is risky, and everyone understands why we need to keep them in check."

"I don't think you are succeeding," Gregor replied. "Those skiffs were sent for us."

"Only for you?"

"Perhaps." Gregor glanced at the other two agents, both older men, both putting on light armor and gathering rifles. "Are they cleared?"

"As much as I am."

"And how much is that?"

Lani shook her head, "Gregor, don't know if you get this, but you're on my planet now. Either you tell me what you know, or I keep you locked away until you do, and whatever mission you came here to complete fizzles away without you."

There was a chance Gregor could fight his way out of here. Lani stood within his jab range, and the other two were strapping their clothes and weapons on. They would be slow to react, surprised. Gregor could down them, then move on.

"What would you do," Gregor said, "If you found something, as you say, out of bounds?"

"Destroy it," Lani replied. "Nothing gets to live on this planet unless it gets our approval, no matter how much Helix wants to believe otherwise."

A confident statement for such a small group, but Lani didn't blink when Gregor matched her stare and hunted for a lie. Most people, when hit by Gregor's dead-set look would wilt under the pressure, begin to babble or shrink away. Lani did neither, and Gregor had to give her a little respect.

"That is what I wanted to hear," Gregor said. "We landed near that base after Helix attacked us on our inbound. The facility is compromised. A creature calling itself Felix grew from some experiment and infested the place."

"You landed near there? Then how'd you get all the way to this city?"

"The tram."

Lani shook her head, "Of course they left it active. Helix has blinders, Gregor. Anything ancillary to their goal and they just miss it. They only have attention for the main attraction, and now they're screwing that up too."

Gregor couldn't argue with that.

"You should go and destroy that base, then," Gregor said, "and let me go back to my mission."

"Nah," Lani replied. "You said you don't even know where your squad is. You're not going to find them wandering around this city blind, so why don't you help us?"

"No."

"Wrong answer. I said this was my planet, which means it's my rules, which means you're coming with us."

'Coming with us' meant heading to the building's rooftop, where a DefenseCorp-branded skiff sat docked and ready. Up a short metal ladder and onto the deck went the four, Gregor helping haul some more cases with weapons Lani figured would be good when it came time to cleanse the base.

Sayers, one of the other agents, whose most defining feature was a cross-forehead scar revealed by the zero hair on his bald head, took the cockpit controls. Wicks, the other, went to the bow to handle the skiff's front cannon while Lani and Gregor wound up sitting in the center. Two more side cannons rounded out the skiff's armament, an aggressive build considering the mission.

While Sayers warmed up the skiff's engines, those electric turbines spinning their techno-whine, Lani attempted to tell Gregor the role he'd play: the guide, leading the other three to this Felix so they could administer lethal punishment and, thus, keep this experiment from getting out of control.

"You want me to lead," Gregor replied. "Okay. I can lead. But I will need my hammer."

"Your hammer?" Lani said.

"My hammer, and my armor. Both are at the tram station. You will take me there, and then we can go hunting."

Lani gave Gregor the quizzical stare he received whenever he talked about his hammer, because everyone inevitably thought he meant a small thing meant for pounding in nails, rather than a masher made for skulls. Also inevitably, after seeing Gregor's hammer, they never questioned it again.

The skiff lifted off into the afternoon yellow, Dynas's haze unchanging and always wet. This skiff's deck had studs, so everyone's boots had some grip as the craft picked up speed, rising over the city and oriented back west, towards the closed tram station and a rendezvous with the virus.

Above and around them, the Black City picked up its pace. More skiffs and shuttles raced into the tower than Gregor noticed from the morning, and the streets below their gliding skiff seemed more full, as if the city's populace had at last shaken off a long night and decided a walk, no matter how dreary, was required. Ponchos, wet suits, and combinations of the two made for bland viewing, like squishy, gray-black bugs stepping through the puddles.

"It really is the worst planet," Lani said. She and Gregor leaned over the skiff's left side, looking. "If the projects weren't so interesting, I'd have left long ago."

"Would they let you leave?"

"Not sure, never asked," Lani replied. "Until now."

"What do you mean?"

"If what you're saying is true, and this outpost really is an illegal haven that Helix is protecting, then this whole thing is compromised." Lani nodded down towards the city. "We're here to protect these people, and everyone not on this planet, from rogue scientists proliferating some bio-weapon beyond what we're investing in. If that's happening, then Helix has blown our contract, and they need to be erased."

"Destroying Felix will not stop the experiments."

"No, but we can, hopefully, slow them down," Lani said. "Then, when you leave, you can take me with you and we'll get the big brass involved. Smoke this place. And get us out of here."

"So you would do this for yourself."

"Damn right, for myself," Lani said as the skiff approached the tram station, with Sayers angling the ship down for a calm landing. "For Sayers and Wicks too. We've been here for years, Gregor, and the mission has held us for this long, but we're ready to be done. Problem is, Defense-Corp won't approve an evacuation until the mission's complete, or the mission's blown."

Why did everyone have to have their own motivations? Was it not enough to simply march into the enemy's ranks and break them down? Bash in a few foes? Gregor hadn't joined Sever to get involved with people's personal problems; if you agreed to a mission, you saw it through and found the joys where you could.

"I can tell you're not a fan." Lani laughed. "Guess what, it doesn't matter."

"Doesn't it?" Gregor replied. "You need me to show you the way."

"And you need us to live," Lani said. "Like everything

else in this galaxy, what we have is a deal. Both of us profit."

Sayers landed on the closed tram station and Gregor led them off. Lani blew the lock off the roof-access door and they descended into the quiet, dark station, to the quiet, dark tram, where three Sever Squad suits sat dark, and quiet.

"Look at this," Lani said. "You didn't mention the extras."

"They aren't yours."

"Don't see why we can't borrow them," Lani replied. "This one looks about my size. Wicks, can you fit into the blue?"

"Mmhmm," Wicks muttered, playing with Rovo's suit.

"They won't work without the codes, or their DNA," Gregor said, beginning to put on his own armor. "Leave them."

Lani cocked her head, and Sayers, standing behind her, whipped out his own handgun. Aimed it at Gregor.

"Then you'll give us the codes," Lani said. "Now. Because we have some clean-up to do, and then a planet to leave behind."

FOURTEEN

Up, Up and Away

THE KART'S control sticks—two, slightly curved like scribbled C's—felt tight in Eponi's hands. Sensitive, quivering as the kart's batteries jumped its jets and leaped the craft a meter above the finished, smooth ground. Around Eponi, the glass bubble cockpit closed and her earpiece crackled as she made connection with one of the galaxy's most famous racers.

"All right, uh," the sound cut for a second. "Eponi? Right, Eponi. Can you hear me okay?"

Forgot her name already. That hurt, but Eponi let the kart's whine wash it away. She held the sticks, she'd be flying the lap. That's what mattered.

"I can hear you," Eponi replied.

The course stretched beyond her, twinkling blue lights glaring out beneath Seleno's red sky, red sand, red mountains. The glossy black pavement between the blue lights would twist and turn, arc over and under terrain as it tested a kart pilot's ability to stay within bounds. To stay, at some points, alive.

"Looks like you've flown one of these a few times, right?"

The contest required some experience to pick this particular prize, and yes, Eponi had that experience. Those nights on the old track, after hours. But this? An official, day-time sanctioned lap run? Never.

"I know how to fly." Eponi said, then ran her eyes across the info screens for the tenth time in as many seconds.

The kart checked out. Green and ready to go.

"Then here's what we're going to do," the voice on the other end, currently sitting number three on the galactic leader boards, said with a hangover's enthusiasm. "Get started, take it slow, and enjoy the ride. Keep it under a hundred, and I'll tell you when to brake and turn. Should be a good time."

Under a hundred? Even the greenest kart circuits pushed three hundred kilometers an hour. Eponi knew there were plenty of people looking to hire the next new racer at the course today. They probably weren't watching her—official tryouts would be coming later, with people who'd worked their way up rather than made a lucky pick with their last race wager.

They probably weren't watching her, but Eponi would make them look all the same.

A small drone, a little ball with a single bright red light, flew and floated in front of Eponi's kart. As she was the only racer on the track, the drone centered itself right in her face, making sure she couldn't miss when its light turned green. And if she did, the kart itself would vibrate, tell her in multiple senses that it was time to *go*.

Eponi exhaled long, slow. She had to keep her nerves down on the track, keep her grip loose and flexible, her eyes looking ahead. Keep the panic at bay. The racers who crashed were the ones spending too much time on the danger they'd already blown by.

"Okay, here we go," said the voice on the other side, already bored. "Nice and easy."

Eponi jammed the accelerator and slammed herself back into her seat as the kart shot forward, the electricity's instant torque shooting the frictionless, floating kart along the track. Eponi managed to keep her grip even as momentum pulled her fingers away. The voice yelled something in her earpiece, but it didn't matter. Didn't register.

She flew. The curves melted away as Eponi fell into instinct, into all those simulator practices she'd run during off-hours, when nobody gave a crap what she did. Those long days coasting the digital stars from one circuit to another paying off now; Eponi had never raced this course in reality, had raced it a million times in a virtual one.

Sometime during the first lap, the voice in her ear had fallen silent. Sometime during the second, someone new had come on, not saying anything more than to keep going, that they were timing her, and they'd tell her when to quit.

"TIME TO GO," Ben said as the shuttle's dash beeped that the cargo hatch had been closed. "We've got what we need."

He'd put away the gun, at least. Decided, apparently, that Eponi wasn't going to pull a deadly trick in this cramped cockpit with enemies all around outside.

"Where are we going, exactly?" Eponi said.

"Up, up and away," Ben replied, then glanced at his wristlet computer. "We're on time to make the meeting. They'll get us out of here."

"They?"

How many people wanted off this planet, and how many lacked a way to do it? Sever's whole mission briefing boiled down to extricating someone from a place that didn't seem all that hostile, yet she had the growing impression that Dynas was not a place anyone wanted to be.

"That's for me to worry about," Ben said. "Just take us up. Once we get out of the atmosphere, we'll catch an orbit and make our rendezvous."

Eponi thought about asking Ben if he'd ever flown before. Quips like 'catch an orbit' didn't help when you were plotting astrogation covering millions of kilometers at ludicrous speeds. Any space-side meet-up needed precise timing, planning, communication.

Then again, none of this was her problem. Ben shooting her for not going along with the plan definitely was.

Eponi primed the shuttle's jets, flipped on the outboard speaker and issued the standard advisory that this particular shuttle would be blasting off shortly and if you did not want to burn up, you ought to stand well away.

The words did their work, and soon Eponi's shuttle had room to hover a meter off the ground, rotate around, and look towards the docking bay's exit. Dynas's yellow, morose sky hung beyond, dripping moisture over the bay's opening. The city's nano-net did its work and clear light came from above. Not a bad exit vector.

"You have the clearances?" Eponi asked Ben. "Or do we just trust that nobody's going to pop a laser up our asses?"

Ben gave her a funny look. "Clearances? What do you mean?"

Eponi's hand drifted over the throttle as she laughed, "You serious?"

The mastermind engineer flushed, a deeply satisfying moment for Eponi, "I . . . don't understand. We loaded the cargo. The shuttle's ready to fly, right? What more do we need to do?"

Two choices. Eponi could stall the shuttle, set it down right here and explain the problem to Ben. Make him understand that sending spacecraft into the air without letting the right people know they were going to be there tended to get defenses triggered. Ben might be able to get the forms filled out, get this whole thing squared away, and Eponi would still be a hostage.

A hostage that Ben had no reason to keep alive once they made their rendezvous.

Choice two, then. Eponi pushed the shuttle's throttle forward, punching up the jets far too high for exiting a bay. The ship blasted out, scorching and blowing over people, cargo, drones and anything else around it. If Ben hadn't made enemies before, he certainly did now.

"What the hell?" Ben shouted as the shuttle blew free from the tower, arcing towards the sky.

"If we're not supposed to be here, we gotta leave quick," Eponi said, adjusting their arc and sending some power to the shuttle's rudimentary defense systems.

No weapons, just some mild armor and avoidance systems meant to keep the shuttle alive long enough to reach protection. The most useless setup imaginable, but here they were.

"I didn't want to attract attention," Ben said, voice tight now, angry.

"Then you shouldn't have picked me to be your pilot."

On cue, the shuttle picked up an incoming hail from the tower. Ben reached to answer, but Eponi beat him to it, cut the call before it started.

"Not yet," Eponi said. "Once they realize it's you and not me behind this, you're cover's blown."

"My cover?"

"Sure," Eponi said. "Right now, all they know is you went on board with a known enemy pilot. I could've taken you hostage. This might all be my plot. When they call back, that's what you say."

Lights lit up on the shuttle's board, one after another, as the tower's defense systems and, likely, some pursuit, focused their attention on the shuttle. Ready to erase the ship from existence.

The hail came again.

"Answer it," Eponi said. "Convince them not to fire, or we're both dead."

Ben looked like he might be having a panic attack. Sweat coated his face, his breath came and went in manic gasps, and the man turned around the cockpit as if expecting to find some hole he could jump through and return to a time when this had never happened.

"Hit the damn button," Eponi repeated, then pulled the shuttle into a steeper climb.

Straight up into that yellow sky, and beyond it, the stars. If they lived long enough to make it that far.

"This is Ben, Ben Taigo," Ben said after he slapped the button, gulping several times through the sentence. "Please don't shoot. Please."

"This isn't a scheduled departure," some tight-laced voice on the other end said. "Any unauthorized flights are to be terminated, unless you can convince me otherwise?"

Eponi shot a glare Ben's way. Remind him who the villain was here. Not him, but her. The pilot taking the shuttle hostage.

"Eponi. I brought her on board, uh," Ben looked wide-eyed at Eponi.

"He wanted me to check the shuttle out, confirm that it looked ready to fly in exchange for some extra dessert," Eponi said, a ridiculous statement. "He looked the other way, and now the shuttle's mine. So let's negotiate."

The other line went silent. Eponi tapped the mute button on their end, looked over at Ben as the yellow sky in front began to darken. Space loomed.

"You ever do anything like this before?" Eponi said. "Because, speaking frankly, you're a terrible criminal."

"I . . . no."

Eponi found it a little sad how fast Ben's bravado had died away. Some people just weren't cut out for a life beyond the limits.

"Shuttle, Eponi," the Helix flight officer resumed. "The craft you're in has no interstellar capabilities. If you return to the tower, we will not fire upon you. No lives need be lost. This can be forgotten."

Eponi screwed up her face. Forgotten? They must really want her alive to offer something like that. What did Eponi have that Helix cared about?

"Sorry, I'm going to take my shot," Eponi said. "Dynas is, literally, the worst. Only coming back if I can't get this thing anywhere else."

"Then take your time," Eponi could hear the sneer in the voice. "When you realize the futility, we will be here."

The call dropped, the target lights did too, and the shuttle soared higher, onward. Ben looking like he was about to pass out. Eponi, flush with the rush, grinning as stars came into view.

FIFTEEN

Fatherhood

Aww hell.

Rovo waged an emotional and factual war. The former would lead to inevitable anger, to a strange despair that a child could be treated like this even on a planet as wet and worthless as Dynas. The latter, the latter would be what Sever Squad would expect. A rational analysis; pick the situation apart and make some sense of what he was seeing.

She sniffled.

Rovo stopped himself from reaching out, from turning around and finding a tissue in the bathroom to offer the girl. He had to stop himself because of what he'd seen in that outpost not long ago. Felix, the disease.

Kashmal, presumably, had a reason for locking this child in the room, a reason for not mentioning her.

Facts. It would have to be facts.

"Can you understand me?" Rovo asked the girl, who hadn't attempted to cross the door's threshold.

She looked, apart from the filth and the ragged gown—Dress? Pajamas? Rovo didn't know kid's clothes—about six or seven, somewhere in the range where she should be able to understand him, and yet be hesitant to leave her safe space, no matter how disgusting.

As Rovo peered beyond the girl, her room truly was a disaster. Crumpled bedsheets—no mattress in sight—and a mealy pillow, a bucket in one corner with a paper roll whose purpose Rovo could, with a stomach-turning frown, discern. The walls had scratches all along them, random patterns and shapes all stopping a little higher than the girl stood. Whether they'd been drawn with a tool or the girl's fingers, Rovo couldn't tell.

"Yes," the girl said, or rather, croaked.

Somehow, on this wet disaster of a planet, the girl was thirsty. Rovo crouched, getting to an eye-level with the girl, and took closer stock. Her brown hair, tangled and long, flowed below her waist and almost to her knees. Dirt smudged her cheeks, but her green eyes were bright and she didn't look malnourished. Kashmal must have been doing the bare minimum to keep her alive, and even simple protein bars fed through a slot were packed with so much fortified nutrients these days that the girl had likely done better than Kashmal himself would have expected.

None of this meant Rovo wasn't going to deliver Kashmal a strong sock to the jaw next time he saw the rat. Leaving a kid, diseased or no, unwanted or no, locked up in a room like this deserved nothing less.

Rovo had sisters. Younger ones. Before he'd leapt to space for financial necessity, he'd patrolled their relation-ships, their health like a shark, seeking out and destroying any potential threats. He'd been good at that, too. Perhaps too good: they'd been happy to see Rovo take a gig on an orbital station and get out of their hair.

"What're you doing in here?" Rovo asked.

"I'm supposed to stay hidden," the girl replied. "Always."

"Why?"

"Because I'm sick."

There we go. Rovo closed his eyes for a long moment. He'd opened the door, and while he hadn't touched her, the air the girl had been living in for weeks—Months? Years?—had wafted all over an exposed head, mouth, nose and Rovo's lungs. Any airborne virus would've found him already.

But maybe she was sick with a cold, a common flu?

"Sick with what?" Rovo said. "Something very bad?"

The girl nodded, sniffled again. Looked down at the floor and her hands as they played with her hair. Rovo's face quirked. This sucked. This was not the plan. Badass mercenaries were supposed to dart in and destroy then beam out the victorious heroes. They weren't supposed to find kids like this.

"Do you know how it spreads?" Rovo said. "Your sickness? Can you breathe it on me? Or do you have to touch me?"

The girl looked up at him, confused, "It's inside." She tapped on her arms. Her chest. "He says it's a part of me, and we have to wait and see what happens."

"Who says that? Kashmal?"

The girl nodded again. A cute little nod, where her chin went all the way to her chest and back up again.

Still, the girl's answer didn't do much to help Rovo decide if aiding her would get himself killed or not. He and the girl stared at each other for some seconds while he put together a different tactic.

"How does Kashmal feed you?" Rovo asked. "Or empty . . . that?" Rovo pointed to the bucket. "Does he come in here?"

"Sometimes."

"Does he wear anything? Like a mask?"

"A what?"

Hmm.

"Does he look like me?" Rovo pointed to his face, then to the little girl. "Like you? Not wearing anything?"

"He doesn't look like me," the girl replied, then took a step forward. Rovo shrank back without thinking. "Are you afraid of me?"

Rovo shook his head, "Not of you. Maybe what's inside of you."

The girl hadn't yet reached the door. If Rovo moved now, he could probably slam it shut in her face. Lock her away again. Or . . . he could assume the virus wasn't airborne. The door wasn't, exactly, an air-tight seal. And if the girl had to touch him to transmit the disease, then Rovo could let her out. Could give her some food, and just keep his hands away from her.

"Do you have a name?"

"Yes," the girl said.

"Can you tell me?"

"Kashmal says I'm not supposed to."

"Well, Kashmal told me you could," Rovo ran along his mental line. "In fact, while he's gone today, I'm supposed to watch you, and to do that, I'm going to need to know your name?"

The girl didn't react for a moment, then slowly smiled in that shy way kids do when they're really happy and really worried because what they're about to say or do means so damn much to them.

"Kaia," the girl said. "That's my name. The one my mother gave me."

"It's a beautiful name," Rovo said. He wanted to ask about the girl's mother, but given where she was, where she had been, Rovo felt her parents were long out of the picture. "Are you hungry, Kaia?"

Another nod.

"Then why don't you come with me and we'll get you some food?"

"But I'm not supposed to leave my room?"

"Kashmal said I get to watch you, remember? Which means I get to make new rules, and I say you can come out, okay?"

Turned out letting Kaia out of her room and into the apartment's kitchen meant unleashing a hungry beast. Rovo scrambled to find food in Kashmal's place that didn't look rotten or potentially lethal, but a few cabinets in, Rovo found some canned soups that served to stuff Kaia enough for the moment.

From there, Rovo kept playing sudden dad, closing off Kaia's room, helping the girl use Kashmal's spitting, hot shower, and then wrapping her in the cleanest blankets he could find. After doing all that, Kaia started to look like a real human. Real enough that Rovo parked her on the couch, told her to sit still, and that he'd be back with new clothes for her.

Not that Rovo had any idea of where to get clothes, or how to get money for them in this city. Compared to Sever's increasingly lost mission, though, this seemed like a challenge he could overcome.

"What're those?" Kaia asked from her couch-blanket fort as Rovo geared up to go, picking up and placing his weapons in his wetsuit.

"They're to keep me safe," Rovo said. "You don't need to worry about them. Nobody's going to hurt you."

Kaia accepted that without much inquisition, partly because Rovo had left his wristlet computer on the couch tuned to some local children's stream. Inane shapes babbled about numbers or letters or something, and Kaia seemed mesmerized.

"Don't move from that couch, okay, unless you need to go to the bathroom," Rovo said, figuring that was safe enough. "And if someone knocks, don't answer unless they say they're me."

Kaia did her trademark nod after all this, and while Rovo couldn't be sure the kid had even heard him, or paid attention at all, he dipped out anyway. Three steps down the hallway and he stopped, turned back, and knocked on the door.

Waited. No sound.

"Kaia," Rovo said, not quite yelling but loud enough to carry through.

"That's me!" came back the girl's response. "You're back already?"

"Nope, just testing you," Rovo said. "You passed!"

Laughter came from inside, and Rovo didn't try to suppress a smile, "Okay, the game starts again right now. Nobody except me."

Kaia giggled again, probably at the computer.

BY THE TIME Rovo made it to the streets, he'd identified two big flaws in his plan: first, he'd left his computer with Kaia, meaning he didn't have any way of looking up a map for where he was, where any stores might be. And second, he'd realized the apartment, with its moldy food, vast amounts of cutlery and more, presented a giant death trap for a child left to her own devices.

He'd also left the briefcase up there, figuring Kashmal's evidence wouldn't help Rovo keep a low profile.

As fresh rain poured around—no longer just humid, Dynas decided to add real water to the mix—Rovo tried to decide whether it made more sense to turn back and wait, or just get the job done quick.

Kaia would need clothes if she was going to get off world. If Aurora and Kashmal came back needing a quick getaway, Rovo bet she wouldn't risk any delays for Kaia. He had to do this now or never.

So Rovo reached out and poked the next person passing by in the shoulder. The man, cloaked in a thick, dark poncho, wheeled away from Rovo, turning with a frightened look, an open mouth.

"What do you want?" the man asked, looking like he expected Rovo to straight up attack him.

"Just trying to find the nearest clothing store," Rovo tried. "I'm new here."

"New here?" the man seemed confused. "I didn't think they were letting anyone else in?"

"Guess I'm special," Rovo said. "Clothing store, where?"

"Oh, uh, head two blocks that way. They have a bit of everything," the man scrunched his eyes. "You work at the tower?"

"Thanks!" Rovo said, stepping by the man and heading along the sidewalk.

Never carry on a conversation past its useful point. Particularly not when you're trying to stay undercover.

Thankfully, Dynas and its terrible atmosphere didn't encourage the man to follow through on his question, and receding splashes indicated he'd given up any pursuit.

Rovo found the smallish store right about where the man had said it was, and unlike some of the more metropolitan planets, or, indeed, the *Nautilus*'s own outfitters, this shop advertised itself under the grim reality that its customers simply didn't have another choice.

Bold, marred white letters on black declared the store

The Loom, though everything inside seemed, to Rovo's unpracticed eye, to be synthetic. Plastics abounded, made to ward off the ever-present water, and while the children's section wasn't large—Rovo shuddered at whomever saw Dynas as the ideal spot to raise a family—there were a few wetsuit-style outfits that'd fit Kaia.

Now, how to pay for them?

The Loom wasn't crowded, but the few people milling through the racks made a successful robbery risky. Rovo could grab the outfit and run, see if anyone cared enough to chase him. Or ask for generosity? He lifted a child's red wetsuit off the rack, turned towards the register, and felt a pistol's business end press into his back.

"Didn't think mercenaries would be buying clothes," a hot voice whispered behind him. "Then again, s'pose that girl does need something to wear."

SIXTEEN

Sever and the Scientist

THIS WAS the strangest damn prison Aurora had ever seen. Not only were the walls and halls a brighter, cleaner blue and black combo than the muck-ridden slime corridors she'd witnessed on other, better worlds, there didn't seem to be many prisoners here. Aurora walked past one empty cell after another, all that pretty glass showing rumpled cots and empty space.

At least till she hit the fifth cell, along the right side wall of a level Aurora had come to understand made a giant square. Cells sat inside and out, and not directly across from each other. That, at least, made some sense: keep your captives from communicating, forming any sort of plan. Escapes were harder solo.

Then again, looking at this one, this hopeless sap stuck in the fifth cell, Aurora couldn't imagine escape being on his mind. The man leaned on all fours, knees on the ground with his hands planted, heaving into a grate in the cell's center. Sickness played an obvious part, obvious because Aurora could see the discolored patches on the man's skin. He wasn't wearing anything other than cursory undergarments, his shoulder-length hair plastered to his sweaty shoulders, twinging with every gasping breath.

After seeing Felix, after witnessing the mutations already wrought upon its people by whomever ran this godforsaken planet, a 'normal' sick person, however severe, left Aurora feeling hollow. Not scared, not disgusted, just . . . detached. Perhaps that's what came with a life like this; exposure to so much awful removed empathy.

That, and the sealed glass cell meant Aurora likely wouldn't catch whatever plagued the man. Felix had indicated his virus required a kind of blood transfusion, an injection to get across, and it didn't take much of a leap to see that what had plagued Felix came from right here.

Aurora amended the mission in her mind, added an optional objective: if she could destroy this place on the way out, or at least cripple it, she would.

"Who are you?" the question came from down the hall, asked by a woman wearing a frazzled, stained lab coat and carrying a large silver case, one that looked a lot like Kashmal's, under her arm.

"Better question," Aurora said, squaring up to the woman in the hallway's center, though several meters sat between them. "Who are you, and what are you doing here?"

The woman screwed up her face, as if not quite comprehending an interrogation in what was obviously her own palace. She looked so at ease with the prison, with what was happening around them, that Aurora didn't need an answer to know this woman drove, or at least helped, these prisoners suffer.

"I don't answer to intruders," the woman replied. "If you would kindly put yourself inside?" she tapped a cell to her right, an empty one, though the scattered sheets and stained floor inside suggested only recently. Some ID badge in the woman's sleeve prompted the cell's door to open. "I will be able to help you soon."

"Don't think so," Aurora replied. "But, on second thought, maybe you can help me instead."

Aurora took a short step towards the woman, who responded with an equal retreat of her own.

"I have two friends that came here, to this tower, yesterday," Aurora said, injecting that steel menace any competent captain learned to employ. "I haven't heard from them, and I'm wondering if you might know what happened?"

"People come to this tower all the time," the woman replied, keeping focused on Aurora, keeping a tight grip on that briefcase. "I don't meet them all. And, sadly, some do disappear."

"Disappear?" Aurora said, continuing to advance as the woman continued to retreat. "Into these cells, maybe?"

Now the woman smiled, "Oh, no. I am helping these. I always know where they are." Her smile dropped away as quickly as it came. "Though sometimes they do not appreciate my work."

"Shocking."

With diplomacy seeming out of the question and Aurora's patience wearing thin, she started another slow step, then burst forward in a sprint. Without armor, Aurora moved faster than she expected—how liberating to fight without kilo upon kilo weighing you down—and her target seemed as surprised, turning to run and tripping over her own boots to fall on her chest, briefcase slipping away and sliding on the smooth floor.

Aurora had her own boot on the woman's back before another breath passed, and her hand on the woman's neck a hot second later, twisting the woman's mouth so that she could speak, breathe.

For the moment.

"Tell me again," Aurora said. "I had two friends. They came to this tower. Do you know where they are?"

The woman coughed. Tried to say something, then coughed again. Aurora let up a little, took her hand off the woman's neck. Not everyone responded well to aggressive interrogation, and Aurora could be patient; the woman wasn't much of a fighter.

"You are one of them, aren't you?" the woman said between further coughs. "Those soldiers that came to Dynas?"

"Sure, one of those," Aurora said. "Now answer the question, or I start breaking things."

"Then yes, yes I do know where one of your friends has gone," the woman said, smart enough not to squirm under Aurora's foot. "He is down below with the others, trying to survive the gift I gave him."

Oh, damn. Sai hadn't seen Felix back at the outpost, he might not know what would happen with this virus, assuming the woman was still injecting her prisoners with the same stuff. Which meant Aurora had to find her friend a cure.

The nice gloves were coming off.

Aurora stepped off the woman, grabbed her collar and pulled the woman to her feet. Pointed to the briefcase, "Tell me there's a cure for whatever you're doing in there?"

"Cure?" the woman said, then shook her head. "There's no cure, because this isn't a disease. I'm making them better, more complete humans."

The woman didn't sound afraid anymore, and that scared Aurora. She'd met cocky scientists before, people so full of their own work that they neglected to realize the threats around them. That made their work dangerous, but gave Aurora a chance: egoists liked to talk about their projects, and the scientist might give away an option if Aurora kept her talking.

That hope died when shouts came from behind, back towards the elevators. Aurora spun around, keeping the woman between her and the half-dozen Helix soldiers, wearing that all-covering body armor she'd seen at the outpost, quick-stepping towards them with weapons raised.

"Let her go and we won't shoot!" the lead soldier said, identified as such, Aurora assumed, by the gold lining around his double-helix patch. "You're outnumbered!"

"I can see that," Aurora said, then whispered to the woman, "Tell them to stay back or I'll snap your neck before they can get a shot off."

"Snapping my neck won't save your friend," the woman replied. "Whatever your reason for being here, I doubt it was to kill me and then die in this hallway."

Not wrong. The woman made a good point. Aurora backed up, pulling the scientist along with her. The soldiers came on, keeping the same distance, repeating their demands without firing a shot.

"Pick up your briefcase," Aurora said as the pair passed by the item. The woman obliged, crouching with Aurora to pick the silver container off the ground. "And keep walking."

After the scientist picked up the briefcase, the lead soldier apparently decided this walking negotiation wasn't going anywhere. He held up a hand, and the back three soldiers turned and began running the other way.

"This floor's a square, isn't it?" Aurora said, keeping up her retreat.

"You're so smart. Are you sure you don't want an injection of your own?" the woman replied. "It would help you, I'm certain of it."

"Keep your needles to yourself."

Aurora estimated a minute, maybe two for the running soldiers to get behind her. Her hostage couldn't cover both sides at once, which made a shot to the back the most likely outcome coming her way.

Not good.

At the hallway's corner, Aurora used the turn to backpedal faster. Another elevator lingered not far down this side, opposite of the larger bank where Aurora had arrived. This one, unlike the standard corporate design of the others, had warning stickers and red lights all around it. An important one, a dangerous one, and possibly an escape.

"Unlock the elevator," Aurora said to the woman, pulling her over to the door.

"Of course," the woman replied. "Though you may not like what you find down there."

The woman obliged Aurora's order, slapping her wrist against the elevator's door and changing the red lights green. Aurora slapped the call button as the soldiers rounded the corners on either side, yelling for her to stand down.

The doors didn't open. The elevator wasn't ready.

Aurora was out of time.

Aurora pushed the woman away, stuck her hands up. The lead soldier grabbed Aurora's hostage while the other two went for Aurora herself, taking her hands and binding them with metal stun-cuffs, ready to numb Aurora's nerves if she made any aggressive moves.

"Stay down, and stay quiet," one of the soldiers said to her. "And maybe we don't kill you."

The woman shook off the lead soldier's help, turned back to Aurora with that devious smile she wore so well, "I'm sorry your plan didn't quite work out, but don't worry. We always have room for more subjects like you. These fine gentlemen will lead you to a cell, and I'll see you in a few hours."

"Looking forward to it," Aurora said as the guards cuffing her lifted and pressed her against the hallway's wall.

All told, Aurora had never been arrested before. This, despite all the hostile invasions she'd carried out, missions that broke local laws with wild abandon. Usually, her enemies just went for the kill shot. Less dangerous that way. A dead DefenseCorp soldier wouldn't come back to haunt you.

And when the elevator Aurora had called opened its doors, Aurora saw her chance to do just that.

SEVENTEEN

Reality Rumble

Sai had never been a leader, a director, a manager of men. He preferred his explosives, his sword and the hands-on work that went with them. Yet, feverish and furious, in a large room filled with test subjects feeling the same, someone needed to step up. Someone needed to steer the plague in the right direction.

Anaskya had gone for the elevator. Disappeared as her large companion met his grisly end at the sharp nails, biting teeth, and slobbering jaws of barely-there humans.

Standing next to the elevator door, wavering in his hazy vision, were Sai's son and daughter. Smiles on their faces, jumping and pointing towards the door. Not real, couldn't be real, but damn did they look like it. The same age as when Sai last saw them, years and years ago. Peppermint ribbons in his daughter's hair the way he'd do it on holidays.

If his kids wanted him to go in the elevator, if his fevered, infected mind saw that as the path, then Sai would take it.

As Captain Happy's last bits were torn away, the Sever

soldier stumbled towards the elevator and slapped its call button. Stuck the man's ID, ripped from the victim's ruined shirt, against the elevator's scanner and saw the green acceptance, the priority override beating out any other callers.

"This way," Sai yelled back to the group, a wet, coughing call that meshed well with how Sai felt. "If you want a chance at a cure, we have to catch her."

Sai couldn't tell how much the other dozen or so victims understood, but most followed the call. Dropped their fleshy bites and meandered Sai's way.

The man that started it all, whose virus seemed more advanced than anyone else's, led the shambling crew in a sashaying run, as if fluid filled his body and slid side to side with every step. The man's red eyes weeped a yellowed pus, while his skin otherwise continued a fast shift towards a darker blue, like a giant, spreading bruise. When he sidled up, as the elevator doors opened, he acknowledged Sai with an open mouth and a hoarse grunt.

"Together," Sai replied, not knowing what else to say.

The DefenseCorp soldier reached out before he could stop himself and put a hand on the other, diseased man's shoulder. Tightened the grip for a second, as Sai would have done to Gregor, or Eponi. He'd known this human wreckage for less than a few minutes, but common purpose forged common bonds.

They went into the elevator and the others poured in behind them. Sai didn't quite know whether they exceeded a weight limit, whether getting this many infected in close proximity would hurt or help them. He did know that his swimming vision, a constant burning throughout his arms and legs, and an occasional, seconds-long hallucination bringing him back home to his family meant Sai was on a dire trip to nowhere good.

The elevator only had one other button. For this, at least, Sai could thank Anaskya. Her desire for direct efficiency gave Sai one less choice to make, one less decision to ponder. He slapped the button, watched the doors close, and listened to the heavy, soaked breathing around him.

From their looks, Sai's motley infected blend came from everywhere on Dynas's societal ladder. Some wore wetsuits, torn and stained, suggesting a life on the city's streets. Easier victims, perhaps, to take. Others, like the doomed man next to Sai, had clothes bearing the double helix logo. Employees sacrificed at the corporation's altar.

By choice, or by force?

Sai guessed the former, courtesy of the latter. An offered bonus or a trip off this world, and when the reality of that choice made itself apparent, a gun shoved against the back to keep people from turning against their initial ideas.

The short elevator ride, and the man's decaying disposition, left no time to confirm Sai's idea.

When the elevator doors opened, Sai tried to make sense of what he saw. Immediately across from him, face pressed up against the wall and wearing one of those cheap wetsuits, was his captain. Two soldiers worked on her, while another half dozen loitered nearby, all looking back towards the elevator, their masked faces no doubt confused at the diseased mass rolling out towards them.

Sai didn't give any order, didn't stride out first and demand each and every guard be turned into grist for his monsters' murderous appetites. The monsters did it themselves.

The ruined man led the charge, catching those black double helix uniforms in his eyes and rushing forth from the elevator with a crazed, coughing roar. Sai pressed himself back into the elevator as the others followed, streaming out into the hallway and diving towards their chosen victims with weeping-eyed abandon.

"Sai!" Aurora called above the shouts, and Sai finally left the elevator to find his commander on the ground, kicking away a diseased woman half-heartedly reaching for Aurora's ankle.

"Lay off her," Sai said, reaching through the blur to push away both Aurora's kick and the infected woman's grab. "The ones with the uniforms, they're the enemy. They did this to you."

The woman looked at Sai, a weathered face starting to show the same dark blue splotches as the warrior man, and she started to say something, when her head simply exploded, burst into flames and melted down as one of the guards unloaded his weapon into her. He aimed at Sai next, when Sai felt a sudden pressure on his left ankle.

Sai hit the floor as the guard's shot blazed through the space where he'd been a second before. Aurora, to his left, reeled back her leg from kicking Sai down, curled, and dove head-first into the guard, her matted, sweaty hair leading a gut-busting charge into the man and knocking him down.

The prison hallway ceiling loomed above him as Sai lay on his back, the fall hitting his chest hard and pushing air away from weakened lungs. He saw Aurora make her headlong charge, hands cuffed behind her back, and knew that he needed to get up, needed to do something.

Between one blink and the next, his mother stood there, smiling down at him, looking just the way she had on the tower rooftop on that terrible day. She leaned forward, reaching with both hands for Sai's, and he took them, felt his mother pull him up, and—

"Sai! Some help here!" Aurora shouted and his mother vanished, replaced a meter away by his captain's struggling form as she tried to keep the guard's gun-hand pinned to the ground.

Right. That's what he was doing. Fighting.

Sai lurched forward and fell on the guard, missing Aurora and driving his elbow into the guard's face with enough force to send the man limp.

The diseased victims were holding their own around the hallway, tackling, biting and tearing at the armored guards. Several of Sai's makeshift companions had been obliterated by laser fire, but surprise and savagery had downed all but two of the guards, who were gang-tackled moments later by the remaining horde.

"Sai, mind getting me out of these cuffs, then telling me what the hell is going on?" Aurora said, cutting through the panicked shouting from the infected's meal.

Opening the cuffs meant getting a badge off their downed guard, something that shouldn't have been so hard, except Sai's fingers had started feeling as big as sausages, and his children kept showing up on the fringes, making it hard to concentrate.

"Sai, focus," Aurora said after he made a fumbling attempt to open the guard's badge pocket on the man's chest. "What's wrong with you? With them?"

"I," Sai closed his eyes. Tried to shut everything away just for a second. Reset. "They injected us with something. It's what they're doing here, in the tower, I think. The point of this whole place."

Sai had to keep talking, had to keep spilling out the words because if he stopped, if his mouth closed, Sai had the sudden feeling that he might not be able to open it again. His fever had to be spiking, that virus sending its heat rushing up and down and all over his body.

"They're going to turn us into something else," Sai continued, sucking in air as he could, and managing to get the guard's ID badge out. Aurora turned her back to him, presented the cuffs, and a sweaty tap unlatched the blue-metal restraints. "Anaskya kept saying it would help us become better, but I don't think she knows what she's doing."

Aurora turned around, helped Sai to his feet, kept her hands on his shoulders. Her face looked clear, solid, real. But then, of course it was. Aurora wasn't like Sai's kids, his mother. Not a hallucination.

"Real?" Sai said after Aurora asked a question that he didn't catch. "You're real, right?"

"About to be a whole lot less so if you don't keep your friends away," Aurora replied, rotating Sai around to face the survivors, who'd gathered around the two of them, looking as distraught, as ruined as Sai felt.

"They're not," Sai looked around, the faces staring back at him ran the line from barely coherent to bubbling rage, but all shared a singular trait that Sai had seen before. "They're not my friends."

"Might want to rethink that before they eat us."

"We're infected," said one of the others, a built-up woman wearing the bloodied remnants of a double helix uniform. "That's all. That's everything. But we're not crazy, just, just angry. And sick."

A sickness in desperate need of a cure. One that, Sai suspected, Anaskya would have. If one existed at all.

"We have to go after her," Sai said. "Anaskya. She's the only option."

"Are you talking about a scientist? Leader of this bunch?" Aurora said. "Because she was here a minute ago."

As soon as Aurora finished the words, the infected group broke and started off along the hallways, calling out for Anaskya's name and getting replies from prisoners still stuck in their cells. Aurora and Sai watched them move, and Sai would have gone after them if not for Aurora holding him fast.

"Sai, I need to know. What's happening to you? Are you compromised?"

Sai relayed the symptoms. Said he felt he could handle standing, moving. That any sustained action would be disastrous.

"And Eponi?" Aurora asked. "Do you know where she is?"

"She turned me in. Saved my life and killed me at the same time."

"She's here then, in the tower?"

"Maybe?" Sai tried to shake his head, but Aurora went right on past his comment.

She explained, in the whip-cracking mission briefing way Aurora had, Kashmal and the briefcase, the objective and the plan to secure a shuttle ride out once Sever Squad had been reunited. Sai caught every fifth word, and even those he let slip away.

Because, truth was, he'd be dead soon, or something so different that the Sai who'd journeyed all this way might as well be gone.

EIGHTEEN

Infected's End

BEING in Sever meant threats had a way of finding you, whether directly like with Lani's gun pointed at his face, or collaterally, like when Wicks attempted to break Rovo's armor's code and almost set off its self-destructive, anti-tamper feature. The suit began a rapid countdown, and Lani, wisely, let Gregor brush by her to enter in a twelve digit string on the armor's keypad, just next to the seam along the armor's left side.

Dying when his own team's power armor exploded wouldn't be the dumbest death Gregor had seen in his time with DefenseCorp, but it would be close. Nothing, though, would top the time he'd witnessed a fleeing prisoner accidentally eject himself into space's cold vacuum seconds before hitting atmosphere. The parachute didn't do the poor man any good.

"Thanks," Wicks offered, standing well back from Gregor. "Forgot they did that."

Agents. Gregor had been thrilled to see Lani at first, figured maybe she'd help him find the rest of Sever, maybe assist in getting a ship off-world. Instead, Lani had reminded Gregor why he liked to avoid DefenseCorp's clandestine service members.

For one, they kept too many secrets. Lani could say all she wanted about destroying Felix and keeping Helix within bounds, but DefenseCorp could've done the same with periodic inspections, a frigate waiting overhead ready to melt down any objectionable material. Embedding agents in the city meant DefenseCorp had other ideas, or wanted to guarantee some investment from this whole venture.

But, did Gregor care?

You take a comet miner with nothing to his name, give him a chance as a muscle-bound enforcer that grows into elite fighting form, you're going to get some loyalty. Aurora might press these agents. Sai might question their real motives.

Gregor had his hammer back, and they were taking him to a place where he could use it. For now, that was enough.

"I give you the codes," Gregor said. "You give the armor back when we reunite with my squad."

"Of course," Lani replied. "Not going to get much done if we're tramping around this city in that."

"If you try to keep it, I will kill you. DefenseCorp or no."

Lani laughed, "Sure. Whatever you say."

The stakes made clear, Gregor supplied the codes and, with Lani and Wicks putting on Aurora's and Rovo's suits, the foursome went back to the station's rooftop, jumped on their skiff and zipped away from the city.

The thick, wet, yellow fog enveloped the skiff as it left the nano net, clogging Gregor's vents and forcing manual cleaning. He showed Lani and Wicks how to do it, cycling the armor's air intake while holding your breath to push that air, and the yellow dust, out the vents. A real pleasure, but, in the process, Gregor realized how little these agents knew about real combat.

"No, never dealt with armor like this," Wicks said after Gregor walked him through the vent cleaning. "Prefer the subtle methods, myself. But if we're going up against something bad, can't be too careful."

"Then if you want to live, let me teach you a few things," Gregor replied.

"And here I thought you didn't care about us," said Lani, no doubt smirking behind her visor.

"My friends will want their armor back," Gregor said. "I don't want to carry it home."

Exploring the DefenseCorp armor's various functions ate up the rest of the skiff ride, until Felix's conquered outpost rose out from the ochre gloom like a dull hallucination. In the day since Gregor had last been here, not much about the outpost had changed.

In fact, nothing had.

"How is this place not crawling with soldiers?" Gregor asked the air. He'd been half expecting this expedition to end before they hit the ground, as any force worth its name should have sent back-up, or even overwhelming reinforcements. "You don't let enemies win on your own turf."

"You do if victory's price is too high," Lani said. "Who knows how many toughs they employ actually know what they're protecting?

Gregor supposed he might revolt too if he found out his friends were being experimented on, turned into walking monsters.

Sayers guided the skiff onto the roof, volunteered to watch it as the other three jumped off and descended on a lift down the outpost's exterior. Gregor realized this must have been how Sai and Eponi made it away.

How were those two? And Aurora and Rovo? Gregor felt fairly safe with this bunch, but was the rest of his squad still alive?

He gripped his hammer tighter, held it ready as they approached a side entrance, one forced open. The big weapon, ready to transmute kinetic force into its strikes, made Gregor feel more secure. Like home, but destructive.

"Before we go in," Lani said as they formed up near the door, with Gregor ready to lead. "Anything else we should know about Felix? What he's fighting with?"

"Don't get close," Gregor said. "Use fire. And don't listen to him."

Wicks and Lani seemed to nod, so Gregor returned to the freakish nightmare he'd preferred to forget, bashing through the thin door with his hammer and heading in.

This hallway, though, was new. Laser scoring etched the walls, along with the occasional silver line from a sword —Sai's katana, no doubt. Gregor saw all this through his helmet's light, as the base's power had apparently failed. Not all that surprising, given the struggle here.

"This was a big fight," Lani said. "How many of you came? An army?"

"Five," Gregor replied.

On the left, they past by the barracks, bunks still sporting sheets and the personal effects of at least some soldiers. Ones either dead or, by now, worse.

Gregor didn't have the base's layout mapped, so he followed the katana slashes, the laser fire. It would, theoretically, bring them back to the conflict's center, where they would find Felix. Or he would find them.

"Didn't bring any shovels, did you?" Wicks said as they rounded a corner and came face-to-face with a rubble wall where the hallway had apparently caved in. "I don't dig with my hands."

"We go around." Gregor led them into a room to the left—an office? Supplies?—then readied his hammer. "Stand back."

It took three thunderous strikes to crack a hole through the walls into the next room, a larger, command-center-esque space. Dead monitors plastered the walls, stood on desks. More important, a door on the far end led to another hallway which . . .

"I hated this elevator," Gregor said.

"Is it as blood-soaked as this place?" Lani asked, looking around the base's center, where the semi-faded, still sticky remnants of Sever Squad's initial foray through these halls remained.

"Felix waited for us below," Gregor said. "Up here, guards attempted to ambush. Neither succeeded. It was annoying."

Give him a straight-up fight any day. Not this cramped quarters, sneaky work. No genetic mutants either.

"Speaking of," Lani said. "You said Felix tended to know what happened around here. Where is our friend?"

"I haven't seen anything unusual," Wicks added. "As fun as this armor is, I'm going to be annoyed if you dragged us all the way out here for nothing."

Nothing, though, seemed to be the trend. The base sat quiet, empty, and without a sound. Not even rats or other vermin made themselves present. As if, after Sever's fighting, the whole base had decided to go quiet.

The emptiness should have been eerie, but given what had happened here not that long ago, Gregor found it peaceful. Like visiting a tomb.

Gregor took Lani and Wicks back towards the power planet, then to the left and through more offices, to where they had rescued Rovo. To where, last Gregor had seen,

Felix's collective mutations had writhed in a massive biological heap, waiting for new blood to add.

Except here, in the empty elevator shaft that had served as Felix's cellular vat, Gregor saw nothing. Only, at the very bottom, a lingering bit of black sludge.

"You're going down there?" Wicks asked as Gregor went for the shaft's sole ladder. "Why?"

"Because if Felix is gone, I want to know."

Gregor descended fast, hammer looped over his back and his hands on the ladder's outside rails, letting him slide down the several stories to the bottom floor.

His armored boots landed with an icky splash, scattering bio-matter around. Gregor knelt down, touched the black-gray stuff with his hand. The mass quivered as his armored fingers touched it. Still alive, then, though it didn't seem to be sucking at him the way it had with Rovo the day before.

"Well?" Lani called from above. "Find anything?"

"Not yet," Gregor replied, standing.

Aurora had said she'd either kill Felix herself or get DefenseCorp to burn the creature from orbit. Now, it looked like she might not need to do either.

Behind him, Gregor heard the slow, grinding sound of an electric door's manual override shoving it open. The Sever turned around slow, drawing the hammer over his head in the same motion.

Standing there, a hunched mass far more gray, brittle than Gregor had remembered, was the reason Lani had dragged Gregor back here.

"Hello, Felix," Gregor said.

"You've come to keep a dying man company?" Felix answered. "How kind of you."

NINETEEN

Nearly Free

HITTING WEIGHTLESSNESS WAS AN ELASTIC MOMENT. Dynas's gravity dipped away in an instant, but Eponi's body reacted to it in swinging sensations as every organ, blood vessel, and nerve adapted to their sudden unmooring. The first time Eponi had felt the sensation, she'd vomited everywhere.

Every other time, she'd succumbed to the manic grin that defined piloting in space. Wonder after wonder after wonder.

"I hate this," Ben said next to her, cradling his gun and looking more green than not.

Some people would never, could never understand what it meant to leave a planet's bindings behind. Others like her? Eponi wasn't lost to the idea that growing up captive to menial jobs and stuck on a backwater world made her sensitive to getting freedom, however imaginary that freedom really was.

She'd left Dynas, yes, but Ben still had her hostage. Though now, in space without another pilot, she had him hostage too.

"You'll either get used to it or you won't," Eponi said.

"I don't belong in space," Ben shook his head. "That's why I took the Helix job in the first place. If things went well, I could stay there forever."

"Then you went."

"Then I went," Ben said. "Spend a day on Dynas and it's already too long."

Ahead, space brightened as stars and planets by the billions popped up in the black. Dynas's home star lay behind them, its light doing little to wash out the distance as Eponi slanted the shuttle to put Dynas between the star and the ship. A little artificial eclipse.

Pointless, unless you wanted to stage a relative meeting place.

As they'd ascended, Ben had mentioned that he didn't have coordinates. Just a name, a date, and a promise. Get to Dynas's shadow and wait, and Ben would find his buyer, and his escape.

"How'd you even make contact with these people?" Eponi asked as she sent the shuttle up to match Dynas's orbit, then turned it to keep the view facing outward. The less she saw of that wet planet, the better. "Some lasers pointed to the sky?"

"Dynas isn't disconnected from the galaxy," Ben said. "Helix needs food, buyers for their products. It's just very controlled. I happen to be one of the people that does the controlling."

"And these people we're meeting, they're going to take us and what you've got back there?"

"That's the idea."

"Why wouldn't they just shoot you, take the stuff for free?"

Ben grinned in that cocksure way overconfident people

had, "The cases are locked. I'm the only one that knows how to open them."

Eponi laughed. Sever ran into countless threats like that. Haughty assholes claiming they couldn't be killed because some weapon, some treasure, some secret code depended on their life. Turned out, you could open anything with enough skill, patience, and, if necessary, explosives.

"You're not taking me seriously," Ben said.

"Definitely not," Eponi replied. "You're either going to wind up dead, or, well, dead."

"Not everyone in the galaxy makes life-and-death deals, you know," Ben replied. "Sometimes people are okay without the killing."

Eponi could allow that her career had jaded her perspective.

Being a kart racer running around the galaxy's fringe, Eponi had been exposed to plenty of deals and compromises, the kinds of things that took place outside the bright lights, the crowds and cameras that made people stars. She sat there as managers and owners and teams and agents pitched away her life, her time for profits. And she went along with it. That was how the galaxy worked, the industry and the life. That Ben had found something similar on Dynas slinging cells for a mad corporation didn't surprise her.

What did?

That Ben didn't think anyone would take advantage of him.

The shuttle blinked a warning, a little red light indicating another craft had entered relatively near space. Eponi had been facing the shuttle outward, planning to at least catch, with the forward facing radar, anything coming from outside the system. This contact, though, came from behind. The ship must've jumped around Dynas, circling the planet in order to approach unseen.

Were they being paranoid? Maybe. Strategic? Definitely.

"Looks like your friends are here," Eponi said.

"Our friends," Ben replied. "Don't piss them off."

"What, you think I might?"

"Yes."

The shuttle they had stolen off of Dynas didn't have the sophisticated radar Eponi was used to. DefenseCorp made sure their ships came ready to scan, see, and pounce on any potential threats. This shuttle only indicated position. Eponi couldn't tell whether the approaching ship was big, small, or deadly. Not that they had any weapons to fight back. Rather than trying evasive maneuvers, any steering or piloting, Eponi left the shuttle hanging and leaned back in the seat. Waiting for the captors.

"Are they expecting me?" Eponi said. "Or am I going to be an inconvenience, one easier to just toss into the vacuum?"

"These aren't murderers," Ben said. "They're just a company, same as the one you work for. Same as the one I worked for. All they want is profit, and something to sell."

"You should really start a new career as a motivational speaker," Eponi replied. "You're making me feel so warm and fuzzy."

Before Ben could reply with anything more than a roll of his eyes, the shuttle shuddered. The approaching ship made its initial dock, latching onto the hatch on their shuttle's side. Another beep and flashing light indicated a secure airlock, ready to transfer over Ben's contraband, and Ben himself.

Personally, Eponi hated those slow interstellar walks. Where only a membrane kept you separated from a quick death. The galaxy was rife with tales about transfers gone wrong: you had the accidental things like a mistaken latch, a sensor reading a close connection when in reality a hairline fracture meant all the oxygen sucked itself out. Or maybe everything looked good, the transfer was going well, and someone thought it was done. Hit a button a minute early and poof, a whole crew gone.

Better to hold for an all clear, so Eponi waited while Ben went back to check. Stayed in the cockpit where she could, if need be, close the doors and seal herself in that tiny compartment. Give herself just enough air to get back to atmosphere if something went catastrophically wrong. If Ben's buyers proved less interested in Ben and his hostage.

Trust was not one of her dominant traits.

"Eponi, can you hear me?" Ben's voice came through the cockpit's speaker.

"Crystal clear," Eponi replied. "You meet your friends yet?"

"They've established the link. Should be over in a minute. I'll talk with them, and let you know what's next."

Which gave Eponi plenty of time to stare at the stars, to count her breaths. To check around and see if there was anything left in the cockpit that could give her some clue, maybe, as to who they were meeting with. What company. Not that she wouldn't find out eventually, but any scrap of information might help.

As stated, Eponi didn't trust anyone she didn't know. Especially companies.

The first time Eponi had left her home on Seleno, the kart racing organization supplied the trip. Eponi had thought she was leaving behind a red mass where so many dreams died or sputtered out, thanks to them. Eponi signed everything they asked her to. She went along with their demands, raced every race she could. And only, only when she met the other pro racers, the ones who had been at this for years and years and years, did she find out how bad she had set herself up. How beholden she was to the arbitrary decisions made by people far more powerful than her.

Even though she had all the talent.

That talent pushed Eponi to start making demands, asking for more cash, better resources. Which all worked fine as long as she was winning, as long as there wasn't someone new that could get the same without all the grief.

She crashed one too many times. Like all kart racers, but, also, because of her demands, not. They decided it wasn't worth repairing her when the next rookie would fly without complaint. And when you're cast out from your life's passion at such a young age?

You wind up flying drop-ship missions for a dangerous company, as part of a dangerous squad.

Speaking of, where were they? Down on that surface. Were they still alive? Would they be surprised to know that Eponi had made the escape, one airlock away from a jump to another life?

She rested her hands on the control panel and leaned forward, trying to find some answer out there. If she went over to the other ship, took that supposed offer and left with Ben, she'd be out. Likely branded a DefenseCorp deserter, targeted with a license to capture or kill if anyone came across her. But Eponi was small potatoes, small game. DefenseCorp wouldn't care about trying to catch her and they'd let her disappear into the dark as so many others did.

No more guns, no more missions, no more armor, no

more strange planets with stranger people and still stranger viruses.

She could ship cargo, send things back and forth until she saved up enough to get her own kart. Not a bad life. Not bad at all.

"Eponi?" Ben said, his voice jarring in. "You still awake?"

"I'm here, where are you?"

"On their ship," Ben replied. "Their taking the deal. They're taking what we brought. And me."

Ben delivered the end with a heavy weight, a finality to it. The kind of tone used in breaking up with someone, or an idea, or dream. Or maybe just disappointing a friend.

"You?" Eponi said, letting the ice formed from his words run through her veins, freezing away any shock. No trust, remember? "Does that mean what I think it means?"

"It means you're free," Ben replied. "Not my hostage anymore."

"Why aren't they taking me?"

"No room," Ben said. "But really, once I told them who we were, they didn't want to make an enemy of your employer. Guess DefenseCorp has too much pull."

"Right."

What else could she say?

"Thanks, Eponi," Ben said. "Thanks for getting me out of there. And now you have your ship. You can go back, and pick up your friends."

In a shuttle that couldn't leave the system?

"Sure. Have a nice life, Ben."

Eponi cut the comm. A second later, the shuttle shuddered again as the latch broke. That airlock seal fell away. The scanners beeped again, tracking the other ship as it blasted off towards the system's outer edge, where it would accelerate out to near light speed or over on its way to some other world, some other life.

Her shuttle couldn't take her anywhere.

No, that wasn't right. The shuttle could take her to the only place she needed to go.

Back down to that miserable world.

TWENTY

Rumble In The Wet

THERE WERE ONLY a few reactions that made sense when you had a gun to your back. There's the first one, which was to surrender. Throw up your hands and hope and pray that the person sticking you up had something he wanted you for, or else you're dead.

Except DefenseCorp forbade that move.

Why? Because DefenseCorp wouldn't pay any ransom, and every time the kidnapper found that out, well, they tended to take their hostages all the way to the grave.

Option two: Try to fight, throw an elbow or slam your head back if the enemy is getting too close and see what happened. See if you could break their nose, make them drop the weapon, maybe grab it and turn it back. In any case, give all you got to the wild hectic scramble to see who could make it out alive in a back-to-nature rumble.

Or option three: Talk it out. Likelihood of success? Low. But, for Rovo, former communications officer for DefenseCorp and master of many languages, perhaps a little higher.

"You put that gun down," Rovo said, forcing steel calm

into every word, "and then you let me turn around, talk face-to-face to figure out what you're doing, and how I can either help you or kill you."

"Doesn't sound like a good deal to me," the guy with the gun said. "Kneel so I can put these cuffs on you."

"Try again," Rovo replied. As he spoke, his eyes surfed the shop, hunting for something more useful and close, something that might help him get out of this alive. He saw nothing, which meant Rovo had to get creative. "Because guess what, I'm not alone. If you don't put that gun away, one of my friends will put a hole through your skull."

"Oh yeah?" The guy replied, hiding a laugh under the words. "I think you're lying."

The man shifted his tone, spoke into something near his chin, to someone not named Rovo. A question beaming to some sort of backup force waiting out in the street. And in that moment, Rovo had the distraction he needed.

The secret about option three? You do it right, and it gave you a great option two.

Rovo crouched and turned, slinging his left arm out in a gut level punch. Crouching removed the man's gun from its lethal aim, and also put Rovo behind a clothes rack on his left, the outfits hanging and blocking the view from the street for any of the man's reinforcements who might've been lining up for a shot.

Rovo's punch hit tough padding, a thick wetsuit, maybe professional grade. Thin muscle beneath that moved at the impact. By the time he pulled his head around, Rovo realized he wasn't looking at a badass experienced killer, but a younger man, wearing a respirator and holding the gun like he didn't know what to do with it.

Was Helix lacking in security personnel? Had Sever, and Felix, wiped out so many that they were pulling in reserves from anywhere?

Either way, the kid didn't seem to know what to do, so Rovo made the choice for him. He straight up tackled the Helix thug, driving him back into the ground. With his left hand, Rovo ripped away the gun and threw it across the floor.

"You stay down, you keep your life," Rovo said, pressing his face close to his would-be captor. "You're in way over your head, kid."

"I'm not a kid."

"Right. Then stay down, man."

The kid didn't, tried to struggle, so Rovo dished an elbow to the kid's temple to lay him out. Another glance around showed any reinforcements taking their time coming in, which meant Rovo didn't want to waste any time getting out.

Rovo ran. He wouldn't call it cowardly, just playing the smart game. As the other shoppers pressed themselves to the sides, stayed out of the way, Rovo got to his feet and ran towards the door, reaching out and snagging a pair of girl's outfits as he ran: little nightgowns. Perfect for any other world but this one.

The sidewalk splashed as Rovo pounded out onto it. Now would be the time for any of the kid's backup to come forward, but nobody waited for him. Maybe the kid had been overconfident, rushed in without backup. The only people on the sidewalk were the usual dregs, muddling through their late afternoon, hunting for a better bit of hope, finding none. A few watched Rovo as he ran by, splashing water as he went. Nobody seemed to react. Because of course, when your whole life is a dour disaster, some real action doesn't even penetrate.

Rovo had to get to Kaia. That much was clear. If they had tracked him to the store, then they would know where he came from, would be going after, well, maybe not the girl. The suitcase? Either way, Kashmal's apartment was compromised.

Wet suits were not good for running. Two splashing blocks later and Rovo had slipped and fallen several times. Every step seemed to squelch the wetsuit into Rovo's creases and remind him of just how good his armor used to be. But in desperate times, you accept desperate measures and Rovo kept moving.

In the block outside Kashmal's apartment, Rovo saw nothing. An empty sidewalk, no stopped vehicles with waiting ambushes. A glance behind showed the kid in the store wasn't pursuing, or had lost him.

And for a moment, Rovo took a breath. Slowed to a walk as he approached Kashmal's door before going in and heading for the elevator.

As he went into the box that would take him up the floors, Rovo tried to put together a plan. He only had one gun. It would take two hands to hold Kaia and the briefcase, and even once Rovo secured them, he didn't really know where to go. No doubt Aurora had gone to the tower, but Rovo couldn't head there.

Take the suitcase and Kaia right to the ones that wanted them? Nope.

Gregor, then. The hammer man might be Rovo's only option. Rovo could try and track Gregor's most likely direction from where they'd split, though that didn't hold much promise either. Rovo wasn't a hunting dog, though even those talents might not help on a planet as wet as Dynas.

So that left the tram station. Where Rovo, Aurora, and Gregor had ditched their armor. If Rovo could make it back there, he could at least get himself suited up. Maybe hold out.

Gregor and Aurora would try to make it back there too

at some point: none of them would leave their armor if they had a choice. Rovo had only worn the suit in the simulator and on this mission and already it felt like a second skin.

The tram station then. Rovo would get there and either die or live long enough to be rescued.

The elevator doors opened and Rovo broke left, towards the apartment. Stopped. Nobody stood in the hallway, but there were sounds coming, loud voices giving commands to someone. Maybe Kaia, maybe to each other. Rovo pressed his back to the opposite wall, then reached and hit the emergency button on the elevator, holding it at this level. That would keep any reinforcements delayed, just a little.

Rovo went forward, step by step, feet crunching into the gripped tile. The one smart concession this planet made to moisture. Rovo held his gun up, ready. Barely breathing.

"They're saying they lost him, that he's probably coming here," said one of the voices from the room, not stressed in the least. "You watch the door, I'll finish packing up the girl."

Packing the girl?

Either way, Rovo didn't wait them to get ready. He dashed the last meter, wrapped around the door and fired as he did so, aiming his weapon at the height of man, not a girl. The first bolt struck one target, in all-black tactical gear. Burned a hole right in his chest and the man collapsed while the other, with Kaia half restrained in some sort of jacket, swung around and put Kaia between himself and Rovo.

"Want to risk hitting her?" The man said, this one older. Helix still had some adults in its ranks, apparently. "She's the one you want, right?"

Rovo didn't see the briefcase anywhere. Maybe they hadn't found it yet. Maybe they didn't know it existed.

"No reason she needs to get hurt," Rovo said. "You can put her down now."

"And why would I do that?" The man replied, his voice calm. Too calm given the circumstances. Rovo tried to sling his eyes around, see if there was someone else in the apartment. "I have time on my side. Yours is running out. Put the gun down and, if you didn't kill my friend there, maybe you live through this."

The man was right about one thing: Rovo didn't have time for talking. He had to take the chance. His enemy wouldn't want to get Kaia killed either, that would ruin their prize. So Rovo charged him.

The man froze up, expecting either a shot or a negotiation. His hands full with Kaia, he couldn't do anything to stop Rovo clocking his face with Rovo's gun handle. Rovo caught Kaia's left hand as the man dropped, steadied her.

Turned her away before Rovo administered a final shot.

"You all right?" Rovo asked Kaia as he took off tight wrap the guards had snared her inside.

She nodded, her eyes tight with something that wasn't quite fear. Maybe stress? Maybe excitement? Either way, Rovo was impressed. At that age, being around a couple of bodies, Rovo figured he'd be bursting out crying. Shrieking for his parents. But then, maybe Kaia didn't have any real parents to scream for.

Kashmal certainly didn't qualify.

"Okay, let's get going. Hit the streets and run," Rovo said. "Ready?"

"I can run," Kaia said.

"Of course you can," Rovo reached beneath the couch and pulled out the briefcase. "Anything else you need?"

"What do you mean?"

"Well, I don't think you're coming back here. Maybe not ever."

Was he supposed to tell that to Kaia? Hard to say. The little girl didn't look like she lived a charmed life. Hard news had to come regularly to someone living in a room like that. In an apartment like this. On a planet like Dynas.

"Can I get something?" Kaia asked.

"Make it quick," Rovo replied.

The girl dashed away, back towards her room and Rovo dragged the two bodies into the kitchen, left them there behind the counter, just hidden from a cursory glance. Not exactly a high-level move, but better than leaving them in the open, where they could be seen through a window. Anything to buy him a couple seconds.

She came back, carried a small ball. A little lion, hopelessly out of place on this world. Mottled yellow, overused. But she hugged the doll like it meant everything to her, and since Rovo was taking away everything else, he let her keep it.

TWENTY-ONE

One Way Off Dynas

THE PRISONER REVOLT on Cassius Five. That's what Aurora could compare this to. Where Sever, at that time fielding a different crew except Aurora and Gregor, dropped in and intentionally allowed themselves to get captured. Once inside, they'd worked to inspire a total uprising that tore apart swaths of Cassius Five's main city. The planet's owners had decided they could do without extending DefenseCorp's contract.

DefenseCorp had decided otherwise.

Of course, leading a whole bunch of disgruntled prisoners was one thing. Breaking out of a high-tech laboratory on a miserable planet with a whole bunch of devastatingly ill science experiments was something quite different.

Aurora and Sai, the latter barely hanging onto his consciousness, gathered all the infected they could find on the prison floor. That meant freeing them from cells, using stolen guard badges to open the glass doorways and convince, when they could, the occupants to come join them. Some were too weak to bother getting up from their cots, and Aurora had no time to play doctor, so she left them without a second look.

Once assembled, the bedraggled twenty of them went towards the elevators Aurora had used, only to find them locked. The call button wasn't working, and swiping a guard's badge only returned an error saying the rank wasn't high enough to override.

"There's another way," one of the other infected, a woman wearing a Helix uniform and looking not quite devastated, said as they huddled around the elevator doors. "You have to have emergency exits, just in case. But they're hidden on this floor, for obvious reasons."

"Well, it's our floor now, so tell us," Aurora said.

Sai nodded, trying to agree, and would have fallen over if Aurora hadn't caught him.

"It's easier if I show you," the woman said before leading them over to a slight indent in a wall in the far right corner, near the prisoner elevator and the remnants from the fight.

The gray steel section was cut out just large enough to resemble a double door, though a cursory glance wouldn't have shown anything. No handle, no button, certainly no exit sign or other indicator. Aurora didn't have to think too hard to guess why: in the event of a real emergency, the people who knew better could decide whether to save the prisoners or not. In a situation like this, where the prisoners were the emergency?

Leave them here. Let them rot.

"So how do we open it?" Aurora asked.

"Try the badge," the woman said. "The scanner's on the right side."

Aurora slapped the ID card against the wall, feeling a little stupid as she did so. It was possible the woman was experiencing some fever delusion, that they were just wasting time. Of course, they didn't exactly have any other leads, so why not.

Given Sai's deteriorating condition, and the increasingly wild looks the other infected were giving each other, Aurora figured it wouldn't be too long before everyone started chowing down on their friends.

Slapping the badge did nothing. No sound, no sign.

"You sure it's this corner?" Aurora said.

"I'm sure," the woman replied. "Most floors in the tower are arranged like this."

"Like a prison?"

"No, like a square. This corner always houses the stairs, I don't know why we'd change here. This floor wasn't always for this."

Aurora gave the woman a closer look. She was a little older, probably not some intern. Her whiter hair, skin, and slightly hunched stance suggested a long career that had burned out by the end. Aurora would've asked what she was doing here, why they picked her for this mad experiment, except there was no time. And Aurora wasn't here to get the full story.

"This is what we do," Sai said, his voice soft enough that Aurora had to repeat his every word the rest of them could hear. "We take all the weapons. Every single one that we have and pile them up. Save one."

The old explosion. Ignite all those laser burning gasses at once, blow a hole in the wall. Not a bad tactic, although the side effect, disarming yourself to fuel the makeshift bomb, wasn't exactly the best plan.

Except the infected had already taken out a bunch of guards with their fists and their teeth, maybe they could just keep that train going. Break out of this the physical way.

"You heard him," Aurora said. "Get the guns, pile them up. Right here."

"These doors are meant to stop fires," the woman protested as some of the infected moved to follow Sai's orders, placing looted weapons on top of each other near the door. "You really think this'll blow it open?"

"Fires and explosions are two different things," Sai said, leaning on Aurora, breathing hard. "It's not the heat that's going to open the door, but the force."

Aurora and Sai moved down the hall while the piling continued, until the infected had jumbled all the guns on top of each other. One pistol remained, handed over to Aurora once the pile was ready. She beckoned for all the infected to stand behind her, halfway down.

"Not far enough," Sai said. "I don't think so, anyway. This could be a lot of shrapnel. Maybe something worse. We should be around the next corner."

"This isn't strong enough to make a shot from that far away." Aurora looked at the little pistol. Meant for close-up duty, inaccurate any range beyond a dozen meters or so. "Someone's got to be closer."

"Then I'll do it," Sai said. "It's my idea, and look at me. I'm not exactly alive anyway."

Aurora hesitated. Self-sacrifice wasn't exactly the Sever code, but in an impossible situation, sometimes you had to make an impossible choice. But they weren't doomed here. Not yet. They could finagle something. Maybe replace one of the bigger weapons with the pistol, take the shot from the end of the hallway and dive behind the corner?

"Sai, there's other options," Aurora said. "We can try something different."

"No, no," Sai said, attempting and failing to point as his arm twitched. "I can barely stand. I'm only going to hold you back. Let me do this, let me do something worth it at the end."

But Aurora didn't give Sai the pistol. Instead, she motioned to a couple of the more sane infected, including the older woman and told them to pull Sai back from the corner. Aurora would take the shot. She could fire and dodge back around the corner, or fall to the floor to limit the exposure.

Aurora didn't have a family. She had nobody waiting to see her. She would pull the trigger

At least, that's what Aurora had planned until she felt hand on her shoulder and turned to see the large man, the brutal one that had led the charge from the elevator.

He was strong, no doubt some sort of security force employee in his former life, but now red blotches and weeping cracks marred his face, blue patches broke out along the scalp as his hair fell in waves. His simple prisoner's uniform bore tears all along a burn where a laser had grazed his leg. Nothing about him looked healthy.

"Let me," the man said. "I'm tired of this damn life anyway."

"I can try the shot," Aurora said.

"And if you miss?" The man replied, his voice weak, whistling. His lungs were falling apart. "You burn energy that we need. That you need. I got this."

Self-sacrifice. A rare trait. But there were objectives that needed to be met, and Aurora understood, saw in the man's eyes a look that she'd seen before: he'd made peace with his choice.

"Anybody you want me to tell?" Aurora said. "Any message you want sent?"

The man tried to laugh but a wheeze came out instead, a cough and he took the pistol from Aurora's yielding hand. "You don't come to Dynas because you have someone you need to tell, because you have something you need to do. Dynas is an end, and I'm ready for it to be over."

"Then thank you," Aurora said, and she moved around the corner with the rest of the bunch. The gaggle of infected bruisers, all clinging to life as some mad virus made mincemeat of their bodies, shuffled back to give her space.

They crouched down, with hands over their ears as Sai instructed. The man, with a final nod back Aurora's way, made one wild, weak shout and ran towards the bundled guns. A deafening boom shook the floor, followed by the crackling fizzle as electric energy seared the air. Alarms, little white lights nestled in the floor's joints, flashed and sounded their horns.

When Aurora turned the corner, a new doorway waited.

The steel sheet had been blown apart, bits and pieces hanging and scattered around the hallway almost all the way to the corner. Black blast scarring coated the walls. Of the man, there was nothing left.

"Right where I thought it would be," the woman said.

Aurora wanted to race up the stairs, get the whole crew moving, but she stopped herself. Sever had an objective here, and, right now, that was getting out alive. Then find Kashmal, get a ship, pick up Rovo and that briefcase and head for the stars. Hopefully they'd find Gregor and Eponi along the way.

Nowhere in that list was a requirement to rescue a bunch of failed experiments. Aurora wasn't supposed to drag a couple dozen infected people off the planet where they could spread to the galaxy or do something worse. Things would, likely, be better if all these infected died here.

Aurora wouldn't call herself heartless, just focused.

"I need to know," Aurora said to the assembled group in the shrapnel-coated hallway. "I need to know what you're infected with. What it is going to do to my friend. And maybe to me."

They stared back at her blankly, a couple making noises that they should be moving and not talking. Until finally that same woman, the one who pointed out the emergency exit, held up a hand.

"None of us know," the woman said. "I mean, we know what the goal is. The whole point of this project. But we don't know what Anaskya infected us with, what it's going to do or how it transmits from one person to the next."

"Wait," Aurora said. "What project?"

Sai, still leaning on her, pressed down a bit, "Aurora, let's just go. They won't cause us trouble. And we might need them."

"None of you are going to kill me right?" Aurora said. "You won't lose your minds?"

She figured she could probably handle anyone that did, but if the whole collective decided to go berserk, that could be a problem.

"Please," the woman said. "Please just help us. Get us out of here."

DefenseCorp objected to freebies. Anyone they helped, anyone that leveraged any resources needed to be charged accordingly. But here? Maybe Aurora could let this slide, just this once. Give them a chance to save themselves.

And, if any of them made it off-world, well, that wasn't Aurora's problem.

"Okay," Aurora sighed. "Okay. If you're following me, then you're obeying my orders. We're going to try to get out of here, and we're going to do it by heading up top.

Find a ship and blast off this wet rock. Either you agree with that and you come with me, or you can go your own way at any point. I don't care. If you try to stop me, or get in my way, I'll kill you. No questions asked."

There were no questions asked. No runaways either.

Aurora led the charge up the stairs, which were just that: Long metal steps in a bland, gray stairway that went on for eternity. Nonetheless, they climbed. The shambling bunch behind her made slower progress, some slipping and falling, others helping them up. A real charitable bunch coming together. It would've been heartwarming, except everyone's degrading flesh and bones and hair made it disgusting and sad.

Two more levels and they heard more noises. Ones Aurora could decipher pretty easily, because she knew them well. Barked orders, the cadence of footsteps with a professional bent. An aggressive set coming their way from above. Aurora held up a hand and stopped the climb at the next landing.

"We can run back down," Sai offered. "We can't take them head-on, Aurora. We have no weapons."

"I'm aware," Aurora said, she turned to the landing's door. Going back down would be the wrong direction. "Let's try this. They won't have locked every door in this tower."

Aurora slapped the guard's badge against the black reader next to the door and this time, unlike below, the badge worked. The door slid away and revealed something bright and filled with glass. A white space, but entirely unlike the cellblock below. Long tables took advantage of the open area, with various cases on each one, some surrounded by machines and whirring monitors. Ventilation ran overhead. Not a soul in sight.

"Come on," Aurora said. "Before they catch us."

They hustled into the new space, their filthiness entirely at odds with the floor's sterile purity. The last one shut the door behind him and silence reigned. Sound seemed at odds with the climate here, the science obviously at work. Aurora could tell this place was a lab, the place where, she could guess, the thing infecting her friend had been made.

"So what do we do now?" Sai said. "They'll find us in here eventually."

"We head to the elevators," Aurora said. "Hope they haven't locked them down."

Aurora didn't say that, given there were no other doors on this floor, locked elevators meant they were all very, very dead.

As they went through the lab, and towards its far side where the elevator bank made itself known with a pair of blazing signs, Aurora glanced at various samples. The monitors and what they read out. Most were indecipherable gibberish, the kind of scientific language only known to those who practice it. But others had labels, designations that were clear and purposeful.

The buyers. The funders. The ones paying for all this. And those names Aurora recognized. Everything from exploration companies, dedicated to finding the next new batch of valuable minerals, to tourism agencies who wanted an easier way to station people on faraway plants, and yes, one Aurora knew would be here, knew deep down had to be involved.

Of course DefenseCorp would be investing in this. Of course they would be paying to see if they could transform their mercenaries into a more effective fighting force.

That didn't make Aurora angry. Breaking Galactic law wasn't a good look, but Galactic law could always be changed. No, what pissed her off, made Aurora clench her fist and grind her teeth even as some of the infected reached the elevator and called out that it was, in fact, working, was that DefenseCorp knew what was happening here and sent Sever in anyway. They had gone in blind for no reason.

Well, Aurora could see now. And she was gonna make it off this rock, dammit. She's gonna make it off and she was gonna make whomever ordered this mission pay. No matter what it cost.

TWENTY-TWO

What Lies Beyond

WHY DEMOLITIONS? That's what they asked him, when Sai first came to Sever. Aurora and Gregor were the only current ones there at that point. The question had come on his first mission, his first flight when Sai was very much a rookie, having only played around the edges in less risky DefenseCorp outfits.

If you wanted the real cash, though, you had to jump into the danger. Which was why Sai picked up explosives. He'd done his homework, looked at the deadliest job in the squad and taken it for himself.

Sai felt he'd do it better than anyone else, and he didn't want to die because someone else screwed up the explosives.

After the infected man detonated the way out through the gun pile, Sai had felt vindicated as Aurora and his infected friends climbed the stairs. All that training had paid off, all the time and effort to blow a wall chunk away to let diseased wrecks make a halfhearted escape.

Better than no escape at all. Better than getting corralled and executed on that prison cell floor.

The lab hadn't come as a surprise. Not like it so clearly stunned Aurora: all the specimens, all this work, all sponsored by supposedly reputable players in the galactic order. Of course someone had to be paying for this. Helix wasn't infecting people for charity. Sai saw the labels and felt a suspicion confirmed, the logic behind how such a city existed on a seemingly isolated and uninhabited planet cleared up.

But as Aurora grew angry, Sai found himself leeching that emotion. She swore up and down about the companies they saw, and those words pierced Sai's infected haze. This was all their fault. He wouldn't see his children again because of these company's vast negligence, their inhumanity.

He wrapped his hand around the beaker, marked for a test the following day. Samples for some strain marked with numbers and letters Sai couldn't understand, but he knew the buyer. The company profited off of mining comets, captured and pulled them to huge stations where the comets would be broken down into their metals. Maybe they wanted someone who could stand on the comet's surface.

Sai's katana had been comet-forged. Provided, likely, by this very company or one of its predecessors. That something so tied to his family had invested in Helix finished bursting the ennui that came from the disease. Could nothing really be pure? Did everything have to be so driven by blind profit?

Was that the galaxy his children would be living in, without Sai to help them?

"Destroy it," Sai said. His voice proved lacking, so he coughed, then repeated the command. Louder. "Destroy it all."

The other infected, milling around the lab, slowly

making their way towards the elevators on the far side stopped at the words.

"Sai, we don't have time," Aurora said. "We can do it later."

"No. There might not be a later, not with everyone behind this," Sai said. "We destroy this now."

He swept the beaker off the table, smashing on the floor. It felt damn good, breaking the glass. Better than ripping the ID off of Captain Happy's body down below, better than tackling that guard attacking Aurora. But nowhere near as satisfying as swinging his sword. Sai might be dying, but he would get the katana back. After he destroyed this place.

"They're just going to rebuild it," Aurora said as more of the infected took Sai's lead, pushed over machines, picked up and launched tools and beakers and instruments around the room.

The silent, sterile place filled with sounds of shredding glass, filled with beeping panicked programs as parameters were pierced and pulverized. Tables overturned and sent their occupants flying. Biological matter, incubating diseases burst free and splattered the walls and floors, rendering the white space splotchy yellow and green. No doubt dangerous, no doubt of no concern to those already damned.

Sai wasn't sure when the stairway door opened, when the Helix forces came through. He was too lost in it, that mindless rage he directed at these worthless, awful instruments around them. The laser fire soon pierced that shell, blazing away in bright beams that lanced the air around Sai, before Aurora tackled him to the ground.

His captain had found a mask somewhere, some gloves too. Sai guessed that as the only uninfected here, Aurora's protection made sense. But in the moment, the covering made her look like someone else entirely. Sai tried a half-hearted push, punch. Aurora had Anaskya's hair, and with the mask, that was enough.

"Sai, stop it," Aurora said, batting his punch away. "Go to the elevators. Now."

She began pulling them along the ground and Sai helped after a second, reconnected with his legs and kicked his boots along the tile floor. They couldn't stand, too many lasers filled the air, the beam's heat washing over Sai as they moved. Screams came too, shouts of pain and rage and despair. Some cut off as soon as they started. Sai saw the other infected being cut down even as Aurora pulled him behind a table, kept pulling them towards the elevators while putting cover in between at every possible moment.

She knew how to be a soldier, how to make use of the battlefield terrain and devise a path to victory even against overwhelming odds. Sai, Sai just wanted to destroy it all. To end himself in a way that didn't involve a slow decay in a cell being poked and prodded, tested and trialed.

"Let me go," Sai said. "Let me die fighting."

"I won't stop you," Aurora replied. "But this is not the place. You're not gonna be a martyr, not for these people."

A few infected made it to the guards, jumped on them as the Helix security forces poured into the room. Before, Sai's team had the numbers. It had the surprise to over-whelm better armed, better armored enemies. But not here. As Aurora pulled them to the elevator bank, Sai crouched behind an overturned white desk, covered with glass and oozing green sludge that smelled like rotting yeast, and saw his momentary friends burn.

No mercy now, no attempt to gather the subjects alive. The Helix team didn't hold back. They pushed away the infected, kicked them down and delivered coup de grace's courtesy of their lasers right to the face, to the chest, to anywhere they could find until the only things left were charred husks. It seemed overwhelming and unnecessary until Sai remembered what they were. What he was.

Sterilize the disease, burn it away.

Behind him the elevator doors dinged. Not cut off yet.

Did he run? Abandon the last few infected throwing things towards the guards, making haphazard lunges even as those bright bolts found their mark?

"Let's go Sai. Now." Aurora spoke with a commander's stance, strong and ordered. Demanding to be obeyed.

Sai had gone into demolitions to save lives. His own included. And when you worked with explosives, you didn't take the reactionary route. You didn't hurry, and you didn't throw yourself into the inevitable out of despair. You had to stay calm, collected, and think about what waited for you on the other side.

The virus hadn't killed him yet and it might not. Those lasers surely would, and now they were turning in his direction.

Aurora tugged at his back, and Sai fled.

TWENTY-THREE

Felix Redux

GREGOR HAD NEVER FACED a foe twice. This was generally because of two reasons: either he smashed them into an indescribable pulp with his giant hammer, or someone else from Sever excised the enemy from the ranks of the living. There were other options to strike an enemy from Gregor's list, ones he disliked. Felix attempted to take one here, standing weak and pathetic, about to die without any fight at all.

The last time Gregor had seen Felix, the viral monster had been leading a mutant horde across the base, consuming living people and turning them into more mindless, flawed experiments. Felix himself had been covered with these growths, and indeed had a whole vat of the stuff, right here in the now-empty shaft.

What had been a nightmare enemy had dissolved to practically nothing.

Even the virus appeared to have left Felix. His growths were gone, his loose skin hung in pale sheets, and his eyes sat hollow in his skull.

"What happened?" Gregor said.

Not out of any sympathy, but curiosity. In the off moments wandering around that wet city, and especially after talking with Lani, Gregor had toyed with and enjoyed the idea of coming back to Felix. Finding him and delivering the smashing that the monster so, so dearly deserved. But this, this wouldn't be delivering a fatal blow to a deadly fiend, but instead squashing an ant.

"The thing with viruses, with experiments, is that you don't know where they're going to end up," Felix replied and offered a weak laugh. "I thought I'd reached the end of the cycle. That things had stabilized. Turns out I was wrong. Turns out Helix just can't stop failing. The virus kept eating and eating."

"And the rest of it?" Gregor said. "The thing in this room?"

Before Felix could answer, noises came from up above. Apparently Lani and Wicks were tired of waiting, and had started coming down the ladder, their clanking boots a ticking clock on the conversation.

"Did you bring the whole squad with you?" Felix said. "I suppose I'm honored. You did say you'd come back to destroy me. I wasn't sure you'd really do it and yet here you are, not even a whole day later."

"They're not my squad," Gregor said. "But they want the same thing I do. You're a mistake, Felix. You shouldn't be alive."

"Oh, I know that now," Felix replied, wobbling around Gregor in a shambling walk. "I thought maybe this would be my moment. After a lifetime spent as a drone in the office mines, here comes Felix's chance. Injected with the perfect dose, reacting the perfect way and here I go, off to take over the galaxy or something like that."

Gregor glanced up. Lani and Wicks were getting closer, their helmets peering at Felix. They yelled a couple questions his way, but Gregor ignored them. He had to decide whether to kill Felix before the other two made it down, or wait and give them a chance to interrogate the viral victim.

"That's how life works, isn't it?" Felix drove on. "All these random events and all you're doing is hoping one of them turns out good for you. Something comes your way that'll take away all of your problems. That's what Helix offered me. How do you say no to that?"

Felix paced, aimless. Gregor kept his hands on his hammer. Despite himself, he waited, listened. Felix's story wasn't all that different from his own, stuck on that comet mining every day waiting for something better. His parents spent their whole lives striking space rock and Gregor had only escaped by punching that idea in the mouth. Just like Felix, he had made a choice he couldn't take back.

Like Felix, that choice would probably kill him before too long.

"It wasn't long after you left," Felix said now. "Apparently the virus needs a lot of calories, new food to eat. I didn't realize, my creations started devouring themselves, the virus started eating me. I can feel it still, dying away inside. Think I might be more virus than person now, and when it goes, I'll go with it."

"You sound like a bad movie," Gregor said. "I can smash your head in, if you want."

"Not yet," Lani said, jumping the last few meters to the ground and landing with a loud bang. "Felix, I'm guessing?"

Felix attempted a turn and fell over. Gregor, shifting his hammer to his left hand, caught Felix's arm, kept the diseased man from face-planting into the ground.

Why had he caught Felix? Pity? Gregor wasn't sure.

"You're no different from the others," Lani said, her helmet doing nothing to hide the disdain. "Gregor led me to believe that something special was happening here. That Helix had finally found a breakthrough. I guess not."

"Breakthrough?" Gregor asked while Felix laughed into a sob. "What breakthrough?"

"I told you. We're here to monitor progress. Helix is doing something that could bring immense value to the galaxy. Or, if they screw up, ruin a lot of lives. Felix might've meant they were close. Now, it just means we'll be stuck here even longer."

Wicks hit the ground behind Lani, slower, more careful. Still learning the armor. That Lani moved well enough said she had some experience with the gear, maybe from a simulator. Or maybe she'd crashed out of DefenseCorp's more active ranks.

"I thought we were here to destroy him," Gregor said. "This is illegal."

"Don't be shortsighted," Lani said. "You have to see how your abilities, your missions might be helped if your body adapted to the target's environment. Think about it. Right now DefenseCorp has to make all kinds of different gear for every biome. Instead, they could just have special troops. Inject a little bit of this and then you're good to go to that icy planet, that lava rock."

Gregor let go of Felix, "I'm fine the way I am."

"Nobody's forcing you," Lani said. "Felix, you're it? Nothing else here we need to see?"

"Not unless you like bodies," Felix said. "The virus wanted more to eat, so it ate everything it could find. It wasn't enough. It'll never be enough."

"That's what I needed to know," Lani said, and she drew her weapon, and pulled the trigger. Once, twice, three times until Felix was only ash.

Gregor stepped back, looked at the burning wreck. Not a fighter's death.

"Do you trust him?" Lani asked Gregor. "Think Felix was telling the truth?"

"I do," Gregor said. "You don't find many liars at death's door."

"You be surprised," Lani replied, holstering the weapon. "Wicks, get going. Do a run through on this level and make sure we're not missing anything. Find something, record it. Felix might not have been what we wanted, but if he took over a base, then he was close."

"Why did we come?" Gregor asked. "If you are here, if you want this to succeed, then why are we on a rescue mission?"

Lani shrugged, "No idea. Let's get back up top. I think you're getting too into the weeds with this one. Defense-Corp is a huge company, lot of moving parts. Not all of them talk to each other."

They started back up the ladder, every hit of their boots on the metal rungs echoing up and down the shaft.

"So what do we do?" Gregor said.

"Complete your mission, I suppose," Lani replied. "Find your objective, get them off world. And then forget this place ever existed."

"We don't work quietly," Gregor said. "We smash and grab. Break things. I know my commander, and I know Galactic law. She won't let this stand."

"She'll have to," Lani said. "She's outranked on this. The people that want to see this succeed sit far above any squad leader."

Authority. What a pain. They always believed they were above everything, that because of some title or some position they had an excuse to shirk common laws, common decency. What Gregor liked about Sever, why he stayed, was that Aurora didn't give a damn about authority. She cared about cash, completing the mission.

And she cared about the squad. Gregor would follow someone like that.

They hit the top of the ladder, climbed onto the landing. Wicks radioed the all clear, that there was some mess, but otherwise nothing remarkable. One room had been burned, looked like. Gregor didn't mention it was him, his hammer, his strike.

"They should have told us," Gregor continued, frustrated partly because he hadn't swung his hammer, because this mission seemed so far from Sever's normal. He wanted enemies to destroy, not mysteries to solve. "Two of us missing already. This is a hostile mission, poorly planned. You could have rescued our man."

"You know why he wants to leave?" Lani said. "I assume he's just tired of being here and because Helix doesn't let anyone off, maybe he got desperate. But now I'm wondering, given the gear you have, he must either have a lot of money-and there's not many that rich here-or he has something that he thinks can pay for what you're doing."

"I don't know." Gregor felt that itch, shifted one hand back towards his hammer. Maybe he could smash the man that had brought them here. "Let's go back."

"Maybe we get to the city, we'll help you find your squad. We know some folks that work for Helix, might be able to check and see if they found your missing members. Maybe arrange something, a deal. They won't let your guy off world, but we might be able to get the rest of your squad freed?

"So we would fail the mission."

"No, your mission's changed. DefenseCorp wants Helix to finalize the virus, to get it working. Now you're on the right side."

TWENTY-FOUR

Starlight Psychology

EPONI HAD the shuttle to herself. In the seconds since Ben had left, since a final click made clear his rescue ship had detached and departed, Eponi had sat in the cockpit and watched on the radar as the ship had dwindled and vanished. It would be accelerating now, getting beyond light speed en-route to some other planet, some other place where Ben's stolen cargo could be put to some profitable use. He'd probably already forgotten about her, his little hostage. His little tool. Just like Sever, Eponi had been pushed into action and now, her job complete, she'd been left aside.

Except Sever hadn't done that. Not really. Aurora hadn't left Eponi behind. DefenseCorp listed Eponi's skills as a pilot and little else, but Aurora had given Eponi a weapon, thrown her in the simulators and had her come with a field team. Nobody, on Sever, held a single role.

Not that Eponi would have minded being left behind. Most of these missions, Eponi would have been content playing out imagined races in a secure cockpit, counting the hours until Aurora and the others returned with the objective and a healthy new cash infusion.

Eponi guessed she could indulge her imagination now. Floating up here, she could hang out with her dreams while she orbited Dynas. Nobody would find her.

She'd never been alone in a spaceship before. Not once. Eponi had to figure such things were rare, right? Who would go into space by themselves? Malfunctions happened. Coordinates were missed without a second check. Any medical problem light years away from help.

And yet here Eponi was, alone. Just like in those kart races, her survival depended on her skills and nobody else's.

She unclipped herself from the cockpit chair. The shuttle would keep spinning around, and barring some interference, some micro meteor or another ship playing investigation, Eponi didn't need to be at the controls. She could take a tour, wallow in the emptiness.

The shuttle didn't argue with her. Ben hadn't locked anything away, though beyond the cockpit there wasn't a whole lot to see. He'd said this was a short range shuttle and he was right. The cargo bay dominated most every-thing back from the cockpit, beyond a small lounge area where handlers might sit. A few passengers could pass the time watching something on the video monitor or play a game on the little board and table that sat between the six small cushioned chairs with gravity belts around them. Had to keep yourself restrained during the inevitable entrance, that rickety crash through the atmosphere that a fully loaded shuttle like this one would make very, very bouncy.

Beyond the passenger quarters, the cargo bay itself loomed empty. Spacious, drab yellow gray metal. The bay doors surrounded by brighter yellow paint, as if warning people that beyond here lay certain death. At least, something to pay attention to, though right now the stripes looked like an odd frame to an empty picture. A few jagged lines on the bay floor hinted at what Ben had taken with him. Leftover, no doubt, from when they were loaded down below.

Because up here, zero gravity reigned.

Eponi kicked off the floor and bounced around off the walls, taking a moment to flip and spin without doing it to dodge some incoming attack. The bay didn't have too much room, a second or two of motion and she hit the opposite wall, but enough. Enough so that for the first time since that skiff had crashed, Eponi felt her heart race a little, her blood rise even as her body told her there was no resistance here. Even as her mind told her she was wasting time.

Right. As if she had places to be.

Back in the cockpit, Eponi confirmed what Ben had said. The shuttle lacked the oxygen, and fuel—the shuttle didn't have enough solar sucking panels to keep it going indefinitely—to get Eponi anywhere. Helix probably kept that intentional, kept major escapes impossible unless you managed to find friends. Or, like the VIP that had called Sever into this mission in the first place, have enough cash stored away to hire your own evacuation.

There were other tactics. Things Eponi could try if she didn't want to go back down to that surface.

That was really the question, up here alone among the stars, that Eponi had to answer for herself. That she kept turning away from.

Going back down wasn't just a philosophy question either. Eponi didn't have any technical codes to get through Helix's landing clearance. Didn't have any weapons to fight back if Helix objected to its stolen shuttle returning home at the hands of a captured, hostile pilot. Even if Eponi wanted to run back to Sever, doing so in a craft like this would likely get her killed.

No, a better choice would be to do something like Ben. Find another ship, get in touch with the passersby and say that she'd found lawbreakers. Monsters. People who wanted to change how humans live and die. That might be enough information to get a pickup, to get someone to stop and drag her away from this place and from this life. Because that was something she had found in those moments with Ben, that she'd seen with him. A change she'd longed for, finally, maybe, here.

Sending out an SOS signal didn't take much effort. Harder though, to direct the alert away from the planet's surface. The last thing Eponi needed was a Helix rescue coming up to grab her. She hoped for a random person, a ship cruising at slow enough speeds to catch the message and be willing enough to come and see what it was all about.

In this galaxy, it took time to get going fast and when your batteries inevitably drained you coasted, soaking solar energy to give your ship a chance to recharge before accelerating again. Slowing down took power too, so convincing any ship to drop its cadence meant getting them the message at the perfect time: charged batteries and time to spare.

"Gotta love those odds," Eponi whispered to herself.

She oriented the shuttles communications array, pointed it away from Dynas and began to broadcast.

"Everyone that can hear me, I'm calling for help. I'm trapped in a short range shuttle above a hostile world, where acts illegal under Galactic law are being performed," Eponi paused. She wasn't used to grand speeches, these words came slowly. She had to think, what would make someone come over and risk their lives to save her? "I know all about these things, and in the right hands that knowledge could bring . . . "

She stopped. Cut the recording. Could bring what? Profit? Fame? Eponi didn't have suitcases full of data, no captured cells or pieces of evidence. It would just be her word. How much was that worth?

Eponi didn't kid herself too much, she didn't say or believe in some greater nobility. That stopping Helix would be an act worth doing in and of itself. She couldn't afford to think that way, and nobody would come to help her if she tried appealing to some sense of cosmic justice.

All Eponi really had to offer was herself, alone and adrift. Who would risk anything for that?

She leaned forward, pressed her face close to the cockpit glass, looking into those stars. She was already starting to feel the decision in her gut, roiling her stomach. There was no fleeing this. There would be no getting out, getting away from DefenseCorp. From this life that she'd fallen into by way of a few too many kart accidents.

The only people that would come and help Eponi without a question, without a reward were still down on that rotten planet. They were still trying to complete the mission, still trying to find themselves a way off the world. Ben had run. Eponi, Eponi couldn't.

"You're so dumb," Eponi said. "They'd better give you a raise for this."

She settled back into the seat, powered up the shuttle's engines plotted out a course back to Helix's city, back to the tower and the landing bay she'd come from. Turned the thrusters up and began to go. The stars swished away and Dynas took over the view.

You couldn't run, not from this life. Not ever.

TWENTY-FIVE

Outdoor Exposure

WHEN THEY HIT THE STREET, Rovo realized he'd made a terrible mistake. With a briefcase in one hand and holding the girl with the other, Rovo himself stood out from the shambling solos wandering the black city's sidewalks. More so, Kaia, with her ragged dress, didn't fit with the wet suit masses. Rovo hadn't taken the time to slip her into his snagged outfits in the sprint away from the besieged apartment.

He'd make a fine parent, one day.

"This isn't fun," Kaia said, standing in a puddle.

Her tone broke Rovo's heart right then. She said the words not like a normal child would, not like Rovo's sisters had back home. Kaia spoke like one who simply stated the miseries of the world around her without any expectation that they would be salvaged by a parent or guardian or anyone else. To her, being soaked was her reality. Best make do and move on.

"Climb up," Rovo said. "You're going for a ride."

Fatherhood had always been a far off delusion, something to be considered if everything broke his way beforehand. Rovo had a career to think about, stars to surf and wild adventures to have and yet, that far off idea realized itself as Kaia clambered up his side to the top of his shoulders where, with one hand, Rovo held her steady or as best he could and splashed along towards the nearest tram stop. Once they made it on a cable car Kaia could sit and they could pretend to be a little family and ride all the way to the tram station where he could get his armor back.

Then he could protect Kaia. Keep her safe until Aurora and Kashmal reached out.

And yet, if Kaia had drawn attention without her wetsuit, she drew even more sitting high over the street on Rovo's shoulders. Eyes everywhere gave them glances, many more than passing. Not that this bothered Kaia: still soaking, Kaia giggled as Rovo maneuvered around a puddle and splashed through a cross-section street.

"Keep hold of my head and don't let go," Rovo said, and Kaia obliged. Her little hands put pressures against his ears through the wetsuit. "I'm sorry you're wet, but I promise we'll get somewhere dry soon."

"It's okay," Kaia replied. "I've never been outside before."

Aurora might have to stop him from murdering Kashmal or at least delivering a hearty dose of angry pummeling. Never been outside? Even in this bleak place, a child should have a chance to get outside their room. To breathe in the moldy air and feel the dead breeze. To understand where they live, and maybe, maybe see some far-off place or ship soaring down from the sky and build their first dreams.

If Rovo had been locked inside his house, even on his comparatively nice planet, he didn't know what he would've become.

Probably nothing, probably no one.

"What does it feel like?" Rovo asked. "Being outside for the first time?"

"Oh I don't know," Kaia said. "But I like it."

They continued tromping along, Rovo scanning for anyone taking more than casual interest. Anyone following them, plotting the worst.

"You sound smart," Rovo said. "Does Kashmal teach you things?"

"He gives me books sometimes. But my friend monkey, he's so smart. He taught me the most."

"Monkey?"

"On my pewter," Kaia said. "He knows everything."

Ha. That made some sense. Kashmal could just slip in a cheap child's toy, one loaded up with endless hours of educational programming and just let the girl go to town. The real question then, was how Kaia seemed so calm, collected. If all she'd been exposed to was her own room . . .

"Aren't you scared?" Rovo asked. "Isn't this strange for you?"

"Monkey always says to be brave," Kaia replied. "So I'm brave."

"That monkey does seem pretty smart," Rovo said.

How nice it would be, if just saying a thing made you that. If you wanted courage, then you'd have courage. If you wanted strength, then you'd have that too. But when Rovo asked for a cable car as they neared the corner, none appeared. None within sight either.

Bad timing.

"We'll wait here until car arrives," Rovo said. "Okay?"

Standing still proved to be a dangerous game. Motion implied action, but by occupying their spot on the sidewalk corner and staying still, Rovo felt more focused attention. People wondering who would be having a child out in the open in this weather. Who would be having a child at all on this world, most likely.

Rovo kept looking around, the buildings surrounding the cable car stop stood five stories tall, pointed roofs trickling water down to the gutters, attempting and failing to keep the flooding to a minimum. Far off spacecraft engines roared their way through the sky while splashing water. Shouted conversations carried between buildings.

Here in the afternoon's middle, the city didn't seem quite as foreboding or miserable, the hazy light sprinkling through the glistening drops to create the rainbows here and there.

Rovo would never call Dynas beautiful, but perhaps it wasn't quite as ugly as he first thought. Perhaps there were a few things here worth admiring.

"That your girl?" A woman's voice said behind him. "If so, you ought to take better care of her. She'll catch a cold or worse like this."

Rovo turned around, a slow move to keep Kaia stable atop his shoulders. A peering woman who looked about as old as Rovo himself, clad in a green and pink wetsuit that seemed to have some concession to fashion, appeared to be the instigator. No poncho for her, just folded arms and judgment.

"I'm just babysitting," Rovo replied. "Forgot the right outfit."

"How do you forget a wetsuit on this planet?"

"Maybe I didn't have enough coffee." Rovo tried to start turning back, but the woman reached out, put a hand on his arm.

"You and I both don't want to see her hurt," the woman said. "We have people covering you from several windows right now. We tried to do this the nice way in the store, but now you've killed two of us." The woman's nice words vanished into an edge. "It's not her fault, so if you hand her to me I'll make sure she gets out of this okay. And the briefcase. Then, at least, you won't be responsible for her death."

This made two ambushes in an hour's time. Rovo had to get better at this, had to figure out what he was missing.

What Rovo definitely couldn't do, though, was keep Kaia on his shoulders. The woman was right about that risk: Kaia didn't deserve anything that might come Rovo's way.

Besides, shifting Kaia around fell right within option one: buy time and look for a solution.

"Okay," Rovo said. "I don't want her to get hurt. Can you promise me that?"

"You don't get to make demands," the woman said. "But we don't want bloodshed. Not here. She'll be fine."

"Then I'll get her down," Rovo said. "Kaia, let's go."

"But I don't want to."

"It'll be okay," the woman said, and she reached up towards the girl with both arms. "Just fall forward and I'll catch you."

"I don't want to, I don't like you."

The woman tried to smile, an insincere one, thin and shallow. Rovo, meanwhile, tried to assess whether he could get to his weapons, whether he could draw and fire them, and which windows the assassins might be using. Odds were slim that would work out. Then a new sound gave him another idea, a way out.

"Come on," Rovo said to the girl, beginning to shift her to one side of his shoulders. "Let's do what the nice lady says. We don't want anybody to get hurt."

"But I don't want to!" Kaia started struggling.

The woman reached forward again, tried to force the

issue by grabbing for Kaia's arms and Rovo pushed her back, "Please, just give me a second. I'll get her off."

The offer worked, if only slightly. The woman backed off and Rovo moved Kaia onto one shoulder then into the crook of his arm holding the briefcase, Kaia's legs straddling the silver metal. As Rovo stabilized her, a swooshing, whirring sound rose up as a cable car slid into place behind them, doors opening with a wet crack.

Rovo jumped back, quick stepping up into the cable car and almost throwing Kaia down the central aisle. Thankfully, the middle afternoon rides weren't as crowded as the morning and the surprised riders gave them space as they shuttled back into the car.

Rovo hoped and received his wish: no hidden snipers attempted any shots, the cable car apparently providing enough cover, enough collateral damage to keep the fire held.

"Careful there sir," said the automated driver. "Please board safely."

"Sorry," Rovo said, scrambling back with Kaia, meshing into the crowd. "Take a seat and keep your head down."

When he turned up front, Rovo saw the woman board the cable car after them, cold fury in her eyes. In the crowd, the woman didn't dare make an open move. She kept eyes on Rovo, her mouth set in the line as the cable car started moving again. The craft continued down the wet streets, with Rovo holding Kaia in his arms, hunched over in a seat with someone else blocking the windows on either side.

Holding on to option one. Buying time until his cash ran out.

TWENTY-SIX

Hot Commodity

THE ELEVATOR ROSE in that steadily speeding way lifts do when they just keep climbing, no floor to stop at. Aurora held Sai, picked him up off the floor after dragging them into the elevator and now she studied him as he swayed on his feet, muttering about the other infected, about how he ought to have saved their lives. Aurora watched the floors climb on the counter to the right of the door, up and out of the negatives and into the soaring positives. Her stomach fell, her ears began to pop as she rose and rose and rose. More interesting, worse even, was that she hadn't entered a number. Hadn't had a chance to try.

Someone had called the elevator.

But that mystery could wait. Speculation wouldn't get them anywhere, and whatever lay beyond the doors when they opened, Aurora would face that with Sai, not alone. She had to get him back, return his focus to the present and find the drive that belonged to every Sever member. At least, every member that lived past their first mission.

"Do you remember when they found Signet Eight?" Aurora said, putting her mouth next to Sai's ear and speaking the words straight and clear. "Those primitive civilizations, always warring with each other. Just happened to be sitting on a whole bunch of valuable minerals and hard metals. Remember that one?"

Sai, for his part, stopped the muttering. Let a single low sob shake his shoulders.

"DefenseCorp told us that our forces were only going in to stop the fighting, to serve as an advance guard for what would be an introduction to the rest of the galaxy. Remember all that bullshit? All the lies they fed us before that one?" Aurora said. It'd been a different team, Sever squad. They had more members then. "They told us we wouldn't need a full arsenal. That they'd be too stunned to see us coming from the sky to fight. We'd have the objective without firing a shot."

Sai listened, breathed. The numbers crept higher.

"They dropped us down, not even with shuttles. Meteor drops. We slammed right into the ground because DefenseCorp thought that would create a better impression. Hundreds of us, all sorts of DefenseCorp squads just bashing around the world. Shock and awe, that was supposed to fix everything. Shock and awe."

"It didn't." Sai didn't so much say the words as breathe them, and Aurora could see his eyes were closed.

"No. It really didn't. You remember how they dropped us in the middle of that battlefield? Those two big armies going at it with their spears and their flinging rocks, those swords made from molten glass?"

"Those swords did look really neat."

"Your katana cut through them like butter."

"I don't even have it anymore. My katana."

Bad move there. She needed to stay away from the sword. Maybe they'd get it somewhere, somehow. Keep Sai's focus on the old mission, not on lost weapons.

"You remember, we were surrounded right away? They stopped the fighting when we crashed. A dozen of us, thousands of them. All spoiling for a fight and now you have these strange invaders coming in," Aurora shook her head, rubbed her nose ever so slightly against the back of Sai's neck. Not about romance, but about love, that deep bond that forms between two soldiers who have depended upon each other for survival. Aurora needed Sai, and Sai needed Aurora and together they would make it out. "Ferris had us all form a circle, and he started talking, as if they could understand him. Trying to explain. And he got hit first."

"They were brutal." Sai at last seemed to put his own legs down, squared his shoulders. "We didn't understand, they fought because that was all they believed. Fight and die and go to your perfect afterlife. The greater the challenge, the greater glory in the great beyond. We were so stupid."

"No, not us. The people who sent us," Aurora said.

"I guess you're right. The people that sent us. Just like here."

Sever had been swarmed on Signet Eight. The warring sides made a spontaneous truce to attack the invaders, as had happened everywhere else on the planet. Sai had made the call, after half their number fell simply do to the pressure. Power armor might protect you from pokes and stabs, might keep you safe from flying rocks, but it wouldn't help you hold firm against fifty charging, strong scaly bodies as they pressed you into the earth and smothered you.

DefenseCorp's bombardment came down through the atmosphere, targeted around them, the lasers and the missiles from the ships above blackening the skies. Sai had dragged Aurora back inside their meteor drop, a tear-shaped, nigh indestructible craft. A perfect shelter to wait out doomsday.

Afterward, Sever found out they weren't the only squad that made the call. Across the world, the natives proved unwilling to negotiate. Capable only of homicidal, endless war. And so DefenseCorp annihilated them, and the mining and extraction companies moved in to claim the prize. Aurora didn't even remember if DefenseCorp expressed any official regret. Aurora knew that she did not. The monsters had tried to kill her, had killed her friends. They deserved what they got.

The elevator doors opened with a *chunk* and a slow swish. On the other side, grinning with a crazed smile, stood Kashmal.

"I found you," Kashmal said. "Right on time."

Aurora wanted to punch the man, but he had called the elevator. Had taken them away.

"They're chasing after us," Aurora said. "We have to keep moving."

"Oh no, I wouldn't worry," Kashmal replied. "Things have changed now. You have him."

He pointed a finger at Sai, and Aurora took another look. Her teammate still seemed tired, weak. Breathing hard and sweating. Hardly an example of an achieving specimen. Of someone worthy of being considered a prize.

"What do you mean?" Aurora asked.

"I'll tell you later," Kashmal replied. "All you need to know now, is that your circumstances changed. You won the lottery, Sai. You and your genes."

Kashmal ushered them out of the elevator, onto a busy floor that, with the sound of starting rocket engines and their high-pitched lines, told Aurora it held a docking bay. Crates and workers shifting them about cluttered in the hallway, and as soon as they left the elevator several more pushed their containers inside and off it went. No mention about the slaughter down below, about the alert and the danger.

Kashmal directed them down the hall. The wide walkway had the polished black floor common throughout the tower, and every so often a door would open into the docking bay, presenting a different ship, a different area. Cargo loading, passengers, fuel, everything else. Kashmal took them to the very end, so that by the time they actually entered the docking bay, they were right near the wide-open exit leading out over the city. A skiff brushed by overhead, holding what looked like a flotilla of guards.

"They're looking for your friends," Kashmal said. "As I understand it, there's one on the loose right now. The one we left at my apartment. They're going to take him and bring him here. How convenient is that?"

"I don't understand?" Aurora said. Sai, for his part, stared around, having lapsed back into silence and whatever battles were waging in his mind. "They were trying to kill us a minute ago."

"The doctor changed her mind. Actually," Kashmal laughed. "It's kind of funny really. She spent all this time, all this effort trying to find a success and then her hand gets forced by some random lab engineer."

"What?"

"I should be sad, because he did what I was trying to do. He made it off world with samples." Kashmal rolled his eyes to the ceiling. "Ben, you're such a miserable pest," Kashmal pointed towards a larger ship in the center of the bay. The only one around that looked truly space worthy. "You get it, right? Everything that's going on here? It's all bankrolled in secret. Viruses made for people willing to pay. But if the stuff gets in the open? If someone else manages to get it out and replicated? Then all this becomes worthless. Now that there are samples off world, Anaskya has to move fast to try to collect before the other companies pull the plug."

Aurora tried to follow Kashmal's assertions. Being the first to get whatever virus was infecting Sai out into the galaxy at large made some sort of sense, even if its intended purpose, modifying the person and changing them into something different, more effective, was against the letter of Galactic law. The laws could be rewritten, could be changed by those with the power to do so. Aurora had seen that plenty of times herself, as DefenseCorp missions had broadened to include the sort of annihilation like the natives on Signet Eight.

Why not play with nature? And why not profit by doing so?

"So why are we here?" Aurora said.

"She doesn't care about you. She cares about him," Kashmal said. "Come on, we've got to get on the ship. Before Anaskya changes her mind."

"And you? You tried to do the same thing as this other engineer?"

"And she would have had me shot, except I promised I'd get you," Kashmal said. "I know, I know, you might be angry. But guess what? We're getting off this planet. The three of us. Right now. And that's worth anything, right?"

Aurora would've strangled him, would have shot Kashmal for what he'd already done, except she had to keep Sai up. Had to keep them moving. Because she noticed guards all over the docking bay, watching the three of them with hands on their weapons.

If Aurora tried to fight back here, no doubt she and Sai would die, and fast. So she kept her mouth shut and walked along, over to the shuttle and up boarding ramp.

The ship was larger, much larger than the shuttle Defense-Corp had given Sever to bounce onto Dynas.

As soon as they boarded, two guards appeared around the entrance and directed Aurora and Sai back, far back, through the steel, gold-trimmed craft. Kashmal disappeared, sneaking off to some other part while the two guards pushed and pointed until Aurora and Sai had made it into what looked like the cargo bay, where crates of food and other provisions lingered.

Not a short journey then.

One other thing stood out in the cargo bay, long and thin and shoved in a corner, smudged but otherwise none the worse for wear.

"Sai, guess what?" Aurora said. "They found your sword."

TWENTY-SEVEN

A Love of Enclosed Spaces

JOIN the ones that save you. That's what Sai had done, after those DefenseCorp soldiers crashed into his apartment, after they cleansed his home planet of the rebels and their endless destruction. Restored order by way of an iron fist, and then handed it back to the plutocrats and corporations that started the whole thing.

Two modes of thinking confronted those who remained: either fight back against a corrupt established order that had proved impossible to defeat, or leave. Sai and his mother chose the latter. She'd taken their savings, their investments and gone off to a less fractious world, and left Sai with his katana to join the harder, faster and more violent life that he'd been so rudely introduced to on the rooftop, stairways, and city streets as his home burned.

But from the ashes so often rises something better. And on that first station, Sai found his eventual wife. Had children and built a good life for himself. Until the galaxy proved again its wildness and his family's planet pulled the DefenseCorp contract. Sai had a choice: take his family into a space-faring life with unpredictable assignments, hopping from world to world, or leave them behind and bring his talents to the higher-earning, active division.

To Sever, and its high-priced adventure.

And where did that bring him? To this cargo hold, filled with illegal contraband meant to be sold off to whomever wanted it, including his own employer. A dangerous thing that could reshape species, that right now was busy reshaping him.

The virus in his body had found an equilibrium, and Sai felt stronger now, almost clear in his purpose. He still drifted from time to time into those hallucinations, as Kashmal and Aurora walked him across the bay and up into the ship, Sai was barely there. He'd spent those precious minutes back home, watching his children learn to play, knowing and understanding why he wouldn't be there when they taught their own children the same.

Come back, Sai. Be present, because if you don't we're not getting out of here.

We?

The slap came fast, sharp. Stinging blood in his cheek that had Sai's eyes popping open and his breath coming in fast. Aurora raised her hand, ready to do it again, when Sai lifted his own arm to block hers.

"I'm awake," Sai said. "For now."

"Better be for always," Aurora replied. "You feel that?"

He did. A vibration lacing throughout the shuttle, one shaking up his feet and knees and back. Without being in a crash couch, a spacecraft lift off would be an adventure. A bruising experience.

"Better brace ourselves." Sai obeyed his own instructions, leaving the open space and pinning himself in a corner, trying to situate his shoulders, his arms so he could hold himself straight as the vibrations increased. Aurora did the same, going opposite him so they stared at each other across crates that contained, in their silver metal forms, the same virus that ruined Sai and so many others in that tower.

"So I think the mission's off," Aurora called across the bay. "I don't know if you noticed, but Kashmal's teamed up with the enemy."

"Aurora, I stopped caring about the mission when she injected me with that virus."

"Priorities, Sai."

"My life takes precedence, Aurora. You know that."

Aurora gave him a sad smile, she knew. They all did. That was part of Sever's charm, where they'd accomplish the mission, yes, but they did so without the callous disregard that so often came from mercenary armies. Cash lay claim to the biggest prize, and keeping each other alive was a nice bonus. To Sever, though, those orders were reversed.

Sai liked to think it was because Sever loved and cared for each other so much. In the tight frantic fire-filled corridors you couldn't help but find yourself friends with the soldier next to you. Willing to give your lives for each other.

Aurora had put it a different way, several missions ago. Keeping Sever unified, alive and carrying on in the same way from one mission to the next, was simply a sound investment strategy. Less downtime, greater returns.

"You don't know where the others are?" Sai said as the vibration shifted, the ship's engines spooling up and lifting them off the floor of the docking bay. "Gregor? Eponi?"

"Gregor and Rovo are in the city somewhere," Aurora replied. "At least, that's where I left them."

"You left them?"

Sai stomach shifted as the shuttle picked up speed, no doubt zooming from the docking bay and angling up towards the stars. Here, in this enclosed space, Sai couldn't tell where he was, what the ship was doing. Only slight twinges told Sai he was flying at all.

Sai would've felt nausea, maybe even thrown up, as most did during the ascent when you had no view of the outside. Except he felt normal, calm. Even his fever had subsided.

"We split up," Aurora was saying. "We had to make a compromise. Kashmal had material that he wanted to get off world. I couldn't leave it unprotected. And Gregor, Gregor threw off the pursuit."

"You left the rookie protecting the valuable goods?"

"I didn't exactly have a choice." Aurora shook her head, stretched her legs a little bit to firm up her position as the shuttle began to shake, getting higher in the atmosphere where those winds and jet streams would knock it about. "What was I supposed to do? Just leave it there? I thought we would be going back to get it."

Sai picked up another note in Aurora's voice, her tone. Tired, yes, but also a little sad and frustrated. This wasn't the way the mission should've gone. Sever wasn't built to separate, they weren't isolated agents trained to take on objectives single-handedly. They were a squad and meant to be a unit. Now they were scattered all across this planet and, soon, above it. Would they ever get back together?

Sai didn't know, and honestly, right then, he had bigger concerns.

Sever definitely wouldn't reunite if Sai and Aurora were taken off to some faraway star. Sold to someone wanting to play experiments with human subjects.

"So how are we getting back?" Aurora said. "Any ideas?"

"Take over the ship," Sai said. "Fly it back down?"

"Wow. I never would've thought of that." Aurora rolled her eyes. The shuttle shook even more, heading into the hardest part of the atmosphere. Just before that freeing release. "How do you want to take over a ship without any weapons?"

Sai looked around. The katana was there, that was nice, though it might not be able to cut through any of the doors here. And when he tried, Sai had no doubt one of those guards would pop in and blast him in the face. So that was a nonstarter. Beyond that, there were the silver cases, all packed to the brim with disease and disaster.

Disease and disaster.

"What's the one thing a buyer wouldn't risk when working with something like this?" Sai said, keeping himself braced but leaning forward ever so slightly to get a better look at those cases.

"Infection," Aurora plied. "You don't expose yourself to something you don't understand."

"Exactly," Sai said. "We have a whole lot of the disease right here."

"And the only one who understands it is on board," Aurora said.

Sometimes the plans unfolded piece by piece, the next step only revealed when they completed the previous one. Often, missions ran on instinct, with Sever dancing through firefights and objectives, each one paving the way to the next. Other times, like when Sai was trapped in a cargo hold with nothing to do but contemplate his own demise, the desperate devising came through in full.

"We're in a sealed container," Sai said. "You release anything here, it's not going anywhere. The shuttle will be exposed and there's no escape."

"You're forgetting something," Aurora said. "I'm not infected."

"Well, here's your chance," Sai said. "With Anaskya on

the ship, she might have a cure. She'll have to bring it out if she gets infected."

All at once, the rumbling ceased. Sai felt his hands and feet drift ever so slightly off the wall and his stomach performed a few flip-flops as gravity fell away. They were in space now, and the virus would have nowhere to go but through the shuttle's closed, recycling oxygen systems. A giant petri dish, filled with unsuspecting victims. Sai compressed, then kicked, pushing himself over towards his katana. With a smooth motion, Sai unsheathed the sword as Aurora watched from the corner.

"You sure about this?" Aurora said. "Because if I get sick and die I will be real pissed at you."

"If you die, I'll probably follow close behind," Sai said. "Besides, we didn't get in this job to play it safe."

Rather than swing the sword into hacking slashes against the suitcases, Sai played the katana's edge against the locks. Worked the sword like a little saw as the ship continued to fly. The katana was sharp and, with every movement, cut a little bit deeper.

When the first case popped open, Sai saw exactly what he expected. Small vials, compressed and vacuum sealed. Ready to be dumped into an air vent for the whole ship to enjoy.

TWENTY-EIGHT

The Reason Why

OFFICIALLY, Gregor wasn't a hostage. He'd simply been re-allocated from his old division to a new one. Assimilated from Sever to DefenseCorp's more secretive branch, the one that blurred the lines between legal and not, that didn't distinguish between objectives and ethics. Lani made sure Gregor felt that line the entire way out of the base, with Wicks carrying Felix's light and decaying body for further analysis back at the city.

Lani had Gregor leading, and every time he looked behind, Lani still had her gun held in her hand, ready to use it. Gregor had his hammer, and figured he could prob-ably get in a swing if he wanted to. Could probably break her and then Wicks.

And then Sayers would run away with the skiff and leave Gregor here to rot with the diseased dead.

DefenseCorp wouldn't care either way. Assuming word of this ever even made it off Dynas. The organization was too large, spanned too many planets and took too many light years to get messages from one side the other to func-tion as any cohesive whole.

Gregor had seen physics' effects on communication play out from his first assignment, when DefenseCorp would issue regulations and rules for new recruits and leaders alike to follow. The recruits, without leverage, would jump to toe the line while local leaders didn't adjust at all. They'd embrace their corrupt positions, send any recruits they didn't like into dangerous missions, and if DefenseCorp ever signaled an audit, the travel time across vast space gave leaders time to hide their actions.

In short, Lani could do whatever the hell she wanted because the consequences were light years away.

"Gregor, you said last time you saw him, Felix was a monster," Lani said to his back as they walked, nearing the base's exit. "You said he had an infected swarm at his disposal, a whole mass of virus waiting to spread. We didn't see any of that."

"You heard him," Gregor replied. "He decayed."

"Or you lied."

"Why would I?"

"I don't know," Lani said. "I don't know why I'm being so suspicious, Gregor, except that it's all lies on Dynas, everyone stabbing each other in the back."

"You think I care?"

They went out the way they came in, through the hole in the side of the building where the doorway had been. Back up the lift to the skiff. Lani kept quiet, and Gregor didn't mind. She was trying to play some sort of game, looking for a deeper meaning. Sever had come here on a simple extraction, get in, get out, and get away. Nothing deeper than that.

"Who was the target?" Lani asked as the lift rose. "And do you know why they are trying to leave?"

"I said they didn't tell us anything."

"Speculate for me."

"No."

Wicks even chuckled at that one, "Don't think you've made a friend, Lani."

"I'm not trying to make friends."

And yet, that's what Gregor had felt back in the apartment. Comrades in arms, kindred spirits both trying to make sure their missions succeeded. Lani had changed when she'd seen the nothing that Felix had become.

Gregor thought he knew why: everyone on Dynas wanted off the world, and that chance seemed to revolve around the virus. If Felix had been a live and healthy mutation, then maybe Lani would have what she wanted. Maybe she wouldn't be so testy with a ticket off Dynas waiting for her.

"What would you have done?" Gregor said as a lift reach the top. "If we found him, infected?"

"Killed him, just like we did," Lani said, but there wasn't conviction behind the words.

"You wouldn't have taken Felix?" Gregor asked.

"Taken him where?" Wicks said. "Back to our apartments? Let him fester there and get us all sick?"

Gregor kept his eyes on Lani, and she matched his hard stare and kept quiet.

"A lot of cash in this virus," Gregor said. "Right?"

"Just get in the skiff, Gregor," Lani said.

Sayers had kept the craft primed, and Lani and Wicks had grown used to their power armor so that they didn't even look all that awkward climbing up onto the craft. As soon as they were aboard, with Felix's body safely secured in the bow, Sayers started the engines whining.

Sayers lifted the skiff, turned it back towards the city. Lani and Wicks went to debrief with the pilot, leaving Gregor alone, free to wander the deck as the yellow fog washed over everything. Dynas's humidity weighed on him, and all Gregor could think about was how badly he wanted to leave this planet. How badly Lani and the others must want the same. Bad enough to do just about anything.

Too few enemies to smash, too little to look at, and the damned pollen or whatever-the-hell kept getting in his vents.

As Gregor made his way to the skiff's aft, Felix's doomed base disappearing into the mist, Gregor felt a crackle over his helmet. A squad level transmission, on Sever's band. At first too static, too far away, but even from here Gregor could recognize a loop. A repeated broadcast put on by someone who didn't have time to stay on band. He moved to the front of the skiff, standing over Felix's body.

"What's going on?" Lani said, moving next to him. "I'm hearing something."

Because of course, the other power armors would already be tied to Sever's frequency. Lani and Wicks would hear it too, but they wouldn't know who it was. They wouldn't be able to tell Rovo's voice.

"At the tram station, requesting assistance from anyone. Helix is coming, and they're going to get us. Top level is clear, streets are marked. The armor's gone. Not going to last too long."

Rovo's voice came through stretched and tired. He needed help. Gregor didn't need to know more than that.

"We have to go back," Gregor said. "To where we found the power armor. He's going to die if we don't."

"Who's going to die?" Lani asked. "Who's making this call?"

"One of my teammates."

"Sounds like he's in trouble," Wicks said. "But we're not exactly supposed to make ourselves visible. Helix doesn't really know we're here. Not officially."

"Wicks is right. If your friend is compromised, we can't go near it."

Ah yes, that's why Gregor hated this branch so much. More concerned with their own secrets than the lives of their other DefenseCorp members. Just a bunch of cowards.

"You didn't hear me," Gregor said, reaching back to the hammer, adjusting his boots to be ready for a boost. "We're going to help him. Now."

Valiant Intercept

THE THING ABOUT DESCENTS, even on a planet as isolated and sparse as Dynas, was that you couldn't just fly a ship down into the atmosphere and hope you wound up in the right place. Planets spun, speeds were relative, atmospheric drag, so many variables.

The shuttle's computers performed most of the calculations, but many required Eponi to at least review the end result. Theoretically, traffic control in the city would designate lanes free to travel, would make sure spaces were clear so that when Eponi came hurtling through the atmosphere at high speeds, she wouldn't run into someone else coming up through the clouds.

But as Eponi punched in those coordinates her computer spat out, as she directed the shuttle around the orbit until that big black city rotated into the right spot for her to return, traffic control didn't say a word.

"Helix control, again, this is shuttle," Eponi glanced at the nameplate, conveniently pasted on the outside and on the control consoles, because everyone understood that pilots went between shuttles like this at random. Pawns didn't get their own ships. "*Valiant.* Yeah, shuttle *Valiant* is looking for a vector to land at the tower. Please assign."

Valiant. What a dumb name for a shuttle like this. Running cargo between ground and space didn't deserve such a name. Something like *Box*, or *Mule* would've been more appropriate. Eponi sat back in her chair and waited. And kept waiting. Before too long she'd have to actually fire the engines to reorient the shuttle or she would lose her chance. Ridiculous.

But hey, in space, she didn't have to worry about getting infected. No diseases in this shuttle. Better bored than dead.

There were a few things she could do while sitting in the shuttle cockpit waiting for Helix to reply. Eponi could search the stars, but the shuttle currently faced the planet and, on the far side of the system's star, Dynas look mostly like a big black blob blotting out a cross-section of the universe.

Without a view, Eponi could fiddle with the controls, check the oxygen levels and make sure nothing seemed amiss. Eponi had already done that five times over, and the percentages never became more interesting. And last, but not least, Eponi could scan the radar. See what other strange objects might be floating into the shuttle's vicinity and guess at what they were. Perhaps an old space station? A satellite? An asteroid on its gradual descent into the planet's atmosphere where it would break and burn into tiny pieces?

Or you might look at your radar and pick up an approaching ship, one flying up out of the black city at a way-too-high velocity. And with a shaky vector, as though the planned path had gone wildly off course. Or its pilot was drunk.

That was interesting. There hadn't been too many

flights space-ward from Helix that Eponi had picked up, though *Valiant*'s scanners picked up small craft buzzing all over Dynas's surface, no doubt shuttling supplies and people to various outposts like the one Sever had landed near. Given the few departures, there wasn't a lot of competition for traffic, but a wild and frenzied flight out might account for why Helix wasn't responding to her requests. Maybe they were too busy dealing with their own disaster.

"Well, might as well see if I can help," Eponi said.

Help, perhaps, wasn't the right word. Descending to Helix meant putting herself back into someone else's chains, and putting that off as long as she could? That only made sense.

She pinged the short range comm, designated the ship heading up and out—a larger ship than her own, considerably so—and sent the message, "This is *Valiant*, reaching out to *Beaker*." These ships and their names. "You're looking a little wobbly there. Need any assistance?"

Her words beamed out across space, zooming towards *Beaker*. Eponi couldn't exactly see the shuttle yet, it had just broken out of the atmosphere and wasn't within the visible range. Nonetheless, Eponi boosted her engines. Re-oriented *Valiant* and started creeping towards *Beaker*. Eponi could call her move a feeling, she could call it a hunch, or she could simply call it curiosity. Or all three.

Just as Eponi got underway, *Valiant*'s comm buzzed, demanding attention, so Eponi slapped the button. Maybe *Beaker* had decided to talk.

"This is Helix ground control," the voice on the other end said. "You're not an approved shuttle, and you're not an approved mission. Return to base immediately. I'll send you the vector. And stay away from the other ship."

"Why?" Eponi said.

"Because you're not authorized to approach it."

"Can you give me anything more than that? It looks damaged. We can help."

Eponi threw the 'we' in her reply to seem less suspicious than a lone pilot bouncing around the upper atmosphere by herself.

"That's a negative. Return to base. Now."

Ground control cut the comm. Huh. They weren't all that pleasant, and Eponi only obeyed people that were nice to her. Or that's what she told herself in this moment, as Eponi redirected her shuttle into a collision course with *Beaker*.

"Hailing *Beaker* again," Eponi said. "Trying to get in touch with you. You still look a little wobbly. Let me know if I can help."

Beaker was more than a little wobbly, and it already veered sharply against orbit, throwing it way off of any flight plan that would lead to leaving the system. More like someone was trying to wrestle over the controls. Or had severely screwed up their calculations. Eponi hit the scan, tried to see if there were any broadcasts coming from the shuttle that might've been on another frequency. And caught one. A wide open signal.

Her mouth dropped open as *Beaker*'s sounds played through Eponi's cockpit.

Screams, shouts. The hard sound of metal things hitting other hard objects, clanks and bangs. Curses and commands. Underneath it all, someone close to the comm just kept coughing. Groaning. Not saying a word, as if they'd forgotten they'd opened the band. That they were broadcasting this everywhere.

So Eponi matched the signal, tried to send something back. Repeated her words from before even as excitement rose. Because *Beaker* was big enough to handle interstellar flight. If Eponi could dock, maybe wait until whatever was going on resolved itself and then make friends with the victors, she might be able to get out.

Or, and Eponi shook her head at this, go back down to the city and take her squad up and out. Actually complete the mission. Be a friend.

Be a hero.

"Eponi?" A hard voice, a woman. One Eponi would recognize anywhere. Aurora's words cut over *Beaker*'s sounds as they started to die out, dwindling to distant sobs. A few pleas. "Where are you?"

"I'm in a shuttle heading your way." Eponi couldn't think what else to say. How was Aurora on the ship? How did she take control? Single-handed? "What's going on over there?"

"We had some disagreements, so I took command," Aurora replied. "Are you able to dock?"

"I can meet up," Eponi said. "We can get you out of there."

"Not just me. Sai's here too. But we lost the pilot. I don't know how to fly this thing?"

Eponi smiled. Just hearing her squad leader's voice brought Eponi's confidence back. She wasn't alone. She didn't need to run. One minute ago she'd had a thousand options, none of them good. Now she had one perfect choice: re-connect with her squad.

"Then listen, and talk to me," Eponi said. "You want to find the radar, and target my shuttle. Once you do that, we can set an intercept and the computers will handle the rest."

"Got it," Aurora replied. "Good to hear your voice Eponi. We didn't know what happened to you."

"It's a story. Sounds like you might have one too."

"You have no idea."

THIRTY

Treasure Hunting

By the time Rovo and Kaia had jumped to the third cable car, the woman following them calmly all the way, Rovo figured he wasn't going to get shot in the street. Helix wouldn't risk trying to pick him off from a distance. They would wait, see what hole Rovo decided to hide in.

Thankfully, Rovo's planned hole had strong armor and plenty of weapons. Helix would let a lightly armed soldier find his arsenal.

"Just hang on," Rovo said to Kaia as they slipped off the third cable car, near the target tram station. Two blocks away from salvation. "We're almost there."

Kaia had performed amazingly well. She pointed at stores, people, and lights, giggling and laughing the whole way. She'd kept that little lion doll in her left hand, showing it every notable thing they passed. Whatever concerns she'd had about being wet, at lacking anything close to proper clothes for Dynas, had disappeared with the adventure.

At first, Rovo felt Kaia's cheer was decidedly at odds with their dangerous situation, but as the cable car rides went on, he began to realize that she had never done this before. Never seen these things that, until now, had only been visible in short bursts outside her window. And in a way, if they were outnumbered and soon to be captured, it felt nice to get Kaia a few fleeting, joyful moments. So when she pointed and laughed, Rovo laughed too. The soldier offered up names and explanations and jokes and even drew smiles from some of the dour folks riding with them.

Rovo could almost pretend that they were a family. That they were being pursued by people who would put a laser in his head didn't stop Rovo from imagining what if this had been a normal day?

Just a father and his daughter out exploring the city.

Not a bad thought.

One that died whenever he saw the woman, always taking up positions near the front of the cable cars so that Rovo and the girl would have to go right by her every time they got off. Always stepping lightly after them, keeping the straight no nonsense expression on her face as she radioed to everyone else their current position. As chases went, this was a methodical one, and Rovo took a deep breath with every inhale and exhale to keep his nerves calm. To keep himself from setting Kaia down, turning around and lashing out at the woman.

Knock her out, and maybe they get away.

But to where? If, by some stroke of luck, the woman was the only one tailing them, Rovo might buy a few minutes. He didn't know where to go with that time, had nowhere to escape to, and carrying a girl and a big silver briefcase wasn't exactly inconspicuous. So instead, during the cable car rides, Rovo put together a different plan. Without his armor, Rovo didn't have many tools, but the small computer attached to his wrist offered one option.

Rovo used the transponder first, beaming out a looping message on Sever's frequency, noting his destination and asking for help. He didn't know where Sai or Eponi, Aurora or Gregor were, didn't know whether they could hear his signal, but it would go out for some kilometers. Tight and light. Maybe, just maybe Rovo could get his squad back together.

They stepped in the puddles within one block of the station. Rovo kept his eyes turning for people on the rooftops wielding weapons, for people walking along the streets who stopped and took any long notice of them, but he couldn't pick out any. Not necessarily because there weren't any—Rovo was hardly a spy, adept at finding undercover enemies—but none were open about it. Nobody wanted to start a public brawl.

"We're going in there," Rovo said as the tram station came into view, the *Closed* sign evident over the main entrance. "You have to be really good now okay?"

"Okay," Kaia said. "What's in there?"

"Treasure. Treasure that'll help us."

"Treasure?"

"You'll see."

At the last crossing before the tram station, Rovo bent and scooped Kaia up, beginning to run. As soon as Helix figured he was going to the tram station, they could trap him. Which meant they would start converging, which meant Rovo only had a few moments to get down there, get his armor on, and set up.

The tram station's entrance had slid shut, just like when Rovo, Aurora, and Gregor first arrived. That seemed like eons ago, even if it was only a few hours. With Kaia in one arm, Rovo swept open the door, stepped inside, and slammed it shut. Aside from the ID card scanner there didn't seem to be any other way to seal the door.

"Where are we going?" Kaia asked.

"To the treasure," Rovo replied. "Not far now."

Kaia didn't look like she believed him, so Rovo scooped her up and ran through the turnstiles leading to the platforms, stepping over and through barriers meant for happier times. He took a right turn, heading past more signs marking the platform closed. Closed because this platform sent the tram to the farther outstation that held far worse things than anyone on Dynas needed to know.

Down a ramp with mottled white tile, the occasional sign on the wall telling people to be careful, to check for their luggage, and to have a nice day.

There it was. The tram Rovo had rode in on, sitting there, defunct. The tram's doors were opened and waiting, and behind them would be the armor and weapons Rovo so badly needed.

Sounds rattled from above, carrying along the station's quiet interior; the tram's entrance being yanked back open. The pursuit on its way.

"Almost there," Rovo said to Kaia, who hugged her doll tight and kept staring around, entranced.

Rovo and Kaia crossed the platform, and then, with a heft, Rovo stepped them both into the tram. No surprise, the tram had zero passengers. The bigger surprise came when Rovo realized the tram didn't lack just people, but the armor too.

Gone. All of it.

Rovo simply stood there while the girl dropped from his arm and ran up and down out the aisle, laughing as if the tram was an amusement park full of interesting and new things, which, to Kaia, Rovo supposed it was. Though, of course, not for much longer. Without the armor, Rovo didn't stand a chance. Helix would catch them, Rovo would be shot and Kaia?

He didn't want to think of what they might do to her.

"Where's the treasure, Rovo?" Kaia asked, crouching and peaking under the seats.

"Looks like someone beat us to it," Rovo replied. "It's not here anymore."

"I hope they're enjoying it, then," Kaia said. "I'm still having fun, though!"

Okay. Breathe, rookie. He'd had moments of panic in his life, but being lightly armed and surrounded by enemies was not one Rovo had lived through before. The odds looked grim, but Rovo was still free. There had to be another way.

Rovo glanced around the platform, and saw nothing except the tunnel. He could run down the tracks away from the city, towards Felix's outpost, which would take who knows how long to get to and, if Rovo got there, what would he do? Be eaten alive by the virus monster?

But what about the other way? Into the city?

"Come on, we're going," Rovo said. "Now."

"But we just got here!"

Rovo ignored the Kaia's protest, grabbed the girl and dashed back towards the side door they used to get in. A laser struck the ground at his feet, just before he stepped on the platform, leaving a black ring where the superheat had pressed into the ceramic. Rovo looked up: the woman, flanked by two Helix soldiers, stared back at him. They had rifles raised.

Ready to deliver.

"I think it's time to stop running," the woman said. "Let the girl go."

Rovo raised his left hand slow. Make like a surrender and then run for it. If Helix valued Kaia that much, they'd never try to shoot him now, when she could be hit. So as soon as his hand got above the shoulder, Rovo kicked right and dashed, holding Kaia in front of him. Not exactly a brave hero's move to use a young girl as body armor, but Kaia wouldn't last long without Rovo, so he did what he had to do.

The woman shouted a sharp command to her Helix forces to hold their fire and not a single laser came Rovo's way as he ran along the platform and disappeared beyond the far edge.

This didn't exactly get Rovo anywhere he needed to be. Turned out tram tunnels didn't have much in the way of useful things. The platform slimmed down to a narrow maintenance aisle, and otherwise the smooth tunnel kept going, the only feature the slight insets that would be glowing had the tram been operating, would've pulsed with the magnetic electricity meant to keep the craft afloat. Now the tunnel was dark, the only light coming from the standard honey-hued maintenance globes overhead.

"Where are we going now?" Kaia said. "I'm tired."

"You can't be tired yet," Rovo said. "The adventure's just getting going!"

On the left, they passed another small inset, this one boasting a sign and a single door. Maintenance. Rovo tried the handle. Locked. Stepped back, drew his pistol and fired a shot at the handle, which melted through. Kaia laughed at the light, and again when Rovo kicked the door open as the Helix pursuit shouted his way from the platform.

Rovo's route wouldn't be hard to follow, but he was simply trying to buy time now. Find somewhere he wouldn't die too fast.

Beyond the maintenance door, Rovo found some slim stairs, concrete and clearly not used very often. With his weapon in his left hand, Rovo tossed Kaia on his shoulders, picked up the briefcase in his right, and moved. Went up the steps three at a time until, quads burning, he came to a landing that offered two choices: keep going up, or break back to the main station entrance. The latter would potentially get onto the street, where they could keep on running.

Except his muscles were getting tired. Helix could keep tracking him and, if Rovo left the station, any possible help wouldn't know where to find him.

"I'm so not good at this," Rovo said, and they kept going up. He passed several doors as he rose, each one locked, but the noises behind him kept Rovo moving. Taking the time to shoot another handle might mean getting caught.

All the while, Kaia kept laughing. Such a cute, delighted noise. Rovo felt his heart breaking every single time.

"I'm going to save you," Rovo breathed as he kept huffing up the steps. "It will all be just fine. Just fine."

The steps ended with a bigger door, this one not locked. Rovo shoulder charged into it. Burst out and found himself on the rooftop. On top of the station, where solar generators had been plugged in around a large landing pad for skiffs. Dynas's wind brushed against his face, as the evening fog began to descend. The rooftop didn't offer any immediate choices.

Rovo would have to clear a dozen meters or more to jump to the nearest building, a distance not even possible with armor boosting the leap.

"No, no, no," Rovo whispered, while Kaia kept pointing at various things asking what they were called.

Trapped. He tried to run to the side of the station, only when he got there, looking down onto the street far below, shots came, fingers pointed, and he saw more Helix guards with weapons raised waiting for them down there.

Totally, utterly trapped.

Rovo set the briefcase down, set Kaia on top of it. And ran back towards the door, telling the girl to stay still. To not move until he said so.

Setting himself up just outside the stairway entrance, Rovo waited. When the first guard came rushing out, Rovo shot him in the back. Sent him sprawling to the concrete. The second guard and the woman didn't follow their friend out.

"Now you've made things so much harder," the woman called from within the stairwell. "I might have tried to make a case for your life. Not anymore."

"Think I would've lost that case," Rovo replied. "I'm out of places to run, but you're going to have to come and get me."

"Don't worry, we will."

But they didn't rush the door. Instead, Rovo heard the telltale whine that, thanks to this planet, he would forever hate. Low-grade engines, skiffs floating in from above. Rovo didn't have to turn to know Helix had them loaded up with soldiers, and that he was out of time.

THIRTY-ONE

Desperate Choices

AURORA HAD TO ADMIT, it felt good having hostages. Normally, Sever stood on the wrong side of the guns. Pinned down, outnumbered and left alone. Forced to break their way out with their own skill and luck. Except now Aurora, guns in hand, watched four Helix guards, Kashmal, and Anaskya while Sai swayed off to one side, heaving and barely keeping his katana off the ground. He'd had some sort of resurgence of the disease; Sai had powered his way through the fight only to start collapsing towards the end, swings going wide and steps turning into stumbles.

Aurora couldn't help but notice Anaskya never took her eyes off Sai, even after Aurora mentioned Eponi's coming shuttle and how Sever was going to head back to Dynas and leave the rest of them up here to rot alone.

"He is regressing," Anaskya said for the third time. "That is so unfortunate."

"You keep saying that," Aurora said.

"Because it is everything I did not want," Anaskya replied. And she did look downcast, her eyes almost welling with tears. "I thought he was the one. That we'd finally found both the specimen and a molecular build that could suffice."

"We met one of yours not long ago," Aurora said. "He called himself Felix. He overran an entire outpost."

Anaskya shook her head while the Helix guards stared at the floor and Kashmal, somehow, kept himself quiet and watched her,

"He will be dead soon, if he isn't already," Anaskya replied. "His version was more destructive, faster acting and more powerful. Building up its host only to eventually tear them down when the host could no longer feed the virus. It was an idea, a short form solution. Shock teams that would subdue the target, before succumbing themselves. But our investors had little taste for it."

"You don't say," Aurora replied. Then she looked at Sai, frowned, "So what's the cure?"

"Cure?" Anaskya said. Then laughed, a heartless thing. "We weren't paid to develop a cure. The change is permanent."

"You better hope it's not, because we've all got it now. You saw what we did to your cargo," Aurora said. At those words, the guards all turned green, and Kashmal look like he might throw up. Anaskya only laughed again.

"Then you've killed us all," Anaskya replied. "Congratulations. You've prevented our escape, and doomed yourself in the process. What a success. What a strong play from your mercenary minds."

Admittedly, Aurora and Sai hadn't considered the fact that there was no cure. That Anaskya would be treading down a one-way road. When they'd released the disease into the shuttle, the idea had been to escape the cargo room, to drive panic and use that panic to overtake the enemy. That had worked, but perhaps at a greater cost. In looking at Sai, Aurora wasn't particularly thrilled at what was coming her way. She already felt the itchiness in her lungs, the virus percolating.

"So you think we're all going to go his path?" Kashmal said, pointing at Sai. "You think we're all going to die now, follow his route? Sweat like him, get that sick? And then we just fall over?"

"It seems probable," Anaskya said. "The aerosol hasn't been heavily tested. There's a chance it may not work, a chance it may fail to hit the critical threshold to turn you into what is happening to him. We used injections on the surface."

"What chance?"

"A slim one."

The plan, Anaskya went on to explain, while Aurora paced and ran through ideas in her mind, was that the buyers could use the aerosol version to simply spray down an army. Infect them all in one shot, and in some cases without even telling them the process was underway. Simple and effective, and much less traumatizing than mass injections.

There was also some thought that the inhaled version might be less difficult to handle than the stronger injection. Might be easier on the body, take less of a toll and still wind up with the super soldier everyone wanted.

"A super soldier for a day, you mean," Aurora said. "Then nothing at all."

She went back to the cockpit, left Sai charge of the hostages, though in truth it didn't seem like any of them had any plans to move. To rebel. What would they get? The clock was ticking and would keep on doing so no matter where the ship went, no matter who flew it.

The radar said Eponi was closing in, Aurora opened the comm back to her.

"Bad news," Aurora said. "I don't think you want to dock with us after all."

The comm crackled for a moment as Eponi breathed back into the mic, apparently processing Aurora's words, which, not surprising. When your commander had you positioned for a rescue attempt and then, after you'd done all the work to line up two ships in active orbit, said that such an attempt was unnecessary, Eponi had every right to wonder if her commander had lost her mind.

"Believe me, Eponi," Aurora said. "We spread the virus across the shuttle. Everyone on board is infected, and it might pass through the airlock into your ship. Anaskya's saying there's no cure."

"Who's Anaskya?" Eponi replied

"The one behind all this. The mad scientist at the center of the experiment. The one I'm going to personally shoot right between the eyes before this virus takes me out."

"What? You're going to die?"

Aurora looked out the cockpit windows, at Dynas's spinning black bulk in the sky. Death hadn't exactly been far from her life for a long time now, always pacing her footfalls and whispering at her ears with every mission. Aurora should have died a dozen times over by now, kept alive only by random chance, endless preparations, and her squamates skills. Now she seemed to have outpaced all of those. Set herself up for the last dance.

"I said there's no cure," Aurora said. "None that we know of. We might live a few days, then we'll burn up. Just like Sai's doing now."

Eponi didn't say anything. What was there to say?

"So what I want you to do is head down to the surface," Aurora said. "Find Gregor and Rovo. Get out of this system. And Eponi, DefenseCorp knew about this. At least some of them did. So I wouldn't trust going back to them either. Take what you can, sell the armor and run."

More silence, then a grim sigh, "Aurora, my shuttle can't leave the system. It's close range only. Even if I wanted to abandon you, I couldn't."

"You don't want to hijack another one?"

"By myself? I'm not a fighter like Gregor. Like you."

"Eponi, you're every bit a fighter as I am. You wouldn't be in Sever if you weren't."

Silence again. Aurora kept watching those stars. Glanced back towards the hallway, towards the sounds of a growing argument in the back. Kashmal's voice kept rising higher and higher. Maybe he was feeling the virus's effects now. Realizing he wouldn't be collecting his big payday. His grand scheme a total failure.

"I'm not going down," Eponi said. "Not doing it."

"Excuse me?"

"You're a fighter, you're saying I'm a fighter," Eponi said. "Then let's fight. I'm about to dock with you, and we're going to find a way to beat this thing. Together, or not at all."

"This isn't some army we're up against," Aurora said, forcing the edge into her voice. That commander's demeanor that she had to adopt whenever someone in her always-willful squad decided to go against orders. "We're not beating this one with superior firepower. Follow the orders, Eponi. Go back to the surface and leave us alone."

"And what're you going to do if I disobey?"

Aurora didn't have an answer to that. She could, though, take Anaskya's ship and steer it away from Eponi's. Push it into a wild dive that would make the ship impossible to dock with. Aurora glanced at the flight sticks, at the cockpit controls. A button maze, coupled with screens that referenced mathematical coordinates Aurora barely understood. But if she kept pressing buttons, maybe she could find something that would work. Something that would save Eponi's life.

Sever's commander began hitting the buttons at random. Slapping at the screens and the keys like a creature that'd lost her damn mind. It felt stupid, it felt amazing. All this frustration brought out on a control panel that didn't deserve it but that had to take it nonetheless.

How dare a life that'd been led with so much vigor, with such hard training, come down to this? Come down to a disease that Aurora had no way to defend against? It wasn't fair, it wasn't right.

As she pounded on the control panel, as Aurora hit one blinking switch after the next, she felt the ship judder and shake. At one point, Aurora gripped a flight stick and tried to turn, but nothing changed. Apparently she'd turned off the engines, set the ship adrift. Aurora tried to figure out how to turn them on, but, stupidly, there weren't instructions for neophytes like her.

Something had changed. A whistling had started throughout the shuttle, a breeze. And a soft alarm began wailing in the cockpit, though Aurora couldn't trace exactly what the alarm was trying to tell her.

How did anyone learn to fly one of these things?

"Aurora?" the voice came from behind her, steady and amused. Anaskya. "Are you all right?"

When Aurora turned, she had a pistol in her hand, ready to lay waste to the doctor. "Where's Sai?"

"Back in the passenger area with the others. Surviving, despite your best efforts."

Aurora shook her head, gestured at the control panel, "I'm trying to kill us before the virus does."

"You might very well succeed," Anaskya spread her hands, showing she had nothing hiding in the active-wear suit she wore. "But it seems you may have found a direction for us to pursue."

"What do you mean?"

"You bled vacuum out of the cargo chamber." Anaskya let slip a sad smile. "All the virus samples I'd been planning to deliver are now floating above a planet I despise."

"Good."

"However, you also exposed that same chamber to extreme cold." Anaskya pulled a hand up to her chin. "I'm not certain, because we could never test these conditions on Dynas itself, but the virus may not survive in such situations."

"Not survive? I thought the whole point was to make soldiers handle extreme environments?"

"But vacuum?" Anaskya shook her head. "No. The negative pressure and the cold are too much. It would kill anyone, but it would also kill the virus. The disease is a rampant, ravaging thing, as we've seen. Stop that rampage with the extreme cold, and it might never start again."

"I don't—" Aurora stopped as the ship shuddered again, a longer and deeper shake than before. A quick glance at the radar confirmed why: Eponi had docked. Guess her attempts to dissuade the kart pilot had failed. One more in the string Aurora had tied to this mission. "So, you're saying we could freeze our way free?"

"Yes. To cure the virus, all we need to do is throw ourselves into space."

THIRTY-TWO

A Cold Cure

SAI HAD BEEN SICK BEFORE, had felt the perilous progress as fevers, chills, and other intergalactic illnesses burned their way through his body. Most, though, had prescribed treatments and, for whatever other failings it had, DefenseCorp invested in curing its soldiers to get them back to the field as fast as possible. So, while Sai had been down before, he'd never been out.

This was something else entirely. Whereas another virus might feel like an invader, this swarmed his systems and made them his own. Sai didn't feel like he was under attack so much as that he had been transformed. The virus had turned him from a human, a father and a demolitions expert surfing the stars for a mercenary company into . . . what, exactly? Someone suffering from hallucinations, someone who weaved from side to side and sought the grip on his sword as his only link to reality?

Yes, that.

But also someone with tears hovering in his eyes, dryness filling his mouth and a permanent rasp in his lungs. However, the muscles along his arms and legs felt harder, stronger. Sai's blood rushed hot in his veins, fulfilling Anaskya's wish for a winter-resistant being.

Good and bad, mixing and mingling with deleterious abandon.

"You're carrying a sword," Kashmal, the VIP they'd come to rescue and who now sat under Sai's blurry watch, said. The man leaned back on a crash couch, next to a pair of the guards that'd survived Sai and Aurora's rapid over-taking of the ship. "You know that, right?"

"It's mine," Sai said, forcing his head up to meet Kashmal's level stare.

The VIP looked flush already, the virus progressing fast through the man's systems. Not surprising, considering how flab and frail the man looked. Like he'd been having a few too many drinks for a few too many years. The guards next to him, while sweating, didn't yet look like they were falling to the disease.

"I gathered," Kashmal said, then tried a laugh. "What I'm trying to figure out is why? Does DefenseCorp issue those now?"

"My family's," Sai said, then wondered why he bothered to tell this man anything.

"Think they'll get it back?" Kashmal said. "After we all die out here? Some salvager's going to find the sword when they discover this ship and say oh, it's this guy's, better sling it all the way to wherever you call home?"

Sai blinked at Kashmal. No, there wasn't a good way for the katana to get back to his wife, his children, and while the thought irked Sai a little, it wasn't a burning concern. He hadn't taught his daughter, his son to use the weapon, hadn't taught his wife. They were destined for different things, probably were already doing them.

Sai could never keep the time dilation straight. Traveling for so long at light speed and over meant simply not aging, while the gravitational mass of his children's world . . .

It didn't matter. If he met them again, Sai would love them as they were, and he hoped they'd treat him the same way.

"Would you shut up?" said one of the guards. "I already have a headache and you're making it worse."

"Talking is my coping mechanism," Kashmal replied.

"Punching you might be mine," the guard said. "Let's find out."

Sai lifted the katana ever-so-slightly, trying not to show how much even that little motion taxed his wrist. Not the muscles, but his mind. Sending movement along his nerves seemed like trying to swim through wet cement; doable, difficult, and dirty.

The ship seemed to respond to Sai's lifted blade, shuddering as if something larger had hit it. Sai only turned when his hostages started looking around him, to the hatch sitting on the side of the passenger area.

A circular door there had been surrounded by thin red lights, indicating in no uncertain terms that this door was shut for a reason. Namely, that opening it once the ship was underway meant the kind of swift, brutal demise one would prefer to avoid.

Now those lights went yellow, and beyond the small window in the hatch—Sai couldn't tell if the window was actually that, or a screen linked to an outboard camera, the latter being less risky and the preferred model on newer ships, but why was he concerned about this? The damn fever had him on another tangent.

What was he wondering about?

Oh. The yellow lights. They were green now. Something had happened. Docking. That's what that meant. An airlock had been attached. Which meant another ship had been up above Dynas, waiting for them.

Anaskya's friends?

Sai shifted his grip, put both hands on the katana and raised it, facing the door. He took one deep breath after another, willing his muscles to tense up, to be ready to spring. Everyone always underestimated the sword's speed in this gun and laser universe. Sai would get his half second to launch the attack and he'd use it.

Until a face appeared that Sai didn't expect to see: curious eyes, hair tied up in makeshift bands, and then a hand waving through the screen.

"Eponi?" Sai said. Had the fever produced another hallucination? This one was so real. "That's not you."

"It's definitely someone," Kashmal said from behind him.

"Sai!" Eponi's voice came through the hatch's speaker, tinny but otherwise sounding like her. "I'm here to rescue you!"

How Eponi had found herself in space above Dynas, Sai didn't know. Didn't really care either—just seeing another friendly face helped salve the encroaching doom. Sai, though, didn't make any move towards opening the door. If Eponi wasn't infected, exposing her to the ship's air would be murder.

"Don't open it," Aurora said, coming back to the passenger quarters from the cockpit, her eyes in that glassy pre-infection stage, but otherwise looking the same confident commander she'd always been. "Eponi's going to help us, but not yet. Not till we clean up this place."

"Clean up this place?" Kashmal laughed. "How are you planning to do that? We're not a decontamination crew."

Aurora turned, pointed to the person following her,

another hostage and the source of Sai's simmering rage: Anaskya. She had on another one of those damned small smiles that said she knew more than you, that she was better than you, and that you were privileged to be sharing space with her brilliance.

"We're going to vacuum the ship." Anaskya folded her arms and let her grin grow wide as the words sank in.

Being haughty after such a phrase seemed right, because Sai couldn't quite believe what he heard. Vacuuming a ship meant exposing it to space, letting all the air get sucked out, along with anything else that wasn't nailed down. Sai had heard the phrase used when attacking—as in, blow a hole in the hull and vacuum the ship—never in casual conversation as a method.

A strategy.

"You're insane," Kashmal, for once, said what the rest of the room was thinking. "We'd all die?"

"Not quite," Anaskya said. "But before you make ridiculous jumps to panic, let me explain."

"She's good at it," Aurora added. "I was about to shoot her, but she convinced me. For now."

"Thank you?" Anaskya quirked an eyebrow. "Now, here is what we can do. Because of the actions of these two, I believe we are all infected. I designed the virus to allow for controlled dispersion, either through injection or, with less success, through airborne proliferation.

"However, we did not design it to spread uncontrolled. Our investors didn't want to create a plague, but an applied method to enhance their employees. As such, you and I being in the same room poses no risk. Only if fresh virus itself is loosed into the air, can we catch it."

Shrugs and bland looks abounded. Sai included.

"Get to the point," Aurora said.

"Fine. I always prefer to understand the reasoning

behind one's actions, but if you would prefer the goal alone," Anaskya breathed, like Sai would before delivering an obvious lesson to his children. "If we kill the virus floating in the air around the ship, there will be no danger to others. If we kill it in our own bodies, then we survive."

"But the vacuum will kill us," Kashmal said. "I thought you'd know that."

"For us, we just need the cold," Anaskya said. "Chill ourselves enough and the virus should die. The body, so frozen, can be brought back with minimal damage if we do so quickly enough."

Vacuum-cleanse the whole ship, then freeze-and-thaw each of them in turn? The whole plot sounded ridiculous. Dangerous and potentially deadly.

Sai dropped the katana and it hit the floor with a clattering metal crash. He looked at his right hand, so covered in sweat that it could no longer hold onto anything. His headache had ramped up, a pulsing pain that blurred his vision with every beat.

He couldn't be picky. Couldn't be difficult. He needed a cure, and he needed it now.

"I'm in," Sai said. "When can we start?"

"I don't see a better time than right now?" Anaskya said. "First, we sterilize the ship. And then, we freeze."

Kashmal, at last, had nothing to say.

THIRTY-THREE

Shock and Awe

THREAT EQUATIONS TENDED to involve stakes. Weigh the potential benefits versus the harm of throwing yourself against the foes presented to you. Gregor, on a skiff with three potential enemies, two of which wore DefenseCorp armor like his own, calculated the threat in forcing them to rescue his Sever squad-mate like this:

Benefit: saving Rovo.

Harm from Lani, Wicks, and Sayers? None.

Not that they couldn't hurt Gregor, not that Lani couldn't land a potentially fatal shot through some crack in Gregor's armor and down the big one once and for all. No, Gregor just didn't register that as *harm*. At least, not compared to loyalty.

You never turned your back on your squad. No matter what.

"I think you're missing the point," Lani said as Sayers hurtled the skiff back towards the city. "You don't command us, and your hammer isn't going to help you."

"It's helped me plenty before," Gregor replied.

"What're you going to do?" Lani raised her rifle,

inspected it without any obvious concern. "Smash us? Say you succeed, do you even know how to fly a skiff?"

"I would figure it out."

Lani laughed as yellow fog swept around her face. All their faces. The skiff rode through the thick mists, gunk again seeping into any little nook it could find in the armor. Sayers, in the skiff's cabin, had Wicks stationed near the windshield, constantly wiping it clear.

Other than the skiff's engine whines, other than their voices, Dynas stayed quiet. Gregor found that one of the oddest things about the planet: noise didn't have a place here. Even in the city, the only constant sound came from splashes. No burning industry, no stiff blowing wind or cries from native animals.

Quiet enough to hear his own teeth chatter against each other as Lani continued breaking down just how trapped Gregor was, "Because, you're no doubt seeing now, DefenseCorp and so many others have too much invested here to let a little VIP request get in the way. And they're going to pay us out, too. Cash you might be able to get your hands on, if you decide to join us."

"I don't turn traitor."

"That's a strong word," Lani said. "Your friend's probably dead already. Just like the rest of your squad. You, though, found us, and I'm able to protect you. We could use the muscle, honestly, because this might turn into a smash-and-grab before too long if Helix keeps messing up."

Why did everyone think Gregor could be bought? Because he carried a hammer and looked so much like the toughs in a stereotypical action film? The ones that could be sent off with a punch, kick, or half-hearted glance from the story's hero?

"We're going to the tram station," Gregor said. "That's the end of it."

Lani shrugged, didn't give any such order to Sayers. Gregor let the skiff buzz on for another few minutes, watching the fog and waiting for Lani to come to her senses. To realize that one DefenseCorp soldier meant more than a mission that had so obviously been blown already.

What were they going to save? A virus that slaughtered its hosts? DefenseCorp couldn't be interested in something that would turn its soldiers into Felix look-a-likes. Melting viral madmen.

The black city rose from the fog instantly. One moment the skiff hadn't passed through its nano net, and all the world was yellow mist, and in the next sat a sopping metropolis, skies buzzing with skiffs and streets shifting with evening commuters riding home.

And right there, right past the city's outer wall keeping Dynas's swamp waters at bay, sat the tram station. A moldering gray mass between residential blocks. And on it, Gregor could see several figures, saw a laser's flash.

"He's still alive," Gregor growled to Lani, the two of them sharing the skiff's bow. "Get down there, now."

"What about the last few minutes made you think I changed my mind?"

Gregor glanced at her. Lani's good cheer at Felix's successful slaughtering had slid into a set face. Her bluff at Rovo's demise had been called by circumstance, and now she had a choice to make.

"You're abandoning your own," Gregor said.

"I'm saving them," Lani replied. "Sayers and Wicks, they're my team. Not you. Not your squad. We go in there and Helix is going to pull our license. We'll get murdered when you leave."

"Then come with us."

"That kills our mission."

"As soon as we get to space, my commander is going to tell DefenseCorp to blow this place to hell," Gregor said. "You won't have a mission."

The skiff coasted over the wall. Either it went down now, towards those figures dashing around on the roof, or . . .

Lani was shaking her head, "DefenseCorp won't do it. They'd be admitting their own role. And you don't know if your commander's even—"

Gregor turned, lifted, and slammed his charged hammer on the skiff's bow. The blow bent and split the metal, sending the craft into an immediate dive. Gregor's boots clicked in, locking him to the slanted surface. Lani and Wicks saved themselves the same way, and Sayers planted hard against the skiff's sturdy windshield as the craft nosed down.

Lani cursed, screamed, and otherwise held on as the skiff descended. Gregor couldn't see what Wicks was doing. Didn't care either. He set his legs, crouched, and waited for the right second.

The tram station rose at them fast, and with it came a better view of the players running around on its roof. One of them, Rovo, snapped off a well-placed shot that took out another figure emerging from the rooftop doorway. Another, a woman, rushed through after the downed figure, aiming Rovo's way with her weapon.

And three others scaled the roof from the far side, near where someone else, someone small, seemed to be sitting.

Rovo didn't see the ones coming behind. He focused on the woman, seemed to be saying something to her. Another second and he'd take a shot to the back.

"Good luck!" Gregor shouted at Lani, and jumped.

His boosted jump made Gregor feel, ever so momentarily, like a superhero. Coasting through the air, high above his landing spot, hammer above his head like a viking warrior from millennia ago, from a planet Gregor had never seen and likely never would.

The trio climbing onto the roof, all Helix guards in that black uniform they wore so well, noticed the skiff. It must have been hard to miss, descending from the sky with its bow all smoke and fire as its electric batteries melted down. Sayers seemed to be trying to keep the thing aloft, slowing its crash with whatever sputtering jets he could get to work.

All that noise and disaster made it difficult to see Gregor plummeting in, at least until he crashed into the middle guard, burying the Helix man into the roof, while Gregor's hammer smashed into the first and sent the ruined man soaring.

Gregor's armor absorbed the landing shock, converting the kinetic energy that should have crumpled his knees and blown his spine into power. Gregor swiveled around to the third guard, who still seemed stunned by the doom that'd just fallen from the sky.

The guard's bad day continued when Gregor knocked him off the roof with a cross swing.

"Gregor!" Rovo shouted from the far side, where he looked to be in a firefight with the woman and another, emerging guard. "Get the girl!"

The girl? Gregor's instincts pieced it together faster than his mind, bringing him around towards the small figure clutching something near the tram station's corner.

What the hell was a girl doing here?

Gregor slotted away his hammer and jumped, used that boosted, kinetic power to fling himself along the roof as the skiff slammed into it, a rippling explosion launching in Gregor's wake. The girl's wide eyes grew even wider as

Gregor flew into her, grabbed her in his arms and cradled her as they dropped off the side of the building.

Rotating in air wasn't easy, but Gregor had done enough drops with Sever and other DefenseCorp missions that he could throw himself forward, surrounding the girl in a protective, power-armor shell as they slammed down into the wet street below, fiery debris following after them.

THIRTY-FOUR

Space Walk

SHE LEFT the airlock to the diseased ones. Eponi caught their attention and then retreated back to her shuttle, sealed the doors, and watched.

The whole plan seemed insane. Expose Anaskya's ship to vacuum and hope that could cleanse the craft? Then individually freeze each and every one of them to do the same?

Eponi kept the doubts to herself as she watched the half dozen members file into the airlock, the elastic gray tube connecting her small shuttle to the larger ship. The membrane billowed out where the people stepped, arguably too many for the passage to hold at any one time, but in zero gravity, weight limits and wind weren't much of a risk.

"We're ready," Aurora said, her voice coming through the shuttle's cockpit. "Open her up, Eponi."

"So long as you realize I'm not responsible for what happens next."

"If this doesn't work, we die, so there's not a whole lot to lose."

Well. Eponi could die if something went wrong. That was something to lose. But she kept her mouth shut.

Before leaving Anaskya's ship for the airlock, Eponi and Aurora had worked to slave over the larger ship's controls so Eponi could operate the ship remotely. Meant more for guiding ships into difficult docking situations than engaging in drastic science experiments, the method did let Eponi see all the various options Anaskya's ship had available.

And there were many. Anaskya had given herself a capable vessel, able to hit post-light velocities for true inter-stellar journeys. Rudimentary defensive turrets nestled beneath armor plating, hidden until necessary, bolstered by extensive reflective paint that would deflect a laser's energy.

In short, this craft wasn't meant to sit in the docking bay on a world like Dynas. It belonged in the fray, diving into contested territory and coming out victorious.

Eponi couldn't suppress a little excitement as she ruffled through the settings, the potential. It would be so fun to fly this thing, and, if everything went well, Eponi *would*. Aurora hadn't come out and said it, but if Sever planned to complete the mission, Anaskya's ship made the most sense to take. Drop their hostages on the surface and blitz off into the starry night.

"Eponi? You there?" Aurora came back over the comm. "It's cold, and we're still dying in this airlock. So any time. By which I mean, now."

"Right."

Exposing a ship to vacuum meant killing any magnetic shielding, then opening a compartment. Eponi had to do this carefully, had to keep the ship's structural integrity together. Spring open the entire craft at once and the sheer forces sucking everywhere might break the ship's supports to pieces.

"So one at a time," Eponi said. The cargo bay seemed a logical starting point, if only because it'd already been opened without major damage. "Here we go."

Eponi flipped several switches, adjusting the view out her own cockpit to one of several hull cameras on the shuttle— standard procedure so a pilot could see what was happening outside—and oriented the view to show Anaskya's craft, lingering there to the side with Dynas's giant glob behind it.

The next switch re-opened the cargo bay over a protesting computer. Eponi watched the tiny flaps open on her cockpit's glass, not a single sound coming. Nothing floated out either, though the force in that bay had to be tremendous.

"We can hear it," Aurora said. "It's roaring loud."

"Only going to get louder," Eponi replied. "I'm going to seal and open the rest of the ship one by one now. Tell me if something goes wrong."

Ships like Anaskya's were built with stops all over them. Thick doors that could seal off whole sections to prevent exactly what Eponi meant to force: decompressing the entire ship. Spring a leak, and you could hope to close off a section and survive until help arrived.

Eponi forced that leak and, one by one, sucked out every room on the ship. Debris coasted out through the cargo bay as she went, everything not nailed down or strapped in shifting and shooting out. Aurora reported some big bangs, no doubt objects not quite able to fit out of their rooms nonetheless making attempts.

The dance ended without any deaths, without any explosions. Eponi retraced her closing steps, finally sealing off the cargo bay. Now came another trick.

The vacuum had sucked all the oxygen from Anaskya's ship. Nobody could breathe in there, so Eponi would have to transfer the air from her own craft over. Which meant she needed to put on a respirator, get herself suited up.

"Going for stage two," Eponi said. "Sit tight."

Respirators were standard issue, and something Eponi had plenty of experience with. Most kart racers did, slapping oxygen masks over their faces while performing more intense races, where hitting high enough g-forces to knock people unconscious was a frequent crash causer. Hopefully Eponi wouldn't be involved in any such maneuvers here, but as she slipped the mask over her face, felt air's first pure brush, that exciting twinge came with it.

She had to get back to racing. And soon.

"Flooding the airlock now," Eponi said. "Get ready to open the passage back into the ship."

"We've been ready."

Of course they had been. Aurora probably had them standing at the door, waiting on her command from the second they'd entered the airlock. Such a tight commander.

Too tight, at times, if Eponi was being honest.

Eponi flipped some switches on the shuttle, adjusting its recycling pumps to redirect one hundred percent of their energy to the airlock, rather than the usual ten or less. Slowly, the shuttle's air would drain into that tube, and when Aurora opened the door back to Anaskya's ship, the resulting pressure would suck the oxygen along.

"So are you happy we took the mission?" Eponi asked Aurora, watching the shuttle's oxygen percentage decline. "That we came here?"

"Not at all," Aurora replied. "Going to ask Commander Deepak for a bonus on this, for all the bullshit we've been through."

"Think we'll get it?"

"Depends on whether I can stop myself from punching him."

"Please do."

"We'll see."

Aurora didn't continue the conversation and Eponi let it die. Watched that dial dip further and further. It felt strange, killing a ship like this. The little shuttle hadn't done anything wrong, had done everything right, really. Yet now they were going to leave it adrift up here, in orbit. Maybe some salvagers would rescue it, restore it to service.

"You'd deserve it," Eponi said, then gave the console a little pat.

She'd done the same with her karts after every race, as if the machines could feel it. Could understand Eponi cared for them, more than she cared for most of the people in her life.

"Go," Eponi said once the dial hit fifty. Half the shuttle's oxygen had flooded the airlock, more than enough to get Aurora's recovery efforts started.

The march back through Anaskya's ship, somehow, worked exactly as planned. Aurora popped the airlock door open and their whole bunch walked in, put on their own respirators for safety, and went about resetting the bigger ship's systems. The only worry came from Sai, who, once outfitted with his respirator, collapsed on the crash couch.

Eponi had almost forgotten they were all infected, all dying.

"Time to come over," Aurora announced a few minutes later, back in her own cockpit. "The airlock's still showing as secure."

"On my way."

Like walking through a house for the last time, Eponi,

with the respirator and oxygen tank looped over her back, went through the shuttle to her own airlock. Pressed in the combination, took one last look at the bland metal that'd been her home for the last few hours in space, and set foot into the elastic membrane spanning pure vacuum.

With no gravity, heading along the membrane felt more like floating than walking. Bouncing on her feet and her hands, Eponi made her way straight ahead, towards the sealed door marking Anaskya's ship.

Almost there.

"Keep it coming," Aurora said. "We're all waiting for you."

Could her commander sense Eponi's fear? Probably. Eponi could feel her own sweat pooling everywhere, felt her rapid breathing as she sucked air in from the tank.

But she made it. Hands hit the airlock door to Anaskya's ship and Eponi entered the same code Aurora had moments ago to pop the door. Only this time, the numbers came back red. Locked.

"It's not opening," Eponi said, forcing calm into her voice. "Aurora?"

"Checking."

Eponi looked around. All gray, pressing in. She couldn't see the stars, couldn't see Dynas. A shut door in front of her, and, back along the membrane the door to her old shuttle. Nothing else. No smells. Nothing to feel. The only sound her lungs squeezing air in and out.

"The ship's saying it can't open the lock because there's not enough air in the membrane," Aurora said. "We have to dump some air back in."

"I'm waiting."

The membrane, though, wasn't interested. A strange sound rose up from the far side, back toward's Eponi's shuttle. It took her a second to parse the rumbling gargle, the grinding frustration coming from her old ship.

The parts. They were still running, but without any air, things were breaking. Eponi should have shut the whole ship down. Should have, but when you were distracted, when you didn't prep ships for orbital stasis, well, ever, you didn't think of what you weren't doing.

Didn't remember what pumps would do with nothing to pump. That they would strain and break and—

The membrane jerked as Anaskya's ship began sending air her way and Eponi's old shuttle caught the oxygen's return. The pressure sent the air howling through the membrane towards Eponi's old shuttle, going against those same straining pumps still trying to push non-existent air back out. That force met at the membrane's connection, and bulged it outward, like a slow-growing balloon.

And when it popped, Eponi would be very, very dead.

New Friends

Rovo saw the rooftop fight playing out in many different ways, most ending with him getting fried as overwhelming Helix forces approached. Kaia would get captured, the suitcase stolen. The mission failed.

In those brief moments where Rovo saw possible success, like after he blitzed the first guard to hit the rooftop, or when he baited the woman who'd trailed him this whole way out into the open and disarmed her with a grab-and-get move, Rovo figured he could get to a stalemate. Bargain his way out and at least survive.

Never, not once, did he bet on a skiff slamming into the rooftop like a giant, fiery knife, slicing and burning its way across the top.

Nor did he expect Gregor, the hammer-wielding madman, to crash down from the sky and deal deathblows to a triple guard set and save Rovo's ass.

But you had to react fast to stay alive, to keep others alive, so when Rovo saw the skiff burning down, saw his own path to Kaia blocked with raining metal fire, he made the yell. Saw that split second cut as Gregor boost-jumped his way to the girl.

Then smoke, shrapnel, and worse blew everything away. Rovo felt a heavy wave hit him, pull him to the ground. Maybe the skiff had swatted him with a large deck chunk, or its armored plating?

"Stop fighting me," someone said, right next to him, and Rovo realized they were pushing back as he tried to get up. "You're not armored. I am."

Armored? Rovo still couldn't see much with the smoke, couldn't move his arms because they were pinned down, so he tried to ask who the hell was on top of him.

Bad idea.

As soon as Rovo opened his mouth, fumes and dust and dirt blew in and set him coughing, hacking up right into what the clearing smoke showed was a visor.

"Are all of you this stupid?" the person—a woman?— said. "Keep your damn mouth shut and maybe we'll get out of this alive."

That they might. Rovo knew they were close to the stairs heading back into the tram station, and somehow the whole roof hadn't collapsed, though it looked like the skiff had slammed its way into being a wall between the two halves.

On Rovo's side, he could see a few bodies—the woman who'd been following him had disappeared—and debris, but little else. No pursuit came running up the walls now, and aside from some approaching sirens and the snap-crackle from the small electrical fires, Dynas seemed quiet. Catching its breath between bursts.

"You can get off now," Rovo said. "Whoever you are."

"Trying to figure out how to do that," the woman replied. "I think the armor's damaged. I can't move the legs."

"Then roll."

Rovo helped, pushing the armor—he recognized the suit now, Aurora's—off of him. As soon as he had space, Rovo stood, then reached over and pulled the gun from the armored woman's holster. Held it up, looked at the cracked barrel, and threw it away.

Guess he'd have to use his scary voice.

"Who the hell are you and why are you wearing that armor?" Rovo said, standing over the woman while keeping his eyes running for reinforcements.

"Name's Lani, and it's not important why I'm wearing the armor," the woman said. "What is, is that you get me up before Helix decides you might still be alive."

"Not till I know what you're doing in my captain's suit," Rovo replied.

Lani slammed an armored fist on the roof in frustration. Rovo couldn't really see her face through the dust-smeared visor, coated with Dynas's yellow pollen. Maybe they'd gone outside the city?

"Now's not the time!" Lani said. "I work for Defense-Corp too, you asshat, and I saved your damn life. What more do you want?"

A lot, really. Rovo would like quite a lot to be explained about this crapshoot mission, but given the circumstances, he supposed he could wait.

A glance at Lani's legs showed some shrapnel damage, but nothing that would disable the legs from moving at all. What would, though, would be the armor's protective mode. Sucked all power into the armor's energy and particle diffusion shields in an attempt to survive a cataclysm like what had just happened.

"Okay, here's what you're going to do," Rovo said, then launched into a series of vocal commands that Lani had to repeat for the armor to unlock.

When Lani finished, the armor went from a stiff block to something like a rag doll, pressing its weight on Lani's limbs and sending them akimbo as Lani found herself able to move.

"Could've warned me," Lani replied.

"Could have," Rovo said. "Let's go."

Though she looked a little wobbly, Lani made it up without much effort. Rovo saw her glance over to the wrecked skiff for a long moment, looking for something, but whatever it was, she either didn't see it or gave up, because she came clomping Rovo's way once he made it to the stairs.

Not that the stairs were going to be much help.

The skiff's crash had broken the tram station's structure, splintered beams and supports and worse, and now the stairs leading back down into the station had collapsed. Where there had been steps, and lights, rubble and sparking remnants ruled.

"Guessing that was our way down?" Lani said.

"It was my way up," Rovo replied. "Now we need an alternative."

The tram station wasn't isolated, but given its purpose, other buildings weren't nestled right up close. No rooftop hops available.

Worse, as Rovo and Lani looked around, the sirens grew louder and paired with a familiar whine: more skiffs, which meant more Helix soldiers.

"Running out of time," Lani said. "Get me out of this armor."

"What?"

"They won't know who we are," Lani said. "At least not me. I can say we were stranded, try to talk our way out of this."

"We're not leaving Aurora's armor behind. She'll kill

me," Rovo said, wondering how true that statement was. Probably pretty close. "And, now that I think about it, where's my armor?"

"Again, not the time," Lani said. "If we can't go down the stairs, then we have to pick a different way."

"Like?" Rovo gestured to the side. "I'm not going to survive a rooftop jump."

"No, we go down the middle."

The crashing skiff had opened a hole in the tram station, then immediately filled it with broken metal, burning batteries, and worse. Still, from the whole list of crappy options Rovo had to work with, picking his way through debris seemed the least bad.

"Fine, but you go first," Rovo said.

Lani didn't argue, and the woman used Aurora's armor to tear a hole in the smoldering skiff's side. They went in slow, testing each step before putting their weight on it. Inside, the skiff was tar-black, with acrid smells that burned Rovo's nose whenever he took a breath. Grating and loose wires hung everywhere, and Rovo cut his hands a half-dozen times trying to keep his grip on sliced up metal pieces.

The skiff's bow had made the deepest smash, breaking through the roof and hanging in the space above the shuttered tram below. Rather than the narrowing point Rovo would have expected to see on any other skiff, the brown metal here broke away into an open hole, as if someone had taken the skiff's front and snapped it off.

"This why you crashed?" Rovo said.

He assumed Lani had been on the skiff, both because he'd seen Gregor in his armor and because if Lani hadn't been on the skiff, then where had she come from?

"We crashed because your friend is insane." Lani made

her way to the edge, looked down. "This is shorter than the roof. The tram's only a couple meters below."

"I know Gregor's insane, but were you letting him fly?" Rovo said, joining Lani at the edge. "Because that would definitely explain the crash."

"He hit the skiff with his hammer and broke it." Lani jumped, landing on the tram with a loud bang.

"Oh." Rovo followed suit, dangling from the skiff's edge first—and adding another cut to his collection—before dropping.

The tram's roof played rough with Rovo's knees, but a bit of soreness wasn't much with all this mess. He caught himself with his hands, rose up and brushed off the wet suit, a wetsuit now so coated with dirt and dust that Rovo figured he resembled a ghost more than a person.

Not that Lani was much better. Aurora would not be thrilled to find her armor as mottled, blackened and scarred as Lani had made it. The white that used to deliver such searing contrast had turned a dusted gray, leaving the suit looking more like a beat-up relic than a death-dealing tool.

Relic or no, Lani didn't wait for Rovo to keep moving. As soon as he recovered himself on the tram, she clomped to its edge and dropped to the track floor. Then kept right on running.

"Where are you going?" Rovo said as Lani went down the tunnel.

"Don't know if you noticed," Lani called back. "But our friends aren't waiting out there."

"Mine are," Rovo said. "And you're not leaving without them."

"Says who?"

"If I get captured, guess who I'm giving up?"

Lani stopped, hunched over, which in the armor looked

like a robot that'd run out of power. The tram station's remaining lights sprinkled a broken white glow over everything, which gave Lani's exasperation the look of a defeated sole.

"You aren't the only one whose lost friends today," Lani said, but she turned back. "How do you know they're even alive?"

"Gregor wouldn't die from a crash like this," Rovo said, clambering down from the tram.

Rovo wasn't sure what *could* kill Gregor. Nothing, most likely.

Lani didn't argue with that statement, and though she muttered curses, sighed, and seemed entirely against Rovo's course, she followed as he went across the landing to the ramp leading up from the station. Unlike the rooftop stairs, the ramp still stood, with pieces coated in fallen ceiling tiles or wall chunks. Rovo stepped over those, kept going up, hoping against hope that Gregor, and maybe the girl, had survived.

At the top, beyond the closed gate, the tram station's entrance sat at a slant. Beyond, the crowded street filtered through in slits and cracks. The sounds, though, came in loud: those never-ending sirens, the skiff whines, and now someone barking loud orders. Threats.

"Something's still happening," Rovo said as he and Lani approached the wrecked entry, keeping low.

"Going to remind you that neither of us have a weapon," Lani said. "So don't start a fight."

"I'll do my best."

As Rovo moved closer, managed to get a better view, he saw why the sirens kept sounding, why the orders were coming in loud.

In the street center, crouched with his left arm around the Kaia and his right holding the hammer, stood Gregor, facing off against Helix forces from every angle. Guards, skiffs, and snipers peering at him from rooftops.

The call came loud and clear. Drop the girl, or both of them would die.

"Lani," Rovo said. "I think I'm gonna start a fight."

THIRTY-SIX

Atmospheric Entry

IN THE TOWER, Sai had faced off against the infected. Those shambling caricatures of men and women who had stumbled towards him, ready to be sliced by his katana. In that moment, Sai had felt strong—even after the skiff crash—and able to handle anything that came his way. He would never be like these people, broken and decaying.

After Anaskya injected the virus, Sai couldn't grapple with the idea that this might be the thing that took him out. He'd be strong enough to defeat it. He could overpower the fevers, the hallucinations, the sudden changing as his arms and legs grew stronger while his head grew lighter. The virus turning him into an aggressive bomb that would detonate before too long.

But his fuse hadn't run out yet.

The airlock's impending collapse triggered alarms throughout Anaskya's ship. Aurora and Anaskya, in the cockpit, didn't have time. Kashmal and the guards, sitting on the crash couch looking confused, didn't have the motivation. Only Sai, sitting on the end with his blade balanced on his knees, had both.

He made a stumbling dash towards the airlock door, the katana clattering to the floor. Not that grabbing the door helped; the potential vacuum had the airlock sealed tight. Sai hunted for the manual release as Aurora shouted to do the same over the comm.

Hard to find a lever when your vision was swimming, when your constant fever turned up into down, long into short, and drifted you back and forth between past and present.

Thankfully, the lever stood out on the airlock's left side, big and red and coated with dire warnings if one was stupid enough to pull it.

Sai was in no mental state to consider the consequences of his actions, so he pulled the damn lever with the strength of a virally-altered madman. Behind him, on the couch, Kashmal cackled with a dire edge that they were all going to die.

The airlock refused to open. Even with the lever pulled, Sai couldn't overpower the vacuum pressure's suck.

"Help me!" Sai shouted, or tried to. His words came out garbled. Shattered syllables wet with his mushy mouth. "Please!"

Sometimes you didn't need words to get your point across. Kashmal and the guards, perhaps stirred by Sai's desperation, perhaps from some realization that their lives might have one last use in them, heaved themselves across the passenger quarters and gripped the airlock, pressing and pulling.

The door moved. Swung with a creak, and when the seal popped, a familiar roar filled the ship. Air sucking out, chill rushing in.

"Hold it," Sai said, making his way around his struggling, drafted helpers to the airlock's edge, feeling the pull on his feet, on his hair.

His ears popped, burst, and Sai's eyes felt like they were squeezing out of his head, but the airlock's slight opening kept the worst at bay. For now.

Sai looked around the airlock's corner, keeping his grip tight. Eponi clung to the other side, folded almost in half. She'd looped her arms through the airlock's outer valve, and though her shoulders looked dislocated, and her eyes had the glassy look of the semi-conscious, Eponi was still there. Behind her, the membrane whipsawed as the split between it and Eponi's shuttle continued leaking air.

Words would be useless over the roar, so Sai tapped the guard next to him, had the man hold on to him with one hand, the airlock with the other. Just enough security for Sai to keep his footing while he reached for Eponi with both hands.

He touched Eponi's arms, grabbed them, and began to pull them free. Behind him, Kashmal yelled something about the pressure, about how if they didn't get the airlock shut soon, their lungs would all burst. The man started laughing again.

Sai unlocked Eponi's left arm, holding it tight with his left, and went for Eponi's right, now leaning most of the way out of the airlock, the membrane more beneath him than the ship. The vacuum tugged at his feet, sliding them every-so-slightly on the floor.

Eponi's right arm came free faster than the first, but as Sai unhooked it from the airlock's circular valve, Eponi jerked back. Sai lunged to grab her and felt his own feet leave the ship's floor.

Only to be yanked back. Planted down.

"I've got you," Aurora shouted behind him. "Reel her in!"

Sai felt a tug, felt himself getting pulled backward until his feet could touch the inside again. After him came

Eponi, and as soon as she cleared, Kashmal and the guards released the airlock door, which slammed shut and locked with a final click. Sai, Eponi, Aurora, and Anaskya—the last link in the pulling chain—collapsed on the floor.

Alive. At least that.

"We can't stay up here," Aurora said a few minutes later, from the cockpit. "The oxygen's too low."

Eponi, weak and leaning on Sai, nodded. "We have to go back to the surface. Pump some fresh air in here."

Her voice sounded slight, her arms—despite Aurora popping Eponi's shoulders back into place—hung limp at her sides. But her eyes sparkled and Sai could feel her heart beating through their suits.

"Can you fly?" Aurora asked her.

"No, but I can tell you two how."

Sai didn't think he was in any state to be piloting a ship, but nobody trusted Anaskya, Kashmal, or the guards to handle it. Instead, the Sever trio sealed the cockpit's door and set the ship in a sharp re-entry, heading right back towards the Black City.

Anaskya's ship had speed where it counted, and they launched down through the atmosphere, rocking and rollicking the whole way.

Dynas greeted them with the same thick yellow fog Sai had learned to loathe since the drop ship had crashed them through the atmosphere only a couple of days before, a time that seemed eons ago already. That yellow fog roiled and split away as they flew into the city's nano net, with the whole urban circle spread below them.

The radio crackled. Began to play a short sentence, with a familiar voice.

"Is that Rovo?" Eponi asked.

"Calling for help," Sai said, parsing the words.

"I tuned the comm to the squad band once we had the ship," Aurora said. "Just in case."

Rovo's call said he needed assistance, said he was at some tram station. Aurora seemed to know where that was, and even as Eponi directed her to open the airways so the ship could refill, the captain tilted Anaskya's ship into a tighter descent.

The city rushed up at them, its wet surface shimmering from above, like looking into a glistening mirror. Beautiful, blinding. Or maybe that was the virus. Hard for Sai to tell what was real.

Aurora's cursing, though, couldn't be disputed. Nor could the subject of the commander's vitriol: several skiffs, a slew of what looked like Helix emergency vehicles, and who knew how many personnel surrounded the burning, ruined tram station. And, more directly, a corner of it, where a familiar figure held a hammer high.

"Is that . . . ?" Eponi asked.

"Damn right it is," Aurora said. "Sai, figure out how to get the weapons on this ship going. We might not be done yet."

The weapons? That, at least, Sai knew how to handle. Anaskya's ship wasn't exactly military grade, but she'd put some teeth on the craft. Sai's fingers played over the console in front of him, sliding energy to the ship's weapons and opening them up. Telling them their targets by swiping his fingers along the images coming from below.

But Sai didn't fire the first shot.

Gregor slammed his hammer down in front of him, the blow shattering the concrete and spraying up a dirt and dust shield as the big man fell back. The surrounding Helix forces began to launch lasers, zeroing in on their target as

Gregor turned his back to them, looking like he was trying to protect something clutched to his chest.

Outnumbered, outgunned.

No more.

The ship's console pinged when they entered range, and Sai didn't wait for Aurora's command to activate the program, sending lasers by the dozen streaming down towards the city, towards the clustered forces.

Against a bunch of skiffs, Anaskya's ship did the job: the bolts sliced down and through the hovering craft, burning out vehicles and sending rooftop snipers scrambling as their posts turned to molten ash. As shots hit batteries and fuel cells, explosions followed suit, billowing out steam and smoke, the rippling noise making it all the way up to the ship as they zoomed in close.

"Kashmal, open the airlock," Aurora said. "And if I have to come back there, I'm bashing your head in."

Aurora's threat, or perhaps the sheer insanity of the situation, worked: Sai saw the light indicating an open door pop on as Aurora swung the ship down into the now-cleared and largely destroyed intersection.

The door was open, the rescue had arrived. Now, as Sai tried to focus his feverish eyes on the surroundings, hunting for targets, there was only one question:

Had they made it in time?

Save The Girl

GREGOR DIDN'T KNOW the girl. Hadn't met her and had no emotional connection to her whatsoever, except that in the second before he reached her with that boost jump, flying along the roof, with his helmet's visor identifying the target and highlighting her for a pristine pick-up, she smiled. Giggled.

Then they plummeted fifteen meters and crashed into the concrete.

And she kept laughing, cradled in Gregor's arms.

What a child.

Gregor had to fight for his own consciousness after the crash, his rattled mind and muscles struggling to identify what the armor had protected and what, now, had been bruised into jelly. Broken into pieces.

His left arm, wrapped around the girl, couldn't seem to unwind itself. Gregor couldn't feel it, so he issued the requisite command to his armor, told it to freeze that limb in place. An option that existed for moments like these; Sever had a habit of breaking bones mid-mission.

His legs still worked, his right arm twinged but shifted. His fingers had feeling. Gregor wasn't downed yet.

"Don't move!" the order came from some speaker Gregor couldn't see—still on his back, watching the dust from the skiff crash fall around him, Gregor hadn't assessed his surroundings. "Don't move or we'll shoot."

The girl laughed again. Said something Gregor lost to a headache's spasm. He blinked the pain away. Focused. Then sat up.

"I said don't move!" The order came again, and this time Gregor saw the speaker, some man standing in front of a treaded police truck, shouting into an old-style megaphone.

Gregor shifted, made sure his trapped left arm revealed the girl still giggling against his chest. Made sure everyone could see launching a shot at Gregor would mean hurting the child.

He didn't have a way out of this situation, didn't have an answer for the assembling fleet facing him—several skiffs, too, pulled up and added their arsenal—so Gregor's only option was to buy time.

Maybe Lani, Wicks, and Sayers would come to his rescue, if they weren't dead. Maybe Rovo could do something, if the crashing skiff hadn't landed on him.

Or maybe Gregor would have to find his own answers.

"Release the child!" The voice tried again.

"Can't," Gregor said back, far too quiet for anyone to hear, but Gregor's lungs seemed a little winded, a little unable to get their breath going.

Across his visor, Gregor's armor brought up his vitals, along with the armor's own health. Damage everywhere, and the armor suspected Gregor might have some internal damage to go along with his left arm. In short, he needed a doctor and the armor needed a technician.

"Are you okay?" The girl asked, a little chirp, and her eyes stared at him with sudden concern. "Are you a bad man?"

Empathy, suspicion. Two opposite asks in the same breath. The things children could do.

"I am fine, little one," Gregor said. "Do not worry."

The armor said he should be able to stand, and Gregor preferred not to die sitting down, so up he rose, slowly and with chips falling away from his metal suit. His bones ached, his nerves screamed that this was a bad idea, but when Gregor had his full height, when he turned to the crowd, the pain washed away.

Facing this many, protecting a child? This was a hero's death. This was a doom he could love.

"We don't want to hurt the child, but if you make any other moves, we'll fire!" The speaker said.

How many bluffs could Gregor call? He'd moved, he hadn't released the child, and now he'd stood up. Clearly they wanted the girl, and wanted her alive.

Gregor grinned, not that anyone could see the smile behind his helmet. Time to test this even further.

"Little one, do not be scared," Gregor said, reaching his arm behind his back to where his hammer sat holstered.

Where it had, no doubt, made his landing a lot less comfortable. Such were the prices paid for carrying gigantic weapons.

Gregor's grip felt solid, and he pulled the hammer up and out of his holster as the speaker shouted again. Threatened again.

Gregor tried to inhale, forced his lungs against his ribs —bruised? Cracked? Broken?—and told the armor to amplify his next words. He lifted the hammer high, its head gleaming in the late evening light, coated with Dynas's ever-present dew.

"You want her?" Gregor announced. "Come get her!"

Perhaps not the stuff of legend, but Gregor wasn't a poet. He was a warrior, and he would fight to his damn last.

The fall had charged the hammer's kinetic energy to its maximum, and Gregor used it now, slamming the weapon into the ground in front of him, splashing up water, dirt, concrete and more beneath it. The debris geyser gave Gregor enough time to turn around, to hunch over the girl as the first shots came pouring in.

They wanted the girl alive, but not enough to hold off forever.

In front, Gregor saw the tram station's collapsing entrance, saw people moving beyond its tangled beams and dangling wires. His armor highlighted their forms, picked them out as allies. Rovo's face, Aurora's armor.

But they didn't fire. Didn't step out to help. Gregor moved towards them anyway, taking one step and then another as the shots began to strike home, began burning through his armor's shielding and superheating his skin.

The little girl began to scream, and not with glee this time.

"Shh, little one," Gregor said as he took another step, felt his upper back flash red as a bolt burned through. "You will be okay, I promise."

He kept repeating the words as he crossed the meters, made it to the tram station's threshold, before his left leg went out. Before Gregor couldn't stand anymore. He knelt fast, buried the girl beneath his burning bulk.

She would live. The little girl must survive.

A rippling boom tore the air behind him. Then

another and another and now screams that weren't the girl's, weren't his echoed around the intersection. More bangs followed, and even Gregor's tortured lungs picked up the ozone scent of laser-burned air.

"Can you stand?" Rovo's voice, next to Gregor now. "We gotta move, Gregor."

"Can't," Gregor replied.

He felt, then saw Rovo shifting his left arm. Winced at the ice-sharp pain that came with it, but the girl was free. Lani, in Aurora's armor, scooped up the child and ran past Gregor, towards the enemy.

He tried to say something, tried to tell Rovo, but Gregor couldn't find the energy.

"Don't worry," Rovo said. "She's taking Kaia to the ship. Where I'm taking you."

What ship?

Rovo slipped himself beneath Gregor's left arm and lifted. Pain spiked through, but Gregor managed to stand, managed to turn around with Rovo to see a giant craft hovering over the intersection, spraying laser fire at the scattering enemies. The surrounding buildings lay ruined, skiffs had slammed into the streets, and vehicles burned.

Rampant, wild destruction. Sever's style.

As Rovo began to walk Gregor toward's the intersection's center, the ship descended, its airlock popping open and a small ramp sliding out. Lani jumped, bounded up the ramp with the girl in hand. After she vanished inside there, face looking out and hands waving them on, stood Eponi.

Miracles upon miracles.

"There's got to be a good story behind this," Rovo said as they trudged towards the ramp, then started up its hard metal surface.

"I will hear it," Gregor muttered, his armor still amplifying his words. "After, perhaps, a nap."

"And a doctor."

"Yes. That would be nice."

In his right arm, grinding against the ramp, Gregor still held his hammer, and he held it tight.

Captain's Orders

ONE SOLDIER in a makeshift medical bay with broken bones and laser burns. Another suffering from a dislocated shoulder and the trauma of nearly being sucked into space. Aurora and Sai taking turns in the improvised vacuum-freezer in the ship's cargo bay, just long enough to kill the virus without killing themselves.

The rookie was the only one who'd come out of the fight without serious harm. And even he was wrapped up caring for a little girl that'd somehow become their charge.

Not to mention Lani, Kashmal, Anaskya, or the two guards still riding along. None of them wanted to go back to Dynas, though for different reasons.

Lani thought her companions had died, her mission failed, and DefenseCorp wouldn't be interested in her services, or her life, any further. She wanted a drop at the next planet.

Kashmal and Anaskya fought over the same goal: how to sell the virus or its applications without any samples, with only their word. Aurora contemplated just letting them freeze to death in the cargo bay, but Anaskya *was* a doctor, and her help was better than nothing with Gregor's wounds.

Kashmal, well, Kashmal could buy passage off the *Nautilus*. That would, technically, give Sever the mission complete. They'd saved the VIP, made it off world.

The Helix guards tossed off their logos and asked if DefenseCorp was hiring.

DefenseCorp was always hiring.

"Aurora, what're you thinking?" Eponi asked as the ship streamed further away from Dynas, picking up speed. It'd get up to and eventually slip into that mysterious physical anomaly that was faster-than-light travel. "Find the *Nautilus*?"

Sever's home ship shouldn't be all that far away. They could swing by a fringe world, drop their human cargo and fly on to meet it. Collect their reward, get their next mission and get on with their lives.

"Is that what you want?" Aurora asked, more to buy herself time to think than anything.

She and Eponi were the only two in the cockpit, though Aurora's thoughts had it feeling crowded.

"What I want, only cash can get me," Eponi said. "But I'd just as soon never go to a planet like that again."

"Yes. I'm tired of them too. Tired of it all, really," Aurora said.

She'd planned, at the end of this, to appeal to Defense-Corp's galactic authority. Ask them to go to Dynas and force the planet's experiments to shut down. But with Anaskya fleeing on this very ship, and the whole city seemingly on the edge of collapse anyway, what was the point?

Push over a toppling tower?

Better to collect the cash for another successful mission,

then reassess her finances. Make that retirement move. Find somewhere calm, peaceful.

"All right," Aurora said. "We're going for the money then. Set course for the *Nautilus*."

With Eponi working on the astro-navigation, Aurora headed back to tell the others. Kashmal, Lani, and Rovo were with the girl, with the rookie holding Kashmal at arm's length and delivering a solid glare to the mission's VIP.

"She's scared because you kept her stuffed in a closet, you monster," Rovo said.

"I kept her there to keep her safe!" Kashmal waved his arms. "What was I supposed to do? Let the one real success Dynas ever produced just walk around?"

"One real success?" Lani asked, standing up away from Kaia and her dusty lion toy. "What do you mean?"

Kashmal looked a little ill at Lani's words, sat back on the crash couch, then ran his hands through his short black hair.

"She's the only one. Been infected since birth and hasn't shown any negative signs. Inside her blood is the answer Anaskya's been looking for."

"Wait," Lani said. "You, of all people, have the only living proof this concept could work?"

"I do," Kashmal said, "because she's my own daughter."

Aurora put herself between Rovo and Kashmal, because the rookie looked like he might drop Kaia and go in for a murderous assault any second. And if he started Aurora wasn't sure she'd stop him. She'd pegged Kashmal as an ass, but this went above and beyond.

"Please," Kashmal said. "It's not, I'm not like that. You've felt the virus," he said to Aurora. "It's broken, yes, but it does make you stronger. More resilient. She wasn't born right. She needed help, but you've seen Dynas. Not exactly cutting edge. The virus saved her."

To Kashmal's credit, the man started crying halfway through the explanation, one that swerved into a longer story. He'd stolen some of the virus, reduced the dose enough that it wouldn't kill a child outright. The doctors claimed the girl wouldn't live long, so Kashmal made the excuse to take her home, let her pass with her family.

But she didn't. Kaia survived, thrived. And nobody could know about it.

"What about the mother?" Rovo said. "Where's she at? Or did you dose her up too?"

Kashmal shook his head, "She's somewhere in the city, down there. She couldn't take the prognosis and left. Couldn't accept it when I told her what I'd done, either. I forgave her that much."

Lani looked down at the girl, still seemingly oblivious to everything that'd been said, "She looks normal enough to me."

As a squad commander, Aurora had to be ready to deal with many different things. Had to be prepared for whatever might come up. Family disputes, however, had so far escaped her list. Whatever she felt about Kashmal's parenting choices didn't, in all actuality, matter. Aurora's job was the squad, her goal was the cash.

"We're going back to the *Nautilus*. Kashmal, you'll provide the other half of your payment when we get there. Then I'm sure DefenseCorp will be happy to let you all buy yourselves passage somewhere else." Aurora delivered the block without a breath, in a stern and level voice meant to brook no opposition.

When she saw Kashmal inhaling, throwing a sick grin on his face, Aurora knew she had failed.

"Your rookie didn't save my suitcase," Kashmal said. "Without it, I don't exactly have any cash." He looked over at his daughter. "She's the only thing I have left that has any value."

"Value?" Rovo shot back. "Helluva way to talk about your daughter."

"He means the virus," Lani said. "What's inside of her."

Aurora's eyes drifted towards the little girl. Defense-Corp would collect on its payment, the company didn't care how. If there was some way to extract cash from Kaia, they would find it.

"You have nothing else?" Aurora asked. "No savings stored away?"

Kashmal shook his head, "You're looking at all of me. And I'm all she's got."

Aurora called the vote an hour later. Sever squad huddled around Gregor's bed, where the big man looked at them with a drug-addled smile on his face.

"Those are the stakes," Aurora said after she'd finished running down the situation. "We go back to the *Nautilus*, Deepak's going to take Kaia as Kashmal's price. I don't know what they'll do with her, but I bet she won't have a fun time while they try to take the virus from her blood. Figure out why it works in her."

"So you're asking us if we want to, what?" Eponi said. "Just not go back? Hide Kaia? Not get our reward?"

"That's the vote," Aurora said. "I'm not sure where else we'd go, what we'd do. But we couldn't go back to DefenseCorp. A mission failed would get too many questions. And I wouldn't trust Anaskya or the others not to tell the truth."

"Give up the girl, or give up our lives?" Gregor said,

then laughed in his broken chuckle. "I can fight and die anywhere, for anyone. Let her live."

Aurora nodded, looked at Sai, still weak from the vacuum freeze and leaning on against the wall. He'd had a longer exposure, necessary to deal with his higher virus load, and looked dry, shriveled.

"I have children," Sai said. "I would never give them up, not for anything."

"One mission in, I don't have much to lose," Rovo added. "I don't want to have Kaia on my conscience."

Back around to Eponi, who bit her lip, shook her head, and sighed, "You know I'm the only one flying this thing. I could take us to the *Nautilus* and you'd never even know."

"But you won't do that," Sai said. "You're not that person, Eponi."

Eponi's glance away showed that she might not be so sure of that, but she nodded, "Okay. I'm in. But what does this even mean? We're turning traitor? We're outlaws?"

"No," Aurora said. "We're dead. To DefenseCorp, to any official, we're casualties. Now we're just a group, working for cash. Like we always were."

"Less orders, more fun," Gregor said. "I like it."

"It's settled, then," Aurora said, surprising herself at how free it felt to cast off DefenseCorp's tight shackles. "We'll head towards the nearest world, drop off our passengers, and figure out what's next."

She looked around the room, caught the nods from all the others. Five fighters, skilled and ready. Not a bad start, at least until DefenseCorp found out they lived, and then, well, then things would get interesting.

But that would be later. For now?

"We might be forming a new group," Aurora said. "Anyone mind if we keep the old name?"

Not a soul objected, and Sever Squad, free and free-lancing, shot off into the stars.

READ *on for an excerpt from* HOPE'S DEBT, *Sever Squad's next adventure!*

An Excerpt from HOPE'S DEBT

No guns on the streets. Aurora laid the command on Sever before vanishing to find them some work. Apparently the captain knew some haunts on the world that she didn't feel like sharing with Sever. Sai would've taken offense at the secrecy, except he had other objectives and getting a bit of off-ship free time fit right in with what he wanted.

Sai had left his wife and children years ago to take up with DefenseCorp. The cash provided had given his family a better life than any possible if Sai had stuck around, dithering away on routine security gigs. With long space travel diluting time, taking the contract meant breaking ties, meant Sai might never see his family again. Even assuming he didn't take a laser to the back.

None of that, though, meant Sai couldn't send messages back home. Before, he could just walk to the *Nautilus*'s communications bay and rip off a sentimental note, or an action-filled, suitably redacted update. Since Dynas and their journey through dead space, Sai hadn't been able to say a word. His family might be sending one message after another to the *Nautilus* and getting nothing in reply.

Fixing that meant finding Wexer's comm station, likely a sprawling mess beneath a large dish busy beaming out data by the petabyte to the intergalactic airwaves.

"You're taking that, really?" Eponi asked Sai as they waited for their turn to leave the ship. Rovo took second after Aurora, and the captain's orders called for a few minutes between disembarking to avoid attention. "Isn't that, like, completely against our goals right now?"

Sai reached over his shoulder, patted the katana's hilt. The long sword rested in a sheath going down Sai's back, something he'd cobbled together during the journey. Normally the blade would slot right in Sai's power armor, but that'd been lost on Dynas.

"I lost the sword once," Sai said. "I'm not losing it again."

"Nobody said anything about losing it."

Sai gave Eponi a level stare. The pilot had set Sai up on Dynas, and no matter how much Eponi claimed Sai would've died without her help, her actions had caused him to lose his power armor, to lose that katana in the first place. No matter the logic, Eponi's trick still burned.

"Take care of yourself," Sai said. "I'll be fine."

Sai's wrist chimed, the timer dinging his turn to ditch the ship, and he took the ramp in long strides.

"It's not you I'm worried about," Eponi said, her words carrying down the exit.

Sai ignored the comment and let Wexer's bright afternoon whisk him away from the docking bay, through the shallow wall ringing the ship, and into the open city. From what Sai had read, Wexer held itself as a stable world, terraformed just enough to kill the volcanic action that'd lead to the blasted landscape. Other than the creamy rivers, Wexer had become one boring rock.

Stability didn't mean beauty: what buildings Sai could see, sculpted from that gray-black rock coating Wexer's surface, were wide and short. Supports buttressed the sides, most painted over with colors, graffiti claiming this or that. Dusty logos showcased corporate outposts mingling with residential huts, everything mish-mashed together.

Wexer rose organically, a desperate rush for the planet's precious metals bringing fortune-chasers and those who profited from them together. Sai saw both in the hawking merchants—they might've left Anaskya's ship, but they were still hunting marks here—and the shadow-eyed humans drifting around.

Aliens mingled here too, more than Sai had seen in a long time. DefenseCorp held a human preference. Mainly, so the company said, because it was more profitable to make weapons, ships, and armor for one species than a thousand. Because of that, Sai still tended to take a longer look at anything with more than two arms, translucent skin, or with a nose that went from face to feet.

As he walked, Sai felt eyes on him too, most trailing from his face to his tied black hair that he'd let grow, and then to the sword on his back. The Sever Squad demolitions expert picked out arms aplenty in the crowds around him, mostly cheap rifles and pocket pistols holstered on waists, but nobody else had a sword like his. That said, with Wexer offering approximately zero security, having your own protection was, more or less, required.

And Aurora had said no guns. Either her memories of Wexer were outdated, or she had a lot of confidence in Sever's looks. Maybe Gregor could stalk a place like this without getting roughed up, but the rest of them?

"Nice blade," growled a man, hooded and hunched over on a big pack. He leaned back against a building's side, a teal-shaded spot advertising mining insurance, and cast a gap-toothed grin Sai's way. "Shame you brought it here."

Sai would've kept walking. The comm station ought to be right around the next block, but the man's words stuck him.

"Shame?" Sai said. "Why's that?"

"Because now I gotta fight you for it."

The man stood, shrugged his shoulders with a sigh that seemed to place the burden for this situation wholly on Sai. The crowd burbling around them noticed something was in the offing, the flow leaving a berth between Sai and the man, a few lookers taking drinks or a snack and posting up around the swordsman and his challenger.

Well, they'd have to be disappointed.

"Sorry," Sai said. "Not tangling with anyone today."

Even if Aurora hadn't said they should keep quiet, Sai had left his random scuffle days behind. His ego didn't need salving by slicing up stupid people on the streets. So he turned, took a step further, and hoped the man would drop it.

Hoped he would, knew he wouldn't.

Sai caught the motion from one of the bystanders: a lanky dude who looked like he'd been scarred by a blast furnace, but nonetheless blew his eyes wide and his mouth open as he watched something over Sai's shoulder.

The gravel ground behind Sai crunched in time with the look, and Sai ducked. The punch, a clumsy one, flew clean over Sai's head. The gap-toothed man took back his blow, gave Sai room to stand up straight, then threw the mercenary an apologetic grin, spreading his hands as if asking forgiveness.

"Don't mean nothing by it," the man said. "It's just there's not many ways to earn a living on this world. Fightin' happens to be mine."

Sai breathed deep to push back the desire to draw his sword and skewer the man right then and there. The wild punch had tripled the number watching them, and a ring had formed around Sai and the man, a classic dueler's court. All the attention on Sai and his katana. Everything Aurora hadn't wanted.

Well. Sai had tried.

"You earn a living by attacking people on the streets?" Sai asked.

"Look around," the man replied. "There's cash to be had. For both of us."

Cries went up around them, calls for bets to be made. Hard cash, with several people shifting through the crowd, announcing odds and, through some application on their wristlets, taking people's bets and moving on to the next.

"Whomever wins, we split our cut," the man said. "Promise not to scrape you up bad."

"So this isn't about the sword."

"Oh no," the man wagged a finger at the katana. "I win, I get that blade."

"And if you lose?" Sai folded his arms.

"If you win?" the man flounced, his dirty jacket and hood somehow staying in place, over to his junk pile. He reached down, picked up a long pole with a single curved edge coming off the top. "I'll let you take this."

The scythe wouldn't be worth it. Sai wasn't a farmer with wheat to cut, and he sure as hell wouldn't be bringing a weapon that large into the packed corridors so many of his fights seemed to require. A scythe wouldn't be much good in a fight like this one either, where the katana's focused point should have an edge.

But, Sever did need cash. With DefenseCorp controlling their accounts, none of them had much for money. Anaskya had floated the food and fuel to get them this far, but now?

"Fine," Sai said. "You want to lose your weapon, let's go."

"There's some spirit," the man said, taking his scythe in his hands. "Figured you wouldn't leave me wanting."

"You might regret that." Sai reached over his shoulder, drew the katana. The blade, polished to gleaming levels, caught Wexer's light.

The crowd around them kept growing, and more than a few called out support Sai's way. More still shouted for the man with the scythe. Now engaged, Sai looked at the man closer, trying to suss out if his adversary was really just a hustler or someone more dangerous. The hooded cloak shaded most of the view, the man's eyes barely peaking out, little sparks that flashed as he made the first move.

A low sweep with the scythe, cutting in at Sai's knees and with enough reach that the crowd drew back a step. Sai, though, went forward, flicking his wrists to the right and sending the katana's blade down to block the scythe. The force of the swing coupled with the katana's sharpness should've sheared the pole in half. Instead, the scythe banged off the sword, throwing sparks and, with its force, knocking Sai off-balance.

The man laughed, set the scythe going in an overhead chop towards Sai's head. Again Sai raised the katana, side-stepped the scythe's sharp hook. This time, when blade met pole, Sai pushed back, shoved the scythe up hard. The big weapon took the man's arms up with it, exposing his chest for a match-ending stab.

Sai sank the katana and went for it, rushing forward from his block to put an end to the fight. The man, far from panicking, kept up his gap-tooth grin. The scythe was back over his shoulder, nowhere near able to block the attack, but the man twisted his right hand, near the pole's base. With a click, the scythe's pole split in two, the bottom half breaking away. From the lower half, a second bright blade stuck straight out as the man brought the new weapon back across his body.

Didn't matter. The half-scythe blade was still too small, still not in position to block Sai's stab. A fancy trick that was just a trick.

Sai thrust, planning to stop the katana's point above the man's heart. The man flicked his wrist again, and the small blade fanned out, thinning itself into a steel half-circle in an instant, just in time to bounce away Sai's attack. The blow still forced the man back a step, but with the space, and with Sai's confusion, the man brought back the original scythe.

"A hook and a shield?" Sai said, stepping back. "Interesting choice."

"I like to think so," the man replied, then cast his eyes around the circle. "Keep those bets coming, folks! You're seeing a show here, take the chance to make some cash!"

Sai took the man's salesmanship and used it to gauge him more. With the scythe split, Sai had reach. The katana ought to be more stable than either of the man's weapons too, winning out in a smashing contest.

But, more important, who the hell was this guy?

Sai couldn't picture just anyone hanging out on a planet like Wexer waiting for fighters to come along. Much less anyone able to hang in there with a weapon like that scythe. Which made the man a mystery.

Which made him even more dangerous.

"C'mon then," the man said, clacking the scythe hook against his shield and sending sparks into the rocks. His wild grin belied his steady stance, his set shoulders. "When I make you bleed, they'll really cheer."

Continue the adventure with HOPE'S DEBT, available now!

Acknowledgments and Author's Note

Helix Strike started as a straight-forward sequel to *Drop Zone*. Aurora, Rovo and the rest would plug right on, blasting away. However, as they often do, more complicated threads emerged in the telling. Kaia, for example, didn't even exist at first. Instead, when Kashmal proved himself a little more complicated than a money-grubbing coward, Kaia turned up as the reason, hiding in a closet, a source of shame and, potentially, salvation.

Giving a massive organization like DefenseCorp a galactic-wide feel is difficult, so when Gregor runs into Lani, we get a better feel for DefenseCorp's many parts that work separate. It's a theme that'll keep on coming up, that in a galaxy so wide and bound (at least somewhat) to physical laws, no company can keep all its parts moving in synch.

Sever Squad will continue, and I'm looking forward to their adventures as much as you are.

Books like these, books of any size, really, are the products of teams. While I do most of the actual production, my wife, family, and friends make my writing possible. My new son, too, provides inspiration I didn't have before.

Matt, a childhood friend dedicated in this book, opened worlds to my young self I never imagined. Whether though computer games, endless imagination as we wandered neighborhoods, or later nights out around Madison, Matt always had a joke ready and a drive to seek out what came next, themes that infuse many of my stories today.

Thanks for diving into these adventures with me, and I hope you enjoy reading them as much as I do writing them down!

About the Author

A.R. Knight spins stories in a frosty house in Madison, WI, primarily owned by a pair of cats. After getting sucked into the working grind in the economic crash of the 2008, he found himself spending boring meetings soaring through space and going on grand adventures.

Eventually, spending time with podcasting, screenplays, short stories and other novels, he found a story he could fall into and a cast of characters both entertaining and full of heart.

A.R. Knight plans on jumping through to other worlds and finding new stories to tell in the limitless borders of our imagination.

Thanks, as always, for reading!

For more information:
www.adamrknight.com

To Matt

Copyright © 2020 by A.R. Knight
All rights reserved.
ISBN:
Ebook — 978-1-946554-59-8
Paperback — 978-1-946554-61-1
Hardcover — 978-1-946554-87-1
Large Print — 978-1-946554-88-8
Published by Black Key Books

This book or any portion thereof may not be reproduced or used in any manner whatsoever without the express written permission of the publisher except for the use of brief quotations in a book review.

This is a work of fiction. Any similarity between the characters and situations within its pages and places or persons, living or dead, is unintentional and co-incidental.

www.blackkeybooks.com

www.ingramcontent.com/pod-product-compliance
Lightning Source LLC
Chambersburg PA
CBHW050337190726

48284CB00007BB/2042